To Trace the Forests Wild

Book Eight
of
The Return of the Tribes

By A. A. Taylor

First Edition

The Rum Lot Publishing
Lowestoft, Suffolk, UK
2025

ISBN- 978-1-918079-22-7
Paperback Edition

Books of this series are available for download on

Amazon Kindle
or
The Rum Lot Publishing
www.rumlot.com

And jealous Oberon would have the child
Knight of his train, to trace the forests wild;
But she perforce withholds the loved boy,
Crowns him with flowers and makes him all
her joy;

Puck ("Midsummer Night's Dream," ii. i)

By William Shakespeare

Book Eight

Freyja

She didn't know it when she started her epic walk, but Lethbridge was 2,643 miles away. But hey, every great journey starts with a single step, and when Freyja closed the door on the only home she had ever known, she didn't look back.

Freyja would never return. She didn't even know why she bothered to close the door. Habit, she guessed.

Alaska's brief and joyous summer was almost there; she could smell it coming, but now, in March, winter was dying of old age. The ice was rotting, and under the snow Freyja could smell green life, coiled to spring to the sun the first minute it could. That was the only spring in Alaska, the leap from dead winter to full summer, and it only took a few glorious days. She wondered if she'd miss it or if the weather in the south was the same as her interior Alaskan home. She would find out.

The dreams had started a few months before, when winter was at its darkest and it was hard to tell the difference between dreams and reality. Even old Jo was in one, only he wasn't old in the dreams. He was in full rude health and rather handsome, really, for a woman who was a man. In all the years they'd lived together, Freyja had never once seen him naked or dressed in anything other than as a man, but she'd always known Jo was physically a female in the same way as Freyja. As a child, it hadn't mattered to her that Jo was physically one thing and mentally another, and when Jo told her to call him "Daddy", that was fine. Freyja didn't know "daddy" was a masculine noun until she was in her teens.

But Jo came in the dreams, happy with his female body and male soul, and even happier to see Freyja, who he loved as a mother-father with all of his heart. But he came with a message, and Freyja listened to Jo as she always had. Jo said it was time for her to go a-roaming and that she was needed in the south. Freyja had lived alone long enough, and just as Jo had been put on this earth to take care of Freyja when she was a helpless baby, Freyja had been put on this earth to take care of others and keep them safe, and she couldn't do that living in splendid isolation deep in the Alaskan interior. It was time she earned her keep and paid back the gods for the gifts she had been given.

And that was all Jo said before he turned and slipped back into the dream forest. Freyja wasn't told who she was to take care of, what she was supposed to do to "pay back," or even exactly where to go but "south". Since she lived in Alaska, just about every other place was south, so that was rather vague, but the other dreams gave hints. One dream had Freyja standing on a road and looking at a sign that said "Lethbridge, 40 km". When she looked the town up in the old *Rand-McNally Road Atlas,* there it was, in Canada and almost on the US border. It was definitely in the south. She never bothered to figure out the distance, but it didn't look too bad. Only about eight inches. A doddle.

The dreams told her some other, practical bits, too. One dream showed her a man with purple eyes and a bad smell, and Freyja fighting him for her life. That was scary and a warning. Be careful.

Another dream showed her meeting a child on the road, and the child running away in fear after seeing her glowing eyes and pointed ears. That reminded her of how she and Jo would go to the town to trade, and Jo always made her wear her hat and sunglasses. It was easy to forget how odd she looked, and the dream told her to remember.

When Freyja was totally honest with herself, she knew she was ready to move on, and the dreams were just a good excuse to make a change. Living alone in the cabin and visiting town every few years was feeling tight. Claustrophobic. Her feet itched. She wandered the backcountry, but while it was beautiful and often fun, it had become repetitive. Been there, done that, as they say in town.

She wasn't worried about the walk; Freyja was very fit and enjoyed the exercise. She wasn't worried about being lonely; the pack would follow her south just like they followed her now. She probably couldn't turn them away if she wanted to. She wasn't worried about her safety because she had the old Winchester and still had a good supply of ammo. And, of course, she had her magic.

In that dream with the purple-eyed man, she'd won the fight, but it was a warning that she could be jumped and to be careful; she wasn't just walking south, she was walking into danger. The dream was saying, "Don't get cocky, Freyja." But danger –

Freyja smiled. A little risk, a little danger. That just made life interesting, didn't it?

When the pack saw her load up the sled, they started to sing and dance, excited to be on the move, maybe even go hunting. She sang back, but then turned serious. Freyja told them that this was a forever journey and that it was for a very long way and that they didn't have to go. Volunteers only.

Everyone volunteered as she knew they would – even the old ones, because they would rather die on the trail with the pack than die at home. In Freyja's opinion, that was a good choice.

Wally

Old Wally could hardly believe his eyes. What was it? Ten years since Freyja last rode into town? But here she was, with what looked like a monster pack of her trademark white wolves.

Dire wolves. The biologists thought they'd brought them out of extinction, but Freyja had them decades before anyone in a biolab cooked up their ersatz copies. Maybe a hundred years.

The woman was nothing if not dramatic, mushing into town on two dog sleds. She rode on one, and the other followed close behind with its own team. Both were pulled by ten huge, white wolves, strung out on a gangline. Following along behind the two sleds were about another six or so free wolves, their pink tongues lolling out as they trotted, puffs of steam coming out of gaping, serrated jaws. They were massive. The outrunners were, Wally knew, just the visible guards to protect their brothers and sisters pulling the sleds. There were probably another dozen or more slinking around the edges of town, waiting and watching.

Everyone on the road stopped to watch, and she pulled up to Wally's store just like she always did when she came in for provisions, flying past the tour buses and parking the dogs and the sleds in between the pickups and family SUVs. Freyja mushed her wolves into the packed parking lot as if she did this every day, and she belonged there.

"Mark!" Old Wally didn't even look behind him; he didn't take his eyes off Freyja. "Go tell your mother Freyja is here and to put on an extra plate for dinner." Mark's eyes were popping out of his head. Freyja! He was only fourteen, but he had heard whispered stories of Freyja and his mother told him that when he was a baby, he had once met her, but he couldn't remember anything. Now she was here. He ran off, but not before running out to the porch and taking another look. *Freyja!*

There were already people gathering around, locals and a busload of tourists, watching the trapper free the wolves from the harnesses and pull the second sled into the parking spot. The wolves yelped and danced, and the steam rose from their hot lungs and made clouds in the frigid air.

A growing crowd of tourists took photos with their phones. Watching an old trapper haul in from the wilds with two dog sleds pulled by the enormous white wolves was a treat, one they didn't expect. Then, she gestured for the pack to go to the edge of the parking lot and wait for her, and like good dogs, the wolves did.

"Wally!" Freyja called him, and then everyone knew it was a woman. She was bundled up in cold-weather gear, and with the hood up on her parka, the ski mask, and mirrored sunglasses, she wasn't male or female, just human-like. But the voice was a clear bell ringing in the cold air. "Are you going to stand there like a lump or help me with these pelts?"

A young woman in a purple ski outfit reached out to pet one of the wolves as he walked by, and he snapped at her. Freyja just shrugged.

"I wouldn't pet'm, lady. They're not tame. And they're hungry." Frightened, the woman backed off.

"Should they be out here with people then?"

"Oh, I don't think you'll hurt'm. I have every confidence that you can keep yourself under control!" Freyja nodded cheerfully. "But if you do go after one, he'll kill you, and there's not much I can do about that!"

The growing crowd murmured and took a step back, which was good enough for Freyja, and she turned to the shop. Where the hell was Wally?

"Freyja!" And there he was, trotting out as fast as his old legs would carry him, along with Mark's dad, Steve and one of the counter guys. "Freyja! Damn you, girl! It's been ten years! I thought you were dead!"

Freyja grinned under her mask. "You know better than that, Wallace, you chucklehead. I just didn't need any of your overpriced and shoddy goods. But now I'm here, looking to trade. Or have you forgotten in your dotage how that works?"

"Nope, I haven't forgotten how to trade, although for ten years you've forgotten how to get here! Your sense of direction is shit! Ten years!" He hugged her and slapped her back, hard, and she hugged him back. Good ol' Wally. Was it ten years? She had totally lost track of time.

With the formal greeting out of the way and insults properly thrown, caught, and hurled back, they got down to the business of unloading the second sled and taking bundles of furs into the store. After a few minutes of haggling, a bargain was reached, hands were shaken, and –

– a tourist rudely interrupted. The guy was in shorts. Who the hell wears shorts in Alaska in March?

"Lady, could you move over a bit to the left? I want to get a shot of you two with the furs." And they heard the whirr of an expensive camera as he crouched down for his photos.

Freyja looked at the man and then looked at Wally. "What's with this fathead? Do I know him?"

"Nah – we're on the tourist trail now, Freyja. We get people flying up from Anchorage in tour groups to see the –" Wally made finger quotes, " – authentic" Alaska. They all think we're actors or something."

"Oh."

Wally smiled apologetically. The tourist with the camera looked a bit peeved; no one was moving.

"Listen, if you don't want your picture taken, just say so."

"Okay, I'll say so. Don't take my picture with your magic soul-stealing box. Begone, witch-man!" And Freyja waved her hand imperiously at the tourist.

Steve snickered.

The man glowered and opened his mouth, but before he could say anything, a tour guide grabbed him by the arm and hauled him out, whispering in his ear. Wally, who was going deaf ten years ago, couldn't hear everything the guide said, but Freyja could. "This is the real deal, and these old trappers are bat-shit crazy. Don't push'm if you want to keep your teeth."

Bat-shit crazy! Freyja was fine with that and gave a cheery wave to the man as the guide dragged him from the store.

"Am I still bat-shit crazy, Wally?"

"Yep, not a doubt in the world, Freyja."

"Thanks to all the gods; I was worried I was losing my edge." She turned to Steve and gave him a hug. "Steve, I see you're man enough to grow facial hair now! Covering your face is a vast improvement! Do you think I can buy a bit of grub? I'm starved!"

And of course she could, and no, her money wasn't any good here, and they all left for the back of the shop where Wally and his family had lived for over a hundred years if anyone was bothering to count.

Freyja

The curtains were all drawn tight, and the only people in the room sitting around the battered kitchen table were Wally, Steve, his wife Meriwa, and Freyja. She was stripped down to her sweater and jeans, and her head was uncovered, showing the world her shock of white hair and enormous, pointed ears. Her eyes didn't glow because she was with friends, but every now and then the darkened room let them see sparks of green fire.

During the Klondike gold rush in 1899, Wally's family moved from Canada to the wild Alaska Territory, and after losing their shirt panning for gold, they sensibly set up a store to sell kit to the miners and trappers and from them made the shirt back and more. No one paid the least attention to theoretical borders back then, and when Dawson City was bursting at the seams and no good claims could be found, stolen, or purchased, many miners tried their luck further afield. Wally's great-great-grandad followed them west to Alaska Territory.

In 1900, ten-year-old Jo's family trekked from the Lower Forty-Five with his twin sister Jane. Like Wally's family, they briefly settled in Dawson during the gold rush boom and then migrated across the border to Alaska Territory after the Klondike's inevitable bust. Their parents, however, didn't set up a store; instead, they staked a useless claim in the middle of nowhere and lived off the land, trapping and panning when they could. After two brutal winters on the claim, Jo and Jane's mother had had enough, and they all moved into the ramshackle town where their dad did odd jobs until the drink staked its own claim on the twins' parents.

When Jane was twenty, she was raped by a trapper and fell pregnant. Jo was already living in the back country as a man, all by himself, panning the family's piss-poor claim and building a cabin. The rape and the pregnancy sent Jane over the edge, and she just never recovered. The trauma of the rape, the trauma of being an unwed mother in 1910, the trauma of giving birth to a very odd baby – it was all too much. She committed suicide the day after Freyja was born, and Jo bought a nanny goat, took the baby out to the deep woods and raised the child as his own.

Wally's grandparents knew all about that sad history of Freyja's birth and didn't see any reason to punish the child for any of that, and they didn't see any reason to be cruel to Jo for living as a man. So they were kind when the little family occasionally wandered into town in the spring to trade pelts, and they gave honest weights to the little bit of gold Jo panned in the summer. Jo and Freyja never forgot the family's friendship, and as Freyja became older (and certainly odder), she doubly appreciated their descendants' discretion. Freyja's secrets were their secrets, too.

Freyja gobbled down Meriwa's excellent chocolate cake as if she hadn't had a slice for a decade, which she hadn't, but in between bites, she told them she was leaving. She didn't tell them about the dreams because they'd think she really *was* bat-shit crazy. While acting as a crazy backwoods trapper to a tourist was funny, she didn't want Wally and everyone else to think she had jumped over the edge from being alone in the wilderness.

"It's time, Wally. I'm heading south, and I don't know if I'll ever be back."

Meriwa took the empty plate and replaced it with the entire cake, blinking back tears and smiling at Freyja at the same time. Her people thought Freyja was good luck and would be sorry to hear she was leaving. She was very rarely seen in the backwoods and only when someone was in trouble. There were stories about Freyja – all good ones. Sometimes they could hear her singing, and that was considered good luck, too.

Wally looked sad, but he nodded. He'd been expecting this. "Ever since the lords and elves came back, Freyja, we knew this day would come. It's for the best, I'm sure. You need to be with your people."

Freyja didn't pause as she annihilated the wonderful cake, but she was taken aback. Lords? Elves? *My people?* What the hell? Jo told her it was time to pay back and help someone; was this what he'd meant?

"Y'know, Wally, I don't get any news out in the backcountry. Why don't you get me up to speed?"

And that's when Freyja learned all about the elves coming back to earth, along with lords and orcs and humans and tribes, and the US and Russia going bat-shit crazy for real and everything. Steve pulled out his laptop and showed her photos and drawings from the internet. Wally told her that while Alaskans in general were staying sane (for Alaskans), the feds in Washington had enacted laws that made Freyja an unperson. She could be thrown in jail with no rights at all if the wrong policemen or border guard thought she was a lord.

Some humans thought that people like Freyja were demons from hell and that they should be killed on sight.

That made Freyja pause the cake-eating, and she looked at her friends. They all nodded. She resumed eating the cake.

"You can contact the Elf Nation, Freyja, and they'll come and pick you up. You don't have to walk south. They'll take care of you. I'll call them for you."

Freyja didn't know what to think; she needed more time to process everything. She certainly didn't know if she wanted to be "taken care of". She had been alone and taking care of herself for most of a century, and she didn't want to be under anyone's control. She'd never lived with a tribe or even a family. Just with Jo, but she had lived much longer without him than with him. Besides, her dreams told her to head south, not east to Europe, where those Elf Nation people lived.

She made up her mind.

"Wally, I'm going to go south like I planned. I have my reasons. But I think it's time I got a phone. Can you set me up? I want to be able to travel and look at this internet by myself, and if I change my mind about the EN, I'll be able to contact them. I guess I can figure out how to do it."

A phone was not a problem; in the shop, Wally sold a complete set-up – phone, field satellite package, solar recharger, extra external battery, all the tech – and Steve left to gather up what she needed. Earlier, the counter guys had paid her for the furs and swapped her gold for loonies, so with that she bought extra ammo, food, and two pairs of new boots; there was plenty left over. She had made some good saddle bags for the wolves, and they'd help her carry some of the extra gear once the snow melted away and she abandoned the sled. Once the phone was set up for her by Steve and she had about fifteen minutes of training, she was good to go.

Freyja thought it would take her about three months to get to the Canadian/US border (the southern one), but who knows, it could be longer. Now she was being told her ears and her other unusual characteristics would cause problems in the US, so she decided to stop in Canada and reassess. Anyway, the dream sign said Lethbridge.

Right before she left, she signed her claim over to Steve, who was stunned. "I'm signing over everything to you, Steve. There's my claim, which is pretty good, really. I can pan a bit of gold out of it, and the cabin is still in good shape. I own a hundred and sixty acres, but now you're telling me that here in the US, I'm not legally able to own anything at all. So it's best if you take it."

He argued, but it was half-hearted, and when Meriwa kicked him under the table, he gratefully accepted it. And with her claim settled, a new phone ("No charge!" Steve insisted), and a loaded-up sled, Freyja hugged everyone, levitated a teacup for Mark to give him something to wonder at, sang a song for the adults, and walked off into the night. She wanted to be far away before the townies and tourists noticed she was gone, and besides, the wolves were getting hungry. If they ate a tourist, that would hold her up.

The Lordfinders

After Freyja left, Wally, Steve, and Meriwa had a big argument about whether they should notify the EN themselves and let them know that Freyja was on her way. If she needed help, the elves would send it, and in their two hours at the dinner table, Freyja couldn't possibly learn all she needed to know about how the world had changed while she was in the backcountry.

Meriwa was pretty sure Freyja didn't know she was a lord until Steve showed her the websites. Whether that knowledge was good or bad didn't matter, she said. It's still a shock to the system to find out there are people like you out there when you've spent all your life thinking you were alone.

Wally was dead set against getting involved. Not only would that get them in Dutch with the feds, who would say they were lord lovers, but for over a hundred and twenty years, his family had kept quiet about the odd trapper and his even odder child, and they weren't going to start squealing now. And since Wally was the elder, his word was final. They said nothing.

In the end, alerting the Elf Nation was moot. The tourists took loads of pictures of the mushing wolves and uploaded them to their social media accounts, and it only took a few of them to notice that the trapper wasn't showing up as anything other than a fuzzy blob. The guy in the store who tried to take photos of the trapper and the trader soon learnt that all of his pics were useless – until he realised he could sell them online to the elf-fantatics.

In Ukraine, the EN intel elves had all the elf-fan websites bookmarked and had long ago coded an AI program that sifted through every social media post looking for real lords and elves; they saw Freyja's blob just minutes after the first pic was uploaded.

By the time Freyja was finishing up her cake, Lord James, Rashid Hadid, and General Jameson (who now lived in Canada) were on a conference call.

By the time she was walking out the door to disappear into the woods, an extraction team was being arranged.

By the time she and the pack were seventy-five miles down the road and bedding in for the night, the US Border Patrol and Homeland Security people tasked with hunting down lords got their first heads up from social media reports that a lord was on the move in Alaska. Since they were given orders by President Meechum to track down and capture American lords, they started looking for her.

The next morning, when Wally walked through the shopfloor to unlock the front door for morning trading, there was a mob of chattering, jostling people milling on the porch waiting to come in to see if the lord was still there (and take photos for their own SM accounts) and buried in the crush were three feds from Homeland Security, flashing badges and wanting an interview.

It was, he told his friends later, a fuckin' mess but pretty good for business. They sold a lot of Wallace Emporium t-shirts to the tourists, and he was happy to unload them. He had overordered.

Everyone working in the shop told the truth and not a syllable more, as Wally saw it. The trapper was an old geezer out of the back country who hadn't been in for ten years. The trapper brought in some pelts, picked up some supplies (which Wally was happy to give the feds a list of), and, after eating a meal, left. No, they had no idea where he/she was going. No, he/she had never told them he/she was a lord. No, they didn't see any elves, not a one.

Wally was very helpful, Meriwa and Steve smiled brightly, the counter guys squinted and said as little as possible, and everyone offered the feds coffee and a free t-shirt. The feds thanked the shopkeepers for the info and coffee, refused the t-shirts, and with that, they left to file their reports and to follow the trail of the sled and the wolves before it got too cold.

Twenty-four hours after Meriwa's wonderful cake, Freyja was well on her way to the US/Canadian border with no idea that the eyes of three countries – the US, the EN, and once they were notified, Canada – were all looking for her, each with their own agendas and each desperately wanting to find this new lord before the others did.

She didn't know there were bounty hunters interested in her, too.

Freyja

At first, Freyja planned to simply follow Rt 5 down to Little Gold and cross the border at the border post there like any tourist, and from there to retrace the route of her grandparents to Dawson in the Yukon Territory, where she'd pick up roads leading south. That would take her about ten days of leisurely mushing, but Wally's information changed things. Maybe it was best now to leave Alaska as soon as she could and not bother with details like official border crossings. She didn't have a passport, anyway.

After consulting the fifty-year-old *Rand McNally,* she decided against heading to the aptly named Border area but to actually cross a bit north, where the forests of Alaska seamlessly blended in with the forests of the Yukon. On a dogsled, she didn't need to follow real roads, and it was better for the pack if she travelled overland, anyway. That brought the Canada crossing to six days, but she'd have to cross the Yukon River, which would be at full flood this time of year. It was doable.

The Ranger

The man with the RumLot business card walked into The Wallace Emporium two days after the feds left and just as the hysteria of a lord passing through town was starting to die down. At first, the counter guys thought he was just another jet-lagged, rather dishevelled, and terribly underdressed young tourist. He walked around the store gawking at everything, taking pics, and even appreciatively patting the massive logs that made up the front.

Back in the day, the building was a massive log barn that was used as a bar/mercantile/post office/bordello and everything else. Then, in the early sixties, when the oil boom took hold, Wally's granddad had it modernised to look just like a lower forty-eight grocery store, complete with linoleum floors, freezers, and false walls in front of the old shelving and fireplace and the huge logs were covered with aluminium siding.

In the last twenty years, every bit of modern plastic and aluminium was carefully stripped away. The place was returned to its 1915 glory, and now it was a tourist's backcountry fever dream. Movie companies even came in for shoots. They were attracted by the huge exposed logs, small windows that brought in just enough light, but didn't let out too much heat, and long, polished wood counters with Edwardian shelving. On one wall stood a massive boulder fireplace that featured in endless Instagram posts and gave Steve no end of fits. It didn't draw worth a damn.

Packed to the ceiling were piles of pelts, blankets, barrels of unknown crap, tools, camping gear, cold weather clothes, vintage vending machines, mugs with pictures of the store, t-shirts, and key rings. And gimme caps. Lots and lots of gimme caps.

The guy bought a gimme cap with "The Lord of Alaska" written on it straight from a carton Janna was still unpacking and asked if he could talk to the owner, a Mr. Wallace.

He was told no, Mr. Wallace was not talking to anyone. Then he gave his card to Janna and simply asked if she would take Mr. Wallace the card.

Wally poked his head out of the back room, waved the guy in, and sat down to tell him to fuck off, but in a nice way, of course. From what he'd read on the internet, you didn't piss off the Elf Nation.

A half hour later, the man left the office none the wiser about anything.

As he left, he stood on the porch and saw a skinny boy, about fourteen, sweeping off a dusting of snow from the sidewalk and asked him where the dogsled was parked when the lord stopped here.

The boy, Mark, was happy to show him. And since the RumLot guy was charming and knew just what to say to a young man, they got into a conversation about lords and elves and how badass they were and the wonders of magic.

"Do you think the wolves are magic?" he asked.

Mark was disparaging. That was a stupid question. "Naw – the wolves are wolves. Freyja just liked the white ones better, and they all interbred. That's what grandpa says. He called it selective breeding."

"Wow, that takes a lot of time to do that!"

Mark shrugged. "Well, she's older than one hundred, at least that's what I was told."

The man nodded. "That makes sense. I guess they'll follow her wherever she goes. She's their pack leader."

Mark frowned down at his broom and started sweeping again. "Yeah, I won't see white wolves any more. She's gone south." Then he realised he was talking too much and said bye and ran up to the porch.

The report was on Jameson's desk as soon as it was uploaded.

"The employees and owner were not cooperative, and although they knew I was with the Elf Nation, and they knew what RumLot Security was, they were loyal to the lord. There didn't appear to be any fear of the lord, but protectiveness. No one was afraid when they spoke to me, just "GTFO and MYOB".

In the parking lot, sweeping up snow, was the owner's grandson. From him I learned that the lord's name is Fraya, that she is over 100yrs old, and "is not coming back" and "heading south." The white wolves are her pack, and she's had them for years. Since she can go overland on a sledge, there is no telling where she plans to cross the border if she plans to get into Canada at all. But "south" and "not coming back" leads me to believe she is leaving Alaska.

Yesterday, there were US Homeland Security people here asking questions. I think they learned less than I did, but they left to follow the sledge's trail. They are looking for the lord.

This morning, a group of elf hunters checked into my hotel. I overheard them bitching that their snowmobiles were late.

Will keep poking around re the elf hunters and Homeland Sec. Otherwise, awaiting further instructions before I leave.

Ranger Bunn"

Jameson looked at the map. Bunn was right; she could cross anywhere, and spotting a black dot with white wolves travelling across miles and miles of forested, snow-covered nothing was not going to be easy. The wilderness of Alaska and the

Yukon reminded sober people just how big the Earth was, and there were vast areas where absolutely no human being had ever crossed over them. Ever.

Given the terrain and her general direction of travel, the most obvious point to slip into Canada was south of Eagle Village. Then she wouldn't have to cross the Yukon River. He sent Bunn to Eagle Village by helicopter. Hopefully, the elves could find a place for him to stay.

The Border Patrol

The Border Patrol helicopter made a wide loop in its sector, looking for anyone mushing cross-country. They didn't fly at night because dogs need to rest, and they didn't think the demon would be travelling in the dark. But once they'd started looking, they'd spotted absolutely nothing that looked suspicious, not even tracks.

They did see about ten guys on snowmobiles who seemed to be moving in the same direction as the demon, that is, to the border.

"They won't get'm," the pilot observed to her spotter. "They're too noisy. He'll hear them and hole up, and they can shoot right by'm and never see'm."

"So you think they're following him? They look like hunters to me." He looked through his binoculars at the snowmobilers. They all had rifles slung across their backs.

"They're not hunting. At least not hunting deer or bear. Any self-respecting fur-ball is miles away from that noise."

"Okay, but what if they're following a trail we can't see from up here?"

She shrugged, banked around, and picked a line in front of the posse and flew down there just to check out the area the fake hunters were aiming for. It was still in their sector.

And they saw him! He was mushing down a small valley as calm as you please, and help-me-Jesus, there must have been twenty fuck'n *huge* wolves loping along beside the team. At first, the pilot thought they were ponies. They were heading due east, straight towards the Yukon River. How he thought he was going to cross it now – it was crazy.

The sniper moved into position. They weren't going to kill the demon, just put him out with a tranq, exactly the same way they would a rogue bear or wolf. Once the demon was out, they'd drop down, secure him, and take him back to HQ. The sniper figured the wolves would scatter when the copter landed, and they wouldn't be a problem. Their boss said that this demon visited humans and they didn't know he was a demon, so he must be one of the weak ones with normal hair and ears and not to worry.

The pilot dipped down, and she saw the demon turn and look up, right at her, but she wasn't worried. They were still well away, certainly out of range of this one's magic. The sniper took aim and fired.

He missed.

That was okay; sometimes it took a couple of shots before they made a good hit. So she swung around and lined up again. The demon took off his sunglasses and looked up, and there was a green flash.

The rotors froze up. The fuckin' blades were iced! The copter made a lazy spin, and it was all she could do to land. The final, sickening twenty-foot drop was totally uncontrolled, with one blade clipping the ground and then, of course, all of them exploded into fragments.

The last thing she remembered was screaming.

Terry

Terry saw the border patrol helicopter go down low. When they spotted the copter, the posse stopped for a second to regroup, and with the snowmobiles on idle, they heard the shot.

"Shit! They got'm!" He was so mad he could spit, so he did. The minute they'd heard about a rogue lord in Alaska, they went into red mode and made it up here in record time, ready to go lord hunting. And now the fuckin' federales got to him first.

He hoped to shit his company wouldn't have to absorb this. His backers were prepared to pay for three missed attempts, and even though this was the first one, he didn't want any.

Then the copter swung around and came back, low and steady. The shot must have missed. Without warning, it spun and disappeared below the trees. A second later, they heard it hit the ground.

The snowmobiles roared back into life, and the posse sped down the little valley and burst through a line of trees to find the copter crumbled up and smoking but still basically intact. A man was climbing out, leaving red streaks on the fuselage.

There was no sign of the lord.

"You three! Take care of these guys! The rest stay with me." Terry grinned; the lord must be very close now. He checked his tranq gun and whooped, and his guys all whooped back; they were pumped up! The adrenaline surged, and they were ready to hunt bear.

Terry was the only one of the posse who had ever had contact with a lord, and the others trusted him, so when he told them to stop and listen, they did. When he told them to go, they did that, too. From their point of view, and most were ex-military, Terry was a top-notch first shirt, which is what he had been in the Royal Army before his little problem with the wuss lieutenant.

No longer in the army, Terry worked for about six months for RumLot Security before they canned him, and during his time in Ukraine, he met several lords. Only one was an Elemental, a little guy named Lord Adem, and whatever magic he did was about as exciting as watching San Marino play football. Nothing to see here, folks.

The lords with coloured hair couldn't do squat. Lord Malachi was a strac dude, and Terry would hate to meet him in a dark alley, but what made him dangerous was all normal stuff. Someone once said he could fly, but Terry never saw him do anything. The vast majority of lords, as far as Terry could see, were more PR magic than real magic. But that didn't mean they weren't valuable, and if his company caught one, Terry knew for a fact that the EN would pay handsomely for an "independent recovery". They just had to get there before anyone else did, including the EN recovery teams, grab the lord, and hand him over to the EN. Hell, he'd even put a nice red bow on'm.

After about three miles, Terry had the guys stop, turn off their engines, and he listened. And heard nothing. But now they could see the tracks of the wolves and the dogsled, and they were fresh, fresh, fresh.

They raced over a hill, and there was the sled, sitting alone in the middle of a snow-covered clearing, surrounded by dense forest. There was no lord. There were no wolves.

He pulled up by the sled and looked at the paw tracks; they all ran away from the sled like a star. The guys pulled up behind him, automatically forming a defensive formation facing out.

"Look!"

And all around them, emerging from the treeline at the edge of the field, were wolves. Big fuckers, contrasting against the dark green of the pines like pale ghosts. The wolves didn't make any sound as they surrounded the posse and paced in tight little circles, watching. They didn't look happy. They looked hungry.

Then, like an audience at a tennis match, the wolves unanimously looked to the south, and Terry saw him, the lord. He was dressed in a motley collection of furs, a parka, and ski pants that completely covered him from top to toe. Only his ski goggles were pushed up on his head, and his eyes were black pits hiding deep in a ski mask and his parka hood. He had an old rifle slung on his back, but he wasn't reaching for it, and for the first time, Terry got nervous.

This guy wasn't worried about them, not a bit. And that copter went down. Maybe Terry should have thought about that a minute before they raced off like a bunch of yahoos. This guy just crashed a copter.

"Hey!" Terry waved. "We're here to help you, not hurt you!" He put down his gun and raised his hands. "We're not Border Patrol! We want to help you get to Canada!"

The lord didn't move. Then the eyes began to glow green.

Shit! It was a woman!

And as fast as the eyes glowed, the snow around the posse began to swirl around them, making a tight tornado with the posse in the centre and forcing them to bunch up even closer. The snow swirled, and if they touched it, it cut razor-sharp and then clumped together. As fast as a thought, they were trapped in a thick tube of ice, twenty feet high and about ten feet in diameter inside. Then the whirlwind stopped, and the trapped men threw themselves against the thick frozen walls, but the ice held fast. One tried to shoot his way through the ice wall, but the bullets just lodged in the ice.

"Stand down!" Terry wasn't going to waste ammo, and shooting was doing no good anyway.

The ice was so cold and so clear that they could see wavy shapes through it, and they could see the wolves running around, sniffing. One peed on the ice, leaving a frozen yellow streak.

"Hey! Lord! We're just here to help! Are you going to let us out? We just want to talk!"

They could see the grey and black shape of the lord walking up to the ice. They could even see her green eyes glowing; the ice was that clear.

"No, I'm not going to let you out. You'll get out on your own. Eventually." Her voice was clear and lilting. Even amused. She tapped on the ice. "Use your noggins, gentlemen. There's a way out."

They watched her shape hitch the wolves back up to the sled, and five minutes later, she was gone.

It took Terry and his guys three hours to dig a hole through the frozen ground and tunnel out of the ice tube, which was slowly melting anyway. Just as the last man was wiggling out of the tunnel, the three guys he left behind at the copter came roaring up.

A rescue copter flew in for the crew, and they had to stay there and give statements before they were allowed to leave. They told Terry the crew said that the lord looked up, and the next thing the crew knew, the blades iced up, and they lost control.

"We're up against a fuckin' Elsa!"

Terry chewed the inside of his lip and looked at the disappearing trail.

"Well, she didn't kill us, probably because we didn't shoot at her. The feds shot at her, and she defended herself. I bet you a beer she could have killed that copter if she had wanted to." He looked at the posse. "We still have a chance. If we go after her and don't shoot but convince her we're friends out to help her, we can get her close enough to knock her out. But if we shoot at her, then all bets are off; she'll defend herself, and she won't be so friendly the second time. I'm for keepin' on the trail but being careful. I don't want to become a man-cicle any more than you guys do. Anyone who doesn't want to stay with the Company can go to Eagle and head home, but you're out of the money. You got five minutes to make up your minds. In or out."

The twelve men talked, moaned, bitched, debated and in the end, four stayed with Terry, and seven opted out. Terry nodded; four was enough, and it meant a bigger share for the winners and the greatly reduced posse moved out. They had an hour and a half to make up some ground and camp before full dark. As they left, one of the Eagle Pass quitters began to sing "Let it Go", and if anyone deserved to be shot and tranquilised, he did.

A few hours later, the five-man posse stopped to camp for the night. As they set up their tents, the man on first watch glimpsed a white wolf. Then they spotted others circling in the distance, howling and yelping.

They made the posse very, very nervous, but Terry told them that if they shot at the wolves, they might as well pack up and go home. If they shot the lord's pets, the get-her-to-trust-us game would be over, and, of course, that made sense.

The wolves didn't come close; they just watched the posse, and in the morning, after a fitful night's sleep, the posse woke up, and the wolves were all gone. Time to move on.

They rode all afternoon, and Terry was starting to worry about their gas reserves. She seemed to be taking some meandering, unnecessary, gas-eating routes on her way through the valleys and ridges. The lord, of course, wasn't worried about gas; she was running on wolf power.

The posse pressed on, chasing the dog sled and the pack of wolves through a light snow that occasionally turned to mist and even a bit of drizzle, and by six o'clock the there was just enough light in the grey sky to crest a ridge and see the lord and her team far below, standing on a sandbar by the boiling, muddy Yukon River. She stood next to the sled with the ten mushing wolves still hitched up, but there must have been forty wolves milling around with her. The sand bar was covered with white fur and snapping fangs.

If she crossed the river, Canada was only two miles to the east, but the Yukon was at its full winter melt fury now, and crossing was suicidal. He took out his binoculars to watch her, and the guys did the same.

Terry grinned at his posse and told them to stick with the plan. She was trapped now, caught between the unfordable river and the posse on the ridge. She'd have to follow the riverbank to Canada, and that meant she either had to go back inland, where there was good snowpack, or leave the sled and follow the river south on foot. Either way, they had her.

Terry was already thinking about how to approach her and sweet-talk the woman into trusting them enough that they could get close. Maybe if he was nice to the wolves –

She stood on the sandbar and looked at the river for a good minute, and then turned back and said something to the wolves. Then she looked right up to the posse; even from the top of the ridge, they could see her eyes snap. The lord waved.

She fucking waved! Not goodbye, but a hi there, nice to see you, glad you finally made it wave. Miguel murmured under his breath, "We're being trolled," and Terry had a nagging feeling he was right.

Turning back to the river, they saw her body glow, and suddenly, out of nowhere, an ice bridge appeared, and from their spot on top of the ridge, the posse felt a blast of hot wind. As soon as the bridge appeared, the lead dog and the team leapt forward and ran across the bridge, followed by an orderly line of wolves. They pelted across the bridge as if they really didn't want to stop and think about what they were doing, and Terry didn't blame them. It took two minutes, tops, for every wolf to get from shore to shore. Then the lord turned, and this time the wave was definitely a bye-bye wave. She strolled across the sparkling ice bridge, just a walk in the park on a sunny day.

"SHIT!!"

They raced down the ridge to the water where the lord had stood five minutes ago, but all that showed that she had been there was a steaming spot in the wet sand. The ice bridge was still standing, and she turned to watch them from the far bank, her eyes glowing bright. Franklin gunned his snowmobile and charged the bridge. Just as he touched it, she shook her head, and the ice bridge exploded in a shower of steam. When the cloud cleared, the far shore was empty.

A wolf trotted out of the forest and lifted his leg and peed in their direction, kicked up some sand towards the posse, and then trotted back into the forest, his white shape disappearing in the gloom.

"That was some world-class trolling," Miguel said.

Terry had to walk away for a couple of minutes; he was so fuckin' angry.

When he came back, he had his map in his hand. "We're heading to Eagle. The other side of the Yukon here is only two miles from Canada, and I bet she's already there by now if the Border Patrol don't catch her, which I'm sure in my bleedin' brain they won't. Not a chance. Once she's on the Canadian side, we can intercept her. Now we have to get to her before the RumLot people do. We can't do anything from here, so let's get cracking and see if we can salvage this operation."

If they were careful, they had just enough gas to get to Eagle.

Freyja

Terry was right, Freyja didn't stop to make camp until she was well into Canada. The border itself was invisible in this part of the Yukon, just a mapmaker's hallucination in the unending pine forest, but since it mattered now, Freyja was conservative in her calculations.

The *Rand McNally* said that due east of where she'd crossed the Yukon River, the border was two miles away, so she went a good four and then stopped and turned on her phone and looked at its map. The geolocation pin that was "Freyja" was well inside Canada, so there shouldn't be problems with the US Border Patrol, and those other guys (whoever they were) shouldn't be able to catch up any time soon. She was safe for now and could tend to other things like feeding herself and her pack and getting some rest.

The wolves told her where a herd of elk was, and she walked out with them and shot two, which would feed the wolves while she fed herself from her provisions and slept. She hadn't done that much magic for years and years, and she was tired to the bone. But she still had enough in her to make a small igloo under the trees and start a fire, and with that done, she trusted the wolves to guard her, so she ate and slept for a good day.

The next morning, she shot three caribou for the wolves to top them off. After thinking about it for a while, Freyja reluctantly decided that when they started moving down to settled country with more people, she couldn't go out hunting for the pack like she did today, and she certainly didn't need them for protection. A fifty-odd super-pack of dire wolves was an attention grabber for one thing. They needed to be fed, or they'd go out hunting for themselves, and that would cause its own set of problems. She knew the ranchers and farmers would shoot them on sight.

She pulled out a nice, calm, family clan of ten and told them to head back to Wallace's Emporium and protect the Wallace family for her. Then she sent back another twenty to her old cabin to guard it. Not that it needed guarding, but it gave the wolves a purpose, and with a job to do, their feelings weren't hurt for being sent back. Besides, she was sure there were pregnant bitches holed up around there, and they needed their pack back. All the wolves were hugged and told that she loved them and to be good, and everyone howled and cried as they left, including Freyja, who sang them a goodbye song to speed them on their way.

Now the pack was still big, but more manageable.

Wendell

Wendell sat in the little bar in Eagle waiting for a replacement passport for the one he'd lost so that he could drive into Canada (not really, but it was a good cover for the locals), nursed his beer, and bided his time. Sure enough, out in the forest, things were happening, and as the news filtered in, he typed reports on his phone and sent them off.

The Border Patrol lost a helicopter. They'd had some cockamamie plan of shooting the lord from the helicopter like she was some animal or something, and when Wendell typed that in, if anyone was looking, they would've seen the muscles in his jaw twitch. The rumours said that they'd tried shooting her and missed, and then the lord had frozen up the rotor and made the copter crash. The pilot had multiple broken bones, the spotter was knocked out but otherwise was okay, and the shooter's arm was crushed in the crash, and he'd probably lose it.

The bartender wasn't very sympathetic. If a freakin' lord was trying to get away to Canada, why the hell were the feds stopping him? And shooting him from a copter? That was pretty low. But he said it in a whisper because, sympathetic or not, being a lord-lover was dangerous – even in Alaska.

A bunch of hunters came in, but Wendell knew they weren't regular hunters. They were the same guys he saw in the hotel when he was chasing down Lord Fraya. The elf-hunters. Wendell knew his elf-fantatics, and 99.9% of them were harmless and rather disorganised souls, but this group caught his attention. They seemed very organised, and there was a military air about them. They were serious hunters. Bounty hunters, maybe.

This group had found the BP copter and, for some reason, ended up in Eagle, waiting for transport back to Anchorage. Wendell sat in his corner all evening, doing his best sad and lonely drunk impression, and listened to them. Yes, they were bounty hunters and talked about the lord and how this one was the real deal, but she wasn't worth the money. Too risky. That ice tube she'd captured them in was serious shit. Terry – now he was a crazy fucker, and while he knew elves and lords from his RumLot time, even he said this one was not to be messed with. But he and some guys were still going after her.

Wendell sent in his report and asked which Terry had worked for RumLot, and a few minutes later, the elves sent back a reply. Terrence Sims, ex-Royal Army and RumLot hire, who didn't make it past the probationary period. Sacked for grabbing one of the female recruits, pushing her into a utility closet, and unzipping. If she hadn't been so good with her own hand-to-hand skills, it could have been rape, but she knocked him out with a few well-placed blows. When he came to, he was told that since he couldn't be trusted around women, he couldn't work at RumLot, and that was the end of his career with them.

He also reported the ice tube thing, but the elf-fanatics didn't talk much about that. Whatever magic the lord did scared them to silence. But she didn't kill anyone, and they were sure she could have. She shook them up and then let them go.

So Lord Fraya was getting pretty close to the Yukon River and the Canadian border. The intel people in Ukraine had absolutely no idea where she was in the vast wilderness, so Wendell waited in Eagle for his fictional passport and news of the lord. She could be passing by him at any time on her way to Canada. There were only five bridges that crossed the Yukon, and they were all south of Eagle.

Wendell would wait.

Mark

Mark woke up, threw on his clothes, and doused his fourteen-year-old body with a manly body spray. He even remembered to brush his teeth. He checked his upper lip for signs of a moustache but didn't see anything.

Mom was in the kitchen making breakfast, and before he could eat a bite, he had to go out and sweep off the store's front porch, ramp, and steps before anyone showed up and compacted the snow into ice. He moaned but grabbed the broom and key and went to do the chore he did every single day when there was snow out. In Alaska, that was a lot of days.

Today, though, the porch already had visitors. Lolling across the porch and even on the swings were ten white wolves. Freyja's wolves.

Mark stepped out on the porch, his jaw slack, and the wolf closest to him turned on his back and begged for a belly rub.

The alpha's belly rubbed, the rest of them bounced over and demanded their own head rubs, and by the time Mark made it back to the kitchen, he didn't smell like cheap cologne; he smelled like wolf.

His mother didn't notice. She was frying bacon.

The wolves never left and were soon known as "Wallace's Wolves" and became a tourist attraction in their own right.

Wendell

Two nights later, the elf-fanatics/bountyhunters had friends drop by the bar, and, blimey, they were furious. Wendell could hear them whispering because, like many people who spent a lifetime (and the last week) around very loud machinery, they all had some hearing loss, and they thought they were whispering, but not really. Especially after they'd downed a few beers and were pissed.

Wendell marked the one called Terry, and when they weren't looking, he surreptitiously snapped a photo with his phone and, of course, attached it to his report. The rest of the report was about the elf-hunters catching up with the lord and her building an ice bridge over the Yukon, and she was probably in Canada by now. Wendell had to smile at the umbrage the men took over her gentle (he thought) trolling of them. No, she wasn't at all scared of them, and they found that deeply insulting.

Terry didn't say much, but he didn't laugh either, and the vicious look in his eye – Wendell had seen that before. You didn't have to be an orc to be an orc, and Terry was an honorary member of the tribe. That opinion went into the report, as well as the news that the bounty hunters had not given up. They were planning to head down 5 to Little Gold and cross into Canada there and set themselves up to intercept the lord as she mushed south. Sooner or later, she'd have to give up the sledge, and that would slow her down. They hoped that as she moved into more populated areas, someone would spot her. Those white wolves would be hard to miss.

Wendell received a message to move on to Dawson City, Canada, and wait with an extraction team that was on its way there. Like the bounty hunters, the EN knew she'd surface sooner or later, and they wanted people ready.

The message was gratefully received. Wendell had sampled all of the delights of Eagle in the first hour he walked into the village, and after four days, the charm was wearing off. A change of scenery would do him good.

Bruce Scott, RCMP

In 1989, the Royal Canadian Mounted Police converted all native constables to regular mounted police status, and the first "real" aboriginal Mounties were assigned to police in the Yukon Territory. Bruce Scott was not one of them; he joined in '92, late enough not to be considered a founding member of the first cohorts but early enough that ingrained prejudice was still a hurdle a First Nations guy had to deal with.

But he dealt with it, and over the years, his successes as a good, working Mountie made people forget he was native, white, or anything other than RCMP scarlet. He didn't climb high in the ranks; that was for people with better educations and political skills, but he was well-respected and occupied a good position as a liaison between his Aboriginal community and the rest of the RCMP and the wider Canadian judiciary. He was the go-to guy for local info in his neck of the woods, especially in investigative work. Now he was at the very end of his career and at sixty-four was looking forward to retirement.

What made Bruce so well-respected amongst his peers was what his boss called his investigative skills, and what his wife called being gawd-awful nosy. Naturally, a curious, friendly man, he knew everyone and everything about the Yukon Territory's Aboriginal peoples. People constantly called and texted him to chat about this or that, and "did he know?" And while most of that was useless chaff, often bits and pieces of info tied together, and he would remember someone who'd gotten drunk in '12 and was thrown in the can for assaulting a woman and how their wife came to a powwow in '18 with a black eye, and now his neighbour's girl went missing. Shouldn't we be talking to him?

Today, he had two totally unrelated bits of information to think about. One was a FYI notice from HQ that a lord was found in Alaska, and he/she might be moving across the border to Canada soon. This was exciting! Lords and elves were all in the south; to think that they might have one in the far north was worthy of conversation. In the Scott household, the young ones couldn't talk about anything else.

Lords! Elves! Magic! Added to that heady brew was a good dose of Aboriginal sympathy for a group of people who were born of the earth and yet were being cruelly discriminated against in the US. Canada was *so* much better, and it was a point of pride now for the youngsters, something Bruce was happy to see.

So Bruce watched the reports come in and read every one. No one in the outside world knew this lord existed until just days ago, when he/she turned up at a general store, looking to reprovision. His RCMP report said the lord was going south. On the way to Canada, the USBP sent out a team to catch him, and he downed a USBP helicopter that was chasing him.

That made the news locally and internationally, and Bruce had already seen his boss on TV making a "no comment" about the reports.

His kids and older grandkids were all up in arms. "Being hunted down like a dog!" Anjij was in tears. All Bruce could do was hug her and say that one day the Americans would come to their senses; everyone does sooner or later. That wasn't true, of course, but she was only twelve. What else could he say?

That was public. The confidential reports told him a bit more. It reported the white wolves, a huge super pack of them followed the lord, and then two days later, he read that he had somehow crossed the Yukon River. It didn't say where, but he did have the geo-location of the downed helicopter. With that number and his knowledge of the area, Bruce had a very good idea of where the lord would end up.

He told his boss, who told him that everyone knew the lord would head down to the Boundary area and cross into Canada there. That made absolutely no sense to Bruce. To get to the highway, they'd have to cross the river again. Why bother? But no, the conventional wisdom said Boundary. His boss, who fancied himself a woodsman, said he'd head south on the American side, where the land was relatively flat and good for dog sleds and avoid the low mountains and hills on the Canadian side.

Bruce looked at the maps. The bend in the river where the lord crossed was absolutely devoid of roads, people, or anything. It was as wilderness as wilderness could get. Yes, it was hillier there, but the valleys would be fine for dog sleds and would actually hold a bit more snow at this time of year.

Bruce also had an ace up his sleeve. He knew a guy who lived out there, an American Vietnam War draft dodger. Old Leo fled the US back in '74 and simply squatted as far away from humanity as he could get. He was still alive, though, and still living out in the backwoods, very near where Bruce suspected the lord would go. The only way to talk to the old coot was by ham radio, and in the days of satellite-linked cell phones, who had a ham radio any more?

Bruce did.

Old Leo was happy to look around once he understood what was going on, which took a *long* while and a *lot* of explaining. He had no idea what a "lord" was, but anyone fleeing the US government was a friend of Leo's, and that was all Bruce really needed to say. He told Leo that this lord guy had a pack of white wolves around and to watch for them. He was a woodsman, so Leo might not see a camp, but the wolves would be roaming. His last words to Leo were *Don't get eaten! I'll have to write a report then,* which made the old man laugh. Leo said he'd go out and call up every day at noon and six with an update until Bruce said the guy had been found somewhere else. And that was fine.

Freyja

The wolf woke Freyja up and told her a man was walking towards the camp. He was alone and very old and seemed to be okay, but of course, Freyja needed to see for herself.

The man's name was Leo, and he was coming to check on Freyja and see if she was alright. He didn't know her name, but he had a friend in the RCMP who called him and said she was running away from the US government, and they both wanted to know if she needed any help. His name was Scott, and he'd told Leo to look for white wolves. As soon as Leo spotted one, he knew the lord was around.

For the first time, Freyja was unnerved. From living in total isolation for years (decades!) to suddenly finding that people knew about her made her feel very exposed. They were making sure she was okay! It was weird.

And now, in the middle of the Canadian Yukon wilderness, she was having a health and welfare check by a total stranger. The last time that happened, she was sixteen, and the government man came all the way out to the cabin to ask Jo why Freyja had never been to school. When he tested her and found she could do her three R's above grade level, he signed her off as graduated from high school and never returned. Lily didn't seem surprised to see him, and Freyja always wondered if Lily was the snitch who'd called the man in. She would've loved it if Freyja had been forced to move to town so she could go to school in the winter, and that meant Jo would have to move to town, too.

But today this old man was very talky (as most of the hermits she ran across were) and sat down at her little fire as if he were an invited duke. So she broke out the instant coffee, some powdered eggs, and a slab of bacon and made them both breakfast.

"So, lady, I left the US and came here in '74 when Johnson was still throwing kids at the Cong. When my number was called up, I just got in my car, piled all my crap in it, and drove as far north as I could get. You could cross the border then, no problem. Now you need a fucking passport!" He drank his coffee and made a face. Instant! "So why are the feds after you? Scott says you were chased out. Something about downing a helicopter!"

Freyja shrugged. "I decided it was time to go south, and it seems that some people find that interesting. I wasn't chased; I was followed."

She sipped her coffee. It needed more sugar, and she dumped four teaspoons in and then a good dollop of condensed milk. Leo winced.

"I don't know why, really. I wasn't hurting anyone, but they sure tried to hurt me! The copter shot at me! So I iced up the rotors to give them something else to think about."

That didn't make any sense to Leo, so all he did was nod. Sometimes it took him a while.

"Well, Scott says you're okay and no worries about being in Canada, but he's fussin' 'bout you. I guess they don' want any border trouble. C'n you talk to him? You can come to my place and use my ham radio."

Freyja thought for a minute and then shook her head no. She didn't want to go to this old man's place. Besides, she was moving on. Now that the old guy had her camp located, it was no longer safe. But this Mountie was a different matter. He'd keep after her unless he was convinced she was no threat to his people.

"I have a phone. He can call me. Why don't I give you my number and you give it to him?"

And so it was done. Leo left, happy with his scrambled eggs, bacon, and bad coffee and a number to give Scott. He had his little adventure, and it would give him something to think about for months. Years!

As soon as the man walked out of camp (gods, he stank!!) Freyja broke camp, and the pack formed up. They had miles to go before they could rest.

Bruce and Freyja

Bruce could hardly believe it. He had the lord's goddamn phone number! Leo had come through and told him the guy was a girl, and that she was okay. The first thing Bruce did was call his wife and ask her to put together a care package for the old guy. Told her to spend $500 on practical stuff, which she thought was a bit excessive, and he thought was not enough. He didn't tell her he'd have to have it dropped by bush air, and that would cost, too. Sometimes the love of your life doesn't need to know every little thing.

He called Lord Freyja.

Holy shit! She answered!

He explained who he was and that she wasn't in any trouble, but that as she got closer to settled areas, those wolves and how people reacted to lords *and* wolves might cause some friction. He was here to help.

Freyja stopped the sled and concentrated on the call. He could hear the wind whistling in the background and the occasional yip of the wolves.

"Thanks for the offer, but I have to be careful."

It was the comment about the wolves that kept her on the line. She knew that any day now there could be a good rain, and as the snow melted, her sled would become a liability. Once she abandoned it, the gear she couldn't carry would have to go on the wolves' backs, and that would cause its own problems. The more she could carry, the fewer times she'd have to stop and buy food. Unfortunately, she ate a lot.

"I need to think about the wolves. I've sent half back home so I don't have to feed them. Will I get in any trouble for shooting caribou for the wolves?"

Bruce paused. Yes, she *could* get in a lot of trouble, but would she really? No. No one was going to arrest a lord for shooting a caribou to feed another endangered species or for survival for herself. But his opinion wasn't the law.

"Canada has some pretty strict hunting laws, but, of course, the wolves don't follow them. As for yourself, if the wolves took down a deer and you put it out of its misery –" Bruce paused. "I would stick with deer if you can." The game she really could hunt with impunity, like rabbits, wouldn't feed a pack of wolves.

He didn't even want to get into licenses, tags, and all that.

"It's feeding the wolves that worries me." Freyja looked at her pack, and Bruce could hear the anxiety in her voice. "I know they're going to be a problem. The people – I can deal with them. Those guys who are following me, they're not going to be a problem."

"What guys are following you?" Bruce's voice was sharp.

"I don't know who they are. But they came up on snowmobiles. Chasing me. Said they were there to help, but I knew they were lying. You can just tell, can't you?" Freyja sighed. "At least they didn't shoot at me! I lost them at the Yukon."

"Listen, Lord Freyja, I think we can deal with feeding the wolves, but people chasing you, that's another thing. You didn't kill anyone when that Border Patrol chopper went down, but if people start shooting at you and you do whatever it is you do back, then that's when I get involved." Bruce rubbed his eyes. "Lord Freyja, if we can meet, just you and me, I'll arrange for a place for you to stay a night or two, and we'll figure this out. You can stay at my place with me and my wife if you want. No one will know, not even my boss."

There was silence on the phone, and for a minute, he thought he had lost her.

"Can I trust you? No one else will know? How do I know I'm not walking into a trap?"

"You can trust me."

Freyja squeezed her eyes shut. If it wasn't for the wolves…

But this Bruce Scott wasn't lying to her. He was telling his own truth.

"I'll call you back," and she hung up.

An hour later, he got a text.

"Where do we meet? I can be in Clinton Creek or Forty Mile tomorrow."

"Forty Mile."

"I'll text you."

Bruce

Nowadays, Forty Mile is a park on the Yukon. Once it had been a town for miners, and that lasted for about fifteen years. Before that, it had been a place the First Nations people used for harvesting.

For two thousand years.

Despite that long First Nations history, it was still called Forty Mile, probably because white folks couldn't wrap their tongues around Ch'ëdähdëk. Sometimes you just have to make allowances for other people's disabilities.

Today, it was a rendezvous point for Mountie Bruce and Lord Freyja and twenty-five lightly domesticated dire wolves.

Bruce was up well before dawn and left Miriam still in bed, snoring away. He had persuaded a friend to sell five dressed deer carcasses to him, and when he got there, he bought one more just to be on the safe side. He was feeding wolves after all. After loading the meat up in the back of his pick-up, he drove the hour from Dawson City to Forty Mile. Luckily, the park was still empty, and the archaeologists, tourists, and park volunteers weren't back yet for the spring cleanup. If anyone had been around, Bruce knew some back trails he could drive up and get a little privacy, but today he was able to wait for Lord Freyja in the visitor parking lot. Just to be on the safe side, he put a traffic cone in the middle of the road. That would stop anyone from barreling in.

So at eight in the morning, when it was just about to get light, he sat in his truck and waited. He could be there all day for all he knew, but Bruce was used to waiting, and he was a patient man. With a thermos of coffee, he was okay.

At two, just when he was waking up from a nap and thinking about having another pee, the phone rang. It was Lord Freyja. A tall figure bundled up from head to toe in a motley selection of old cold-weather gear, she was standing about ten feet away, looking in his window with her phone to her ear. Just as she opened her mouth to say something, a wolf jumped up against the car to look in, his huge head and gaping jaws filling up the window and scared the living shit out of Bruce. Through the passenger window, Bruce saw a sea of wolves surrounding the truck, excited and circling, and a couple jumped up against the pick-up to look at the meat in the back. The truck shuddered. They were already drooling.

Bruce waved, but didn't get out. He rolled his window down a bare inch.

"Lord Freyja? Pleased ta meetcha! Hey, I'd love to get out and shake hands, but I have six deer in the back for your pack, and I probably smell like deer meat. Is it safe?"

She nodded and grinned. At least he thought she smiled, but it was hard to tell with the hooded parka and the ski mask. She yelled something at the wolves, and they all backed off, whining and grumbling, then politely arranged themselves in a big circle, their tails thumping like really mean-looking dogs.

Bruce got out, and before he or the lord said or did anything, they fed the wolves. He opened the tailgate and jumped in and laboriously slid each deer to her; she tossed the eighty-pound carcasses around the circle like they were nothing. When all six were dispersed, she said something to the wolves, and in unison they attacked the meat like – well – wolves.

They stood there, sharing the last of his coffee, watching the wolves gorge, and chatted. He chatted; she listened. She didn't talk much. It was really quite normal, thought Bruce, other than the fact that he was talking with someone who could toss around eighty-pound dead weights like they were basketballs and crash helicopters with a look. No wonder the men chasing her didn't scare her. She scared *him*.

"So, are you going to take me up on the offer to spend the night with Miriam and me? Still stands. You can have a hot, home-cooked meal and a shower, and we can talk about how to keep the wolves fed on your journey."

Freyja looked around. No human had been to Forty Mile since winter; she could smell it. It was pretty deserted, but it was a good place, a place of resting, and the pack was now well-fed. They would play a bit and then sleep it off. They'd be set for days now.

"Thank you, Bruce. I'll take you up on your offer, and I hope Miriam doesn't mind. I could really use a bath. Do you think she'd mind if I threw some clothes in her washer?"

It only took a few minutes for Bruce and Freyja to haul the dogsled to the back of the museum building and for her to get a backpack together. She spoke to the wolves in that weird language, and she said later that she'd told them to mind their manners and not attack anything and that she would be back in two days. They were used to her going off for weeks at a time, so there were no problems with them missing her.

Now Bruce had a problem. He hadn't told Miriam he was bringing someone home for dinner and to spend the night. She loved company, so that part wasn't a hitch. The problem was that she loved guests so much she nagged him constantly about what they liked to eat, who they were, and all that, to the point of distraction. Bruce certainly couldn't tell her he was bringing home a lord, the magical woman she'd heard about on the news. That would blow her mind.

So he made an excuse to Lord Freyja that he had to take a pee and went behind the building and called Miriam to tell her he was bringing home a guest. She was a bit funny, distracted, but she said Fine, no problem, and that was good enough for Bruce. He hung up fast before she could ask any questions.

It was about four when they pulled out of the Forty Mile parking lot for the hour-plus drive back to Dawson's Creek. All Freyja brought was a backpack and her rifle. Good Mountie that he was, Bruce made sure it was unloaded before he put it in the gun rack. The thing was practically a museum piece but perfectly maintained, and he wished he had some time to look it over. Bruce asked her to put her seatbelt on, and then he had to show her how to do it.

Freyja was apologetic. "I've never been in a new car before. The last time I was in a car, there were no seatbelts."

"This pick-up isn't exactly new, but all the cars since the '80s have had seatbelts! That must have been an old car!"

Freyja thought for a minute. "It was back in '53. I was taking my dad's body back to the cabin, and the undertaker drove me."

Bruce didn't know what to say to that. Then his mind started doing math. If she were around in '53… "It must have been tough losing your dad when you were a kid."

"Oh, it's tough any time, isn't it? I was forty-three, but y'know. It's your dad."

Bruce couldn't help himself. "You were born in 1910?"

Again, he didn't know how, but he knew she was smiling. "Yeah, I'm an old codger. Workin' on my second century now."

"Shit!" And he was silent for a bit. "Well, I've just turned sixty-four, and I hope I have twenty or thirty more years to go. I understand lords live forever. Shit. That's a long time."

"I didn't know what a lord was until this week. I didn't have a phone or the internet, but since I got one, I've been reading the websites, and I seem to check all the boxes. There's a lot of weird stuff out there about'm. I don't know what's true or not, but that Lord Cadence of the Elf Nation said she will live forever, so that's supposed to be true. Ten days ago, I thought I was just a freak of nature. A one-off."

"No, you're not a one-off. I've never met a lord, but they do exist. I've never met an Italian, either, but everyone says they're real."

Freyja chuckled and then looked out the window. Bruce drove on.

When they pulled up to his neat wood-frame house, all the lights were off, which was unusual. Normally, Miriam would have the kitchen porch light on, and he was sure she'd be waiting for him and their guest. But no, the place looked buttoned up tight.

Damn, she even had the door locked! Fumbling with the key in the lock, he turned to Freyja.

"I really expected Miriam to be home." And he swung open the door.

"SURPRISE!!!"

The lights snapped on, scaring the shit out of Bruce and Freyja. She dove off the porch. Inside Bruce's family were screaming and laughing. A big banner was over the kitchen table announcing to the world, "Happy Birthday, Bruce!" And it was all flashing lights, balloons, and party hats.

"GODDAMN!! WHAT'S GOING ON HERE?"

Miriam was laughing so hard she couldn't talk. In a panic, not sure what was going on, Bruce spun around to look for Freyja, but she had vanished.

"Damn, Miriam, you scared the shit out of Freyja! She's run off!"

He leaned over the porch railing and saw her crouching behind the truck. "FREYJA! It's okay! My damn fool family –"

Miriam burst out of the door, and Bruce had never seen her run so fast. For an old lady of excellent poundage, she could really move.

"Freyja! I'm *so* sorry! We didn't mean to scare you!" She grabbed the derelict her husband dragged home and was all soothing apologies. "It's Bruce's birthday! He didn't know we were going to have a surprise party!"

Miriam looked back at Bruce, and her face fell; he had *that* look. The "I'm going to blow up any minute" look. He almost never lost his temper, but he was losing it now.

The kids and grandkids were now at the door, and no one was laughing anymore. Something was bad wrong.

Through gritted teeth, Bruce's voice was low and dangerous. "I promised Freyja on my honour that no one would be here but you and me, Miriam. She trusted me. Now, look, half the tribe is here."

"I'm so sorry –" She turned to Freyja. "I didn't know he promised you that. When Bruce told me he was bringing a guest, I didn't think – I thought a party was okay. It would be fun."

Freyja looked at Miriam, the slowly incandescent Bruce, and the stricken faces of the gathered family. She shuffled her feet. What's done was done, and he didn't know; she could hear that in his voice. *Anyone* could hear that in his voice.

"I'm okay. I'll stay on two conditions. Bruce promised me that no one would know I was here. Can all of you keep me a secret? It's important."

"Sure!" "Lips sealed" Everyone nodded. Jesus, Dad must have brought home a crime victim or a battered woman or something! Maybe she was in the witness protection program.

"The second is that I have a slice of cake. Is there going to be cake?"

Miriam hugged her. "There's always cake, sweetheart." And with that, they went back into the house, and Bruce celebrated his sixty-fourth birthday with his family and one very strange guest.

Standing in the crowded kitchen, Freyja asked Miriam if she could take a bath. "I haven't washed for a week, and I'm sure I smell like an old dog." The rest of the family had already started their party and pretty much ignored Freyja, which was perfect. Freyja was escorted upstairs by all the kids and a still apologetic Miriam and was shown a bedroom and the bathroom.

"Miriam, can I talk to you for a minute? Privately?" The kids were shooed downstairs, and Freyja started to undress. "I'm going to need your help."

The parka came off, the boots were removed, and Miriam saw a woman's body dressed in an old grey sweater and ski pants.

Then Freyja took the ski mask off.

The two women looked at each other.

"Do you think your family can handle me, Miriam? Or should I stay up here? You can tell them I'm very tired and just want to go to bed."

Miriam gulped. No wonder Bruce was upset. Then she pulled herself up. She was Canadian First Nations, dammit, not some darn holy roller American! Freyja was a guest in her house and was certainly not going to be confined to the spare bedroom.

"I think my family will be very happy to meet you just as you are. You clean yourself up, dear, and come down when you're ready. Do you need anything? Shampoo?"

Freyja's eyes glowed bright green. Then she grinned because if she didn't smile, she'd have to cry.

"Shampoo is great. Some extra-large Q-tips if you have'm."

It took a second, then Miriam burst out laughing. How could she not?

Back down in the kitchen, Bruce was still pissed, and the kids were doing their best to jolly him up. "Kids," of course, is a relative term. Asin, the oldest son, was forty, and his wife Janet and their own kids, Anjij (12) and Bruce, Jr. (8), weren't exactly babies. Then there was Leah and Bill and their three kids. And lastly, little Minwaadizi, who everyone called Mimi, who was so pregnant she was about to pop, and her husband, Rich and their two toddlers. So fifteen people in the Scott clan filled up the kitchen and spilt into the living room where the kids ran riot.

Miriam walked down the stairs, and immediately the room went quiet. Her face (and, bless her, Miriam could never hide her feelings) was a picture. She held up her hand for silence and cocked her head, listening. Then everyone heard the toilet flush, and a second later, the old pipes creaked, and the shower started up. Then she nodded. "Your father has something to say."

Bruce scowled, "I don't know what I can say, Miri. I prom –"

"She took that ski mask off, Bruce. I saw her. She'll come down without the mask."

Janet put her hand over her mouth. Oh god, the woman was beat up – or deformed – Even the kids went quiet at that point, sensing something was wrong, and the babies ran over to Mimi and Rich.

Bruce nodded, looked at his hands, and then turned to his family. "I suppose all of you have read in the papers about that lord who escaped from Alaska –" And the room erupted.

A half hour later, when Freyja stood at the top of the stairs and looked down, she saw five sets of eyes staring back up. All the kids were sitting cross-legged at the base of the stairs, waiting, eyes glued to the upstairs landing. When she appeared, Little Bruce screamed back to the kitchen, "She's here!" and jumped up and down like someone had just scored a winning goal.

Then all the kids were jumping and clapping, and Freyja descended, laughing.

"What an entrance! You make me feel like Cinderella in her ball gown!" And she got to the last step and sat down on the stairs. "So tell me your names, and you each get one question." The adults stood at the kitchen door and stared, open-mouthed.

If they had secretly wondered if Dad was going crazy with this lord thing, there were no doubts now. This woman was a lord, complete with white hair and huge, pointed ears like a lynx. She was beautiful, a very tall Viking with laughing, tip-tilted green eyes, and cheekbones that could cut glass. But beautiful or not, she was certainly not human-looking, not with those ears and the subtle green glow of her skin that teased a human's eyeballs. Her eyes glowed bright, just like the drawings on the internet.

The kids told her their names, and a few asked questions; the rest had attacks of shyness.

"Can you wiggle your ears?" Yes, and she did, and they giggled and squealed.

"Can you do magic?" Yes, and a pillow from the sofa flew over their heads, and she grabbed it like a football, eliciting gasps from everyone.

"Can you give wishes?" No, and she shook her head sadly. No wishes. Freyja wasn't a fairy godmother, unfortunately.

"Does doing magic hurt?" No, but it sure tires me out.

And that was the end of the questions and the beginning of a lovely and unforgettable family party.

By the end of the evening, Freyja had all the cake even she could eat, and the Scott clan was fully invested in keeping her secret just as she had hoped.

Terry

Terry and the posse had been in Dawson City for three expensive days, and it didn't help that the guys who weenied out and went to Eagle drove up, whining that they couldn't book transport out to Anchorage because all the press people had sucked up the bush planes and copters. Now the chickenshit bastards wanted back in.

When the news came out that a lord trying to escape to Canada had downed a US Border Patrol copter, it didn't take long for the press, along with friggin' elf groupies, to snap up the few hotel rooms that were open during off-season. That jacked up the prices for everyone, so to keep expenses down, Terry booked an absolute rathole at the very edge of town. The fekkin place even charged for wi-fi. Who does that anymore?

No one would talk to them about the lord except for people who didn't know crap. When a girl at one of the tourist traps told him that someone had seen the lord flying over the town on her broom, he gave up. Terry didn't know if the slag was sincere or pulling his leg, but he had suspicions his leg was getting longer by the minute. Shit, he hated women, especially smart-ass women. They were useless except for one thing, and he wasn't getting any of *that* lately either.

He was chasing a smart-ass woman who was laughing at him.

Killing time in the freezing parking lot with an early morning vape, Terry waited for the guys to form up so they could go to breakfast together. Then they'd poke around town and listen to rumours and try to get a heading on the lord so they could intercept her. They were ready to grab her. Rumours said she was going south, and Dawson was the logical route for the roads south, although no one knew what was meant by "south". Southern Canada? Mexico? South America? Antarctica? It could be anywhere, but Terry guessed she was going to Ottawa to the EN embassy there. She obviously didn't have any way of contacting them. Coming from the backwoods, the stupid bitch probably didn't have a phone, and she might not know how to use the internet. Women were ignorant that way. If she did, she'd already be in the UK.

Maybe she had another lord to pick up, a friend. Maybe she was looking for elves. Who knows?

Looking up, he scanned the parking lot to see where the hell those lazy sods –

There was a flash of white in the treeline. A second later, emerging from the trees behind the hotel, a white wolf trotted across the parking lot, as bold as you please, and headed down the road into town.

SHIT!

Terry jumped in his truck and slowly, cautiously, stalked the wolf down the street, making sure he always kept it in sight but not getting too close. Being a wolf, it didn't stick to the road but cut across lawns and parking lots, taking the most direct route to wherever the big beast wanted to go. Terry almost lost it twice, but then, a block or two ahead, he'd see it. It was going home. And home was where the lord was.

The Recovery Team

Wendell walked into Bontons for breakfast and waved to the girl behind the counter, who shyly waved back. He had been in for breakfast twice now, but they didn't know he was Elf Nation, and when he walked over to the EN table, they looked at each other and raised an eyebrow. Another one!

Bonton's had a reservation system even for breakfast, but good gods, it was worth the trouble. Someone in Lowestoft had put in a standing breakfast table reservation for RumLot and didn't hide who they were. Sometimes it was better just to go public and see what shit stirred up, and Jameson thought now was a good time to get the town behind them.

If Lord Fraya showed up, they needed to find out fast, and now the Dawson City grapevine was on full activation. Unknown to the grapevine, the elves in Ukraine were listening to every local phone communication that tripped the AI filters. A lord was somewhere in the area, and the Elf Nation was coming in force to find him or her. If she were here, a townie would know it. If a townie talked on a phone, the EN would find out.

The Elf Nation reservations meant that Bronton's was on full staff today because no one wanted to stay home if something exciting was happening. It also meant that the press, who were starting to dribble into Dawson City, were hanging around, too, and despite the March tourist doldrums, the hotels and restaurants were packed.

Jameson was sitting at the table, a half-eaten breakfast pushed to the side, and flipping through his tablet, but he stopped long enough to jump up and give Wendell a bro-shake and a grin. Right behind him, Maksym and Darnya were seated at another table, working on their own breakfast; they were still undercover. Maksym looked tired. Darnya just looked happy.

Wendell had barely put his bum on the seat when the waitress trotted over to get his order. Then Jameson looked over Wendell's shoulder and said, "Miss, just hold up a minute. We have two more coming." Then he winked at Wendell. "Showtime!"

Berke and Judy walked in, waved to Jameson, and made a big, huge, noisy greeting fuss, getting everyone's attention. No one could miss Judy even if they wanted to. She was in full snow-bunny mode in a bright pink ski outfit. She looked exactly like a Chinese Barbie doll.

The restaurant employees knew who had reserved the table, but Jameson really wanted to stir up attention and get some good mindwaves for Judy to read. The couple sat down and took off their ski hats, and their ears popped up like antennas.

OMG, *lords* were in Bronton's! Two of them! Real ones!

Berke was starving, and while Judy wasn't a bacon and eggs girl, she did like the pastries. They ordered every item on the breakfast menu. Wendell hoped they'd left him some food because the waitress was so excited talking to the lords that she forgot to take Wendell's order.

The guys talked, and Judy looked like she was paying attention, but she was scanning for information. Then she hit pay dirt. A cook received a text just as Judy was scanning.

A white wolf is running down the street! Weird! I brought the cat in.

While the guys talked about sports crap, and Berke pretended he knew what they were talking about, she texted the message to their WhatsApp group. Maksym and Darnya got up to leave, and Judy kept scanning.

Terry

He pulled off the road about a block away, slumped way down in his seat, and messaged the posse. He'd found her. The house was off the road a bit, a nice two-story, wood-frame house painted yellow. It had a big front porch and a picket fence that was pretty, but didn't keep out crap because it just went along the front and didn't attach to anything on the side. On the porch, two white wolves lolled and dozed, waiting for the lord to come out.

He looked at the wolves; they would be a problem, and he thought about how to get them out of the way without alerting the lord. If she felt in danger, she'd do some magic shit on them, so surprise was the only way they'd get her. The whole sweet-talking thing was out the window because that took time. With the town heating up with press, groupies, and probably the fucking RumLot pricks, time was one thing they didn't have. This was going to be a full-on mugging.

She'd get darted, and once she passed out, they'd throw her in the back of the pickup and bug out. Anyone who got in the way, whether it was a wolf or a human, would just have to take the consequences.

Freyja and the Scotts

She loved to cook, and she loved to watch hungry people eat, but Miriam had never seen anyone eat like Freyja. Bruce had his two eggs, ham, and toast, and that was enough. Freyja had an entire carton of eggs fried over easy, a full pack of bacon, a huge bowl of oatmeal, and even then, she looked longingly at Miriam's

Danish. As he always did, Asin had dropped off Anjij and Bruce, Jr. on his way to work, and they would walk to school after breakfast.

Bruce debated just keeping the kids in the house for the day until Freyja was long gone, but they promised on their honour not to breathe a word to anyone, not even their best friends. Freyja seemed happy to see them, and she talked more freely to the kids than to the adults, so Bruce let it go. He'd learn more listening to the kids ask questions, and boy, now that they weren't shy around her any more, they asked a lot.

"Why is your hair white?" Because I'm very old.

"Can I touch your ears?" No, because it tickles and feels funny.

"Can you fly? On the internet, people have seen lords fly." No, I think lords must have different things they can do that they're good at, like some people can play basketball and others can draw.

"What are you good at?" I can hear really well, I can sing really loud, and I can make things hot or cold.

"Why don't you stay here and live with us? We'll take care of you!" At this, Freyja smiled. "I don't need anyone to take care of me; I'm fine. I've lived alone and taken care of myself for over eighty years! But now I have to take care of other people, and that's in the south."

And she wouldn't talk any more about that.

Instead, she asked her own questions, asking about the kids' school, what they did for fun, and other distracting topics. When she asked him about his school, Bruce, Jr ran to the living room to dig out a school newspaper from his backpack and immediately ran back.

"There's some big white dogs on the front porch! Two of them!"

Freyja sighed. "They've followed me. They're my wolves. I'll go tell them to go back to Forty Mile."

"What's their names? Can we pet them?"

"I don't know which ones are out there, so I can't tell you the names. And no, don't pet them until I'm out there. They won't hurt you, but they're not used to kids and being petted. But you can take them a bowl of water if you want. They'd probably like that."

Bruce, Freyja, and Miriam sat at the table and chatted over another cup of coffee while the kids ran to get a basin and fill it with water to give to the wolves.

A piercing scream.

Bruce had never seen anyone move so fast. She was a blur, and Freyja burst through the house and out the front door.

When he got there, she was in the front yard, and a man was there, holding Bruce Jr by the neck and with a rifle pointed at Freyja.

"Well, you *are* here! Now, if you cooperate, I'll let the ki —" And Anjij ran up and kicked him in the leg, her furious little face a mask of red rage.

"YOU LET HIM GO! LEAVE FREYJA ALONE!!" Another man leapt over and grabbed her, yanking her back, and she kicked and screamed. Bruce had never felt so helpless in his life. He scanned the yard. Six armed men were circling the lord and the kids.

"Now we have two kids. Like I said, if you –" And he froze.

Freyja turned and looked at the man holding Anjij. He froze. Anjij kicked him, and his leg broke in two, and he toppled to the hard ground, shattering like a porcelain figurine.

"BOSS!!" One of the men shouted at the centre hostage taker holding Bruce, Jr. The boy wrenched out of his grip, breaking the kidnapper's arm off, and he toppled over, too, shattering into a million pieces.

Freyja spun and looked at the guy who was yelling. By now her entire body was covered in a green glow, and he froze– and one of the remaining men shot her.

She twisted, and Bruce saw her eyes roll up. Then she said something in the strange language and fell to her knees and passed out.

The wolves howled with all the fury of the Banshee. Bruce had never heard anything like it, but they didn't go to Freyja. They leapt over the porch railing and went for the three remaining men who shot at them wildly and scrambled back to their cars.

From between the parked cars and out of the brush emerged the rest of the wolves who had been hiding and resting, awaiting Freyja's call. Chasing the doomed men down like deer, the hellhounds grabbed one and savaged him. Running for their lives, the other two rocketed down the street, the wolves chasing behind. It didn't take them long to catch up and even less time to rip their prey to shreds. There was no sound; the men didn't have time to scream, and the wolves were too intent on the kill to yip or howl.

There was no point in running after the men; they were finished. Bruce looked back, and Miriam was clutching both kids to her chest, hiding their eyes, so he ran to Freyja, who was on the ground, her body glowing and traces of something that looked like St. Elmo's fire flickering over her body.

Miriam screamed to Bruce, "Don't touch her! She's hot!" And like the sensible woman she was, she yelled at Anjij to call 911, told Bruce Jr to get inside the house, and she dashed in to get her oven mitts.

Bruce didn't know what to do. But Miriam did.

The Lords

Judy was finishing up the last croissant when she froze.

"She's been shot!"

"SHIT!" They all leapt up and exploded out the door to their cars, leaving the rest of the diners stunned by the sudden scramble at the EN table.

"Where!?" Wendell threw himself in the driver's seat, and everyone piled in.

Judy frowned, and she began to glow. In the meantime, Jameson called the intel elves to see what they knew.

"Emergency Ambulance called –" And they had an address; it was only a few blocks away, but then Dawson was a small town.

Judy was listening to the entire town now, and Berke saw the intense concentration it took to filter through all the noise.

"They don't know what to do. A kid is screaming on the phone to 911. I can hear her. She's flaming."

Jameson yelled into his phone to get Sarah and Adem ready, and then they screamed past a man lying in the middle of the road. Or parts of a man. The wolves were very thorough.

Wendell swerved around the body and drifted through a 90-degree turn, and they flew past another body. Then, in front of them, a small group huddled around a glowing, green mound.

Berke and Judy ran to the group while Wendell and Jameson secured the site. Darnya and Maksym squealed up and secured the other end of the road. They'd have a crowd gathering in any minute. In the distance, they could hear sirens.

Bruce looked up from where he was kneeling by Freyja, and by God, there was another lord! Two of them!

"Don't touch her! She's too hot!"

"Yeah, we know. We have oven mitts, and my wife took out the dart, but we don't know what to do. She's having some sort of fit." Bruce stood up and stepped back. He was just in the way now.

Berke nodded. "We'll take care of her.

Judy ran off to stand in the middle of the road, her little body glowing now almost as much as Freyja's.

There was a tremendous boom, making Miriam scream and everyone jump; two of their windows cracked from the concussion.

Bruce looked at the little lord, and standing next to her were two *more* lords in what seemed to be nightclothes. A hugely pregnant woman who was glowing green and a short man. He did something because he flashed blue, and at the edges of Bruce's eyes, he could see ripples in the air.

Elves! Two appeared in a shower of sparks, and then the man and the pregnant woman were gone.

Two seconds later, all hell broke loose – if having masses of elves port in was hell. Flashes of gold, fearsome, grim elves everywhere; then more flashes and snaps, and a whole platoon of soldiers – human ones – armed to the teeth and in RumLot battle dress ported in with a guy in chinos and a white shirt yelling at them to secure the area. Bruce watched them just appear out of nowhere, running in with organised chaos, commanders yelling and pointing, and everyone seemed to know what they were doing.

Bruce told his boss later that it all just took minutes. One minute, he was bent over the flashing lord, and the next, his entire house was protected by an armed perimeter of soldiers. Every time he looked over at the road, it seemed more soldiers were pouring in.

Lord Althea and the EMT crew both ran up to Freyja at the same time, and it was all Bruce could do to hold the humans back so they didn't touch the still-flaming lord.

Freyja was flashing and sputtering, having some sort of epileptic fit. She'd calm down for a second, and then her back would arch, she'd scream in pain, and she would spasm into another attack. Althea, who was also in a pyjama top and jeans and bare feet, grabbed Freyja's head and held it down, and she began to glow.

"She's having some sort of allergic reaction to the dart."

"We have EpiPens." The EMT was hesitant. She had no clue what to do, but Althea looked up and frowned, thinking.

"Bring it here. All you have." The EMT ran back to the ambulance and brought back five pens; Althea slammed one into the lord. "I don't know if this will work. Lords don't have allergic reactions, but it's all I can think of for now."

"Tuân does," Berke murmured, and Althea looked up. "Yes, he does, doesn't he! Mould allergy."

Almost immediately, Freyja settled a little, and Althea gave her another injection.

"Okay, let's move her. Berke, can you pick her up?" And with that, Berke carried Freyja to the elves, and Miriam and Bruce watched them disappear. A minute later, all of the lords were gone.

Two minutes later, some of the human soldiers started a managed retreat towards the elves and winked out. And as fast as they'd come, elves and soldiers were gone.

Miriam looked at Bruce and let out a great shuddering sigh. "Well, that's a morning to remember. I guess I'll go take care of the kids. I don't know whether or not to send them to school. I need to call Asin. I guess you need to talk to those guys."

Bruce looked at her. "What guys?"

"All of those really angry police and Mounties over there being held back by the EN people."

He looked, and outside of the perimeter, which the Rumlot people had somehow hardened with metal barriers as well as soldiers, was a huge crowd. In the crowd, he recognised some faces.

Bruce sighed. A mountain of paperwork. He could see it now.

He went over to talk to them.

Freyja

Freyja opened her eyes and saw a ceiling. She wasn't used to waking up and seeing a ceiling, and its bland white expanse was a bit confusing until her eyes focused and her brain caught up.

She heard a tiny sound and turned her head. An elf.

The little woman looked like an elf, at least like the ones Freyja saw on her phone when she looked at the elf sites. This was a rather matronly-looking woman in a striped dress and a starched white nurse's apron, just like the nurses Freyja used to see when she was a kid. In between her huge ears balanced a little starched white nurse's cap with a gold star embroidered on it.

"Good morning, Lord Freyja! I see you're awake! Can you eat a bit? You'll feel much better if you do."

"You're an elf."

"Yes, I am. And you are not. We're both in your room in Aelfeham House, the lords' home in the Elf Nation. Now, can you sit up by yourself, dear? Should I call for help?"

Freyja sat up. The nurse elf, whose name was Sister Marjorie, was soon accompanied by three others, and they all chattered in the same language Freyja used to talk to the animals. Of course, the animals used very, very simple words, and these elves did not, so it took a while for Freyja to understand them, but if she didn't try too hard to parse what they were saying, it got easier.

They brought her bowls of a very good soup, bread, and a big plate of fruit and cheese, and she ate it all. With the last bite, she started to nod off, but then she jerked awake and said, "Marjorie! Is everyone at the Scotts okay? Can you tell me if the kids are okay?"

"Yes, dear, everything is fine. Everyone in the Scott clan is happy and proud that they helped you. They wish you well, and you can call them up later if you want, but they're asleep now. Time zones and all that."

Freyja nodded and lay back on the pillow and slept.

Jo and Freyja

"You can't stay here, you know." Jo looked sad, but otherwise seemed in perfect health, just like he did when he walked out of the forest in Freyja's last dream. "Sometimes you just can't stay where you want to because you have responsibilities somewhere else."

Freyja looked at the ceiling. She didn't even know where "here" was or why she'd want to stay, but she was feeling better, and she supposed she'd be getting out of bed pretty soon. Maybe today.

She looked back at Jo, who was sitting in an armchair at the side of the bed. Normally, Sister Majorie sat there, but the elves didn't watch her all the time. They just came in when they brought in food or helped her wash or go to the bathroom. They all seemed very busy.

"I'll have to find a way to get back to Dawson and pick up my stuff."

"You just tell one of the elves, and they'll take you back to the Scotts. They'll do whatever you say if it's sensible and you're kind to them. That's what elves do. Elves take care of lords; lords take care of elves."

Freyja looked at the ceiling. "You didn't want to stay with me, did you. You wanted to go with Lily."

Jo looked at his hands. He didn't say yes, but he didn't say no either.

"You were my responsibility. I took you, so I had to take care of you. Lily loved me, and I loved Lily. But you couldn't live in town, and she wouldn't live in the backwoods. *Wouldn't* and *couldn't*. Two powerful words."

"I'm sorry, Jo. I really am. You were a great dad – the best. And I'm a freak of nature who kept you –"

"*No, you are not!* Don't ever say that. Don't even think that." Jo was angry now, but he always got angry when Freyja said something about not wanting to be whatever it was she was. Jo accepted what he was, and he always expected her to accept what she was.

God or gods or whoever decided such things had made them both the way they were, and it was their job to take joy in their gifts and work around the shortcomings. Fighting who they were was childish at best and evil at worst.

"You've been given great gifts. But better than your gifts, you have a good soul. I'm so proud of you, and I don't regret a minute, not a minute, of raising you. Yeah, it would have been nice to have a normal life with Lily. But she and I managed, and when you got old enough, we could be together more often. We had good times."

He calmed down again and looked at her, his hazel eyes crinkling as he smiled, the way they always did. "A normal life. I don't think either of us even knows what normal is. But I had a very good life, all told. But it's time to give back, to make a fair trade for the gifts. To balance the books. It's all about Balance, Freyja."

He cocked his head. "Would you give back your gifts, Freyja, if that was the way to balance the books? Would you give back forever life, your magic, the wonders you can do and see, to be a normal human?"

Freyja looked at the ceiling again and smiled to herself. "No." She looked over at Jo. "No, I like being a freak of nature. It can be a lot of fun sometimes."

He nodded; he knew as much. Jo had seen the joy she took in her magic.

"Okay, Jo, point taken then. I owe – so how do I pay back the debt? How do I balance the books?"

"You go back to Canada to take care of your people, you protect the elves there, you wake more up. And while you're doing all that, you have a happy life. That will balance the books."

Freyja sat up and looked at her dad. He was fading.

"Wake up elves! What do you mean? How can I do that?"

He faded, and all that was left were his words hanging in the air.

"You'll figure it out."

Freyja, Chi, and Gary

The Breakfast Room was almost empty when Freyja walked in. She stood in the door, leaning on a cane, and took it in. A happy, large, sunny butter-yellow room with a buffet along one side, two double doors leading in on the other, an elaborately carved stone fireplace with a low table and cosy armchairs in front, big windows overlooking a lawn, and the rest of the room was filled with a long, long table and chairs.

Sitting at the table were two lords. Men in red uniforms. They were arguing over something, but in a friendly way. Something about food rations and how much they needed to allocate to get the most points.

She walked in alone.

When Freyja woke up that morning, she had her usual breakfast, and when she said something about getting up and about, Sister Majorie was quite adamant. No, Lord Freyja needed at least one more day of bed rest, and tomorrow a physiotherapist would come by and help her walk around.

So after Sister Majorie and whoever was helping her got Freyja cleaned, toileted, fed, and otherwise fussed over, and they bustled away, Freyja simply got out of bed, grabbed the cane that was left so she could get to the toilet, and hobbled to the wardrobe to look for clothes.

All the wardrobe held was a uniform, a pair of jeans, a t-shirt, and underwear. A very fancy, to Freyja's eyes, red wool uniform with lots of buttons and beautiful embroidery on the sleeves and down the seams of the slacks. She didn't want to wear that rig at all. It felt like a commitment somehow, and besides, it looked hot and itchy. She grabbed some panties, ignored the bra (she didn't wear those, anyway, no matter what Lily used to say), and put on the jeans and t-shirt. That was enough, and properly dressed, she opened the door to the hall and went exploring.

And that's how she ended up at the Breakfast Room's door. She had wandered down long, long halls of closed doors, and somehow she knew that the rooms were private. Other people lived behind those doors, and Freyja didn't test them. She found stairs and then smelled food and followed her nose to big double doors that stood wide open.

Another step in, and the men, both lords, looked up. One, a little guy, grinned at her and waved. The other man, much taller, with bushy red hair, looked at her, and his mouth made a little O, obviously surprised to see Freyja.

The little guy jumped up. "The new lord! Hello and welcome! My name is Lord Chi, and I'm one of the Old Farts. I'll explain that later, but I don't fart often, so don't worry. This is Lord Gary, and he's not old, just useless. I heard your name is Lord Freyja!"

Lord Gary looked at her and awkwardly waved. Oh stars, she was the most beautiful woman he had ever seen, even prettier than Vrt, probably because she was unbonded. He could smell her status even though she was very clean, and her special scent was just a faint whisper of perfume. She was a full lord, with magnificent, *sexy* ears, and a thick, bright-white braid that went down to her waist. And there was real power behind the vivid green eyes; they could both feel it.

Freyja smiled shyly and nodded. "Pleased ta meetcha both." They were the first lords she had ever met. Two men like her. Freyja didn't know what to say, so she looked at the buffet, which to Chi's eyes looked pretty well cleared out. But to Freyja, it was abundantly full, over the top even.

"Would anyone miss it if I took a bread roll?"

Chi laughed, "No, the elves would be happy for you to have a snack. Take what you want, that's why it's here. Do you need any help?"

Freyja smiled and shook her head. Chi and Gary watched as she picked up a plate. Gary wondered how she was going to manage the plate and the cane and was just about to offer to help her when she let go of the plate, and it simply levitated next to her.

The woman's eyes didn't even glow. The plate followed her down the buffet, and rolls, meat, deviled eggs, all sorts of food just flew up and landed neatly on the plate. It was a virtuoso performance in a place where Elementals lived and ate, and magic was an everyday occurrence. Chi had never seen anyone do that. Oh, most of the white-haired lords could levitate a salt shaker down the table or make a plate of cake float towards them if they were too lazy to get up and fetch it themselves. But he'd never seen anyone make multiple bits of food dance around at the same time while levitating a plate, *and* off to the side, making a cup of tea. And her eyes didn't even flicker.

She sat down at the table, the heaped plate and tea floated to where they belonged, and she smiled at the men.

"Lord Chi, Lord Gary. Do you have a minute? I'd like a little company, and if you would tell me about this place, I would appreciate it."

That was all the invite they needed. Freyja ate and listened, and the two men talked until they were hoarse.

After having her fill of Chi's jokes, half of which she didn't get, and when Gary started to talk about online gaming, Freyja suddenly said she was really, really tired and gave her goodbyes and went back to her room, where she took a nice nap until lunch.

At noon, the elf didn't bring in her lunch but came in and announced that since Lord Freyja was feeling better, she could eat in the Breakfast Room with the other lords. After lunch, if she was still awake, an elf would be in to talk about "important things".

"What's important?"

"Sex," the elf said and wouldn't say anything else. That was for the expert to discuss.

Anja

Anja stood outside the lord's door and read the note. It was hard to read. Her English wasn't great, and Lord Jack had scrawled the note very quickly. He was usually much better at this.

"Anja, Lord Alizah is dropping an egg. No cleaning or visits of any kind. Please come back in five days. – Lord Jack"

Well, if the lord was giving her some time off, she wasn't going to quibble. "Doing" for the lords was a wonderful job, and the last thing Anja wanted was to jeopardise it. Cleaning the lords' penthouse was easy; they were tidy people, and the lords were lovely. All she had to do was clean for a couple of hours every day and keep her mouth shut. If they hadn't insisted on living up high, the elves would be doing the work, and Anja would still be stocking shelves at Tesco.

And, thank you, Mother Mary; she was paid silly money for her discretion. Money that kept her daughter in Leeds and her son in Poland, comfortable with good allowances.

Dropping an egg? Poor Lord Alizah must be on her period, something that had never happened before. Anja shrugged and returned to the ground floor and left to visit her daughter and grandkids in Leeds. She didn't say anything to the rotation of Warrior Elves who guarded the building's entrance. Lord Alizah's monthly curse wasn't their business, and Anja was paid to keep secrets.

Caddy and Kyrylo

Normally, new lords were Caddy's business, but Jameson's report piqued Kyrylo's interest. While Freyja was having an overwhelming lunch in a jam-packed Breakfast Room, he and Caddy were having a quiet cup of tea and a private discussion about the new lord in their kitchen. Ivana and Rurik were playing cars under the kitchen table, so that made a bit of noise, but it was easily ignored.

Kyrylo asked Caddy what she thought about this new woman.

"Jameson writes that he had a long talk with the Mountie, Bruce Scott. He was pretty forthcoming; he and his family are squarely on Team Freyja, and they want her to be safe. The elves think she's an Elemental, and from what she demonstrated in Dawson and Alaska, she's pretty strong."

"Unlike Berke, she's not shy about showing it either." Caddy frowned and scrolled through the transcripts. "It's strange. On the one hand, she wants to be kept a secret, but then she tells the Scott kids she *can hear really well, I can sing really loud, I can make things hot or cold.* She didn't care that the Scott family saw her ears. She confronted the bounty hunters twice when they were chasing her. She didn't have to do that. I'm sure she could have thrown them off her trail or sent the wolves after them. But she didn't want to kill them, and it was easier to make that ice cage and bridge. She just wasn't worried."

"Berke spent seven hundred years keeping an entire clan of lords secret, and he did a lot of roaming with humankind. He trained himself to be discreet in a dangerous world. Freyja, it seems, was kept in a safe place, not one hundred per cent isolated, but…" He looked at Ivana and Rurik. "Like these two. Curated experiences, it seems. She has no fear of people she has learned are okay, but was taught to be cautious. She knows she's powerful, but I really doubt she knows all the risks in the human and orc world. She wasn't careful enough when she ran out to save the kids. She's not warrior-trained. Berke was."

He looked at Ivana and Rurik again. "I doubt that she even knows what an orc is."

"She didn't put on the red coat this morning. The elves say she was told by the nurse to stay in her room one more day, and she just went a-roaming anyway and ended up listening for two hours to Chi and Gary."

"Oh *shit!*"

"Shh!" She pointed under the table. "Yeah. No kidding. Jack and Alizah seem to be off the grid, so no one has talked to her since she woke up." Caddy fretted. "I really need to get a lord manager for Aelfeham House; we're buckling under the strain of new lords."

"Well, we'll have to get someone to talk to her, become a friend, someone she'll respect. Berke and Judy?"

"I'm thinking about Adem. She says she sings. Why is singing an ability on par *with making things hot or cold*? He plays an instrument and is an Elemental." Caddy nodded. " Let's get them together for a little sing-along; maybe we can go drop in on them."

Kyrylo nodded. "Sounds like a good start. I just want to make sure we have all of our Elementals ready when the shit hits the fan. We need to know what she *can* do and what she's *willing* to do."

"Well, she's not 'ours' yet, but I hope we can get that changed. We haven't lost one yet."

"OH SHIT!" Rurick yelled from under the table, and there were sounds of cars crashing. Then Ivana started yelling, "Oh Shit! Oh SHIT! Oh Shit! Oh SHIT, Oh, oh, oh, oh Shit..." in the *Jingle* Bells tune.

Caddy looked at Kyrylo and made a face, trying not to crack up.

"You and your potty mouth!"

Freyja

After her nap, it was time to eat again, but before she could go to lunch, the elves insisted that Freyja take another shower, which was now getting excessive. Did they think she got stinky that fast? But the elf stood at the door and had a "don't give me any grief" expression on her face, and Freyja just didn't think another wash was worth the effort to fight over, so she showered. Then, with fresh clothes from the skin out, she was allowed to go back to the Breakfast Room.

The place was packed, and for the first time, Freyja understood – really understood – that she was not a freak of nature, not a one-off biological sport, but part of a species, a tribe. Here, she wasn't special; she was normal.

There were no humans in the room, just elves and lords, and the lords came in all skin colours and sizes. But the common characteristics of everyone were the blue or green glowing eyes of a lord. Not everyone had huge ears, but about half did. And if they did, they also had white hair.

When she walked in, a few looked up and smiled and immediately turned back to their meals and their friends. But most just went on with whatever they were doing; they were getting food from the buffet, talking with friends, arguing, laughing, and a group in front of the fireplace was playing cards.

For the first time in Freyja's life, she walked into a crowded room and no one stared, but also no one took care of her. She didn't know what to do, and everyone else certainly did. For the first time, she worried about what others *like* her thought about her. She wasn't just an oddball to humans, but now she was an outsider, an oddball to her own kind.

She had never in her life been to school or church or any meeting where she was the new guy in the group; the closest she'd come had been going to Bruce's birthday party, and the Scotts had all been determined to make her feel at home. This mob wasn't hostile, but they already had their little groups. She didn't know it until later, but everyone assumed that Jack and Alizah were there somewhere to take care of this new lord and show her around. They were always with the others. Freyja wasn't their problem, and they were all occupied.

The Breakfast Room was hot, it was noisy, and it was overwhelming. There were smells she didn't understand. She didn't see a free place to sit and eat.

So she turned around and walked back out.

Her bedroom was down some long halls, and Freyja didn't want to go sit in there, so she turned left instead of right and found an outside door that led to a terrace. Lounge chairs were arranged around a small fire, and she gratefully sat down and listened to the quiet and her own chaotic thoughts.

Freyja was disappointed in herself, and she really didn't know why. Walking out of the Breakfast Room felt like a defeat. It was like she had chickened out, but what was she afraid of? She looked into the fire and sighed. Maybe, when lunch was over, she would go back when it was much less crowded.

"Lord Freyja, are you okay?" It was one of the housekeeper elves. She looked at him and smiled. "I'm fine."

She didn't look fine to him, and he frowned. "Do you want a beer? People who come out here always ask for a beer. It's a thing." Freyja nodded, and a minute later she had a Molson in her hand, and the elf brought her a hamburger. Somehow, that made her feel a lot better.

_____

Brenda

The housekeeper elves manning the buffet told their line manager that Lord Freyja had walked into the Breakfast Room and no lord said boo to her, no one was friendly, no one was watching out for her, and she left. Who was mentoring her? She was out on the terrace by herself, and the elf who was shadowing her was sure she'd had a panic attack, although she said she was fine.

The manager called up Brenda and wanted to know what the hell was going on; she had an Elemental lord sitting on the terrace having a panic attack, and the other lords were shunning her. Who was her mentor? Her staff didn't want to be around a lord who was cracking up, especially an unknown Elemental!

Brenda texted Caddy and asked who Lord Freyja's mentor was. The woman was not doing well, and Brenda needed someone to talk to her. But Caddy was in a meeting with the two elf clans in Denmark who were having a trade dispute and wouldn't be available for a couple of hours.

In the meantime, Brenda told the Aelfeham House clan to assign a warrior elf to shadow Lord Freyja, and if anyone needed a lord's help, to contact Lord Berke or Lord Köke. They knew how to handle lords.

_____

Freyja

After lunch, Freyja wandered around Aelfeham House, poking her head in any room that didn't give off "private" vibes.

She knew she was supposed to meet an elf to have a talk about sex, but had no idea where she was or how to contact her.

As she was wandering down still another long hall, an elf popped in just inches in front of her, and she almost tripped over the little woman. The elf didn't bother to hide her irritation. "Lord Freyja! You have a Lord Lesson *right now*! Sylvia is waiting!"

"And how am I supposed to know how to find this Sylvia? Where is she?"

"She's waiting in the Lesson Room! Where's your mentor? Hasn't anyone set up your phone with the scheduling app?"

"What mentor? What phone? What app?"

The elf face-palmed herself. "Well, that explains *a lot*. We'll fix this. In the meantime, I'll take you to the Lesson Room."

The lesson was really, really interesting. And disturbing.

Freyja learned all about lord reproductive biology, elf reproductive biology, pheromones, Scent, bonding, and how to avoid accidental bonds. She learned about men.

In turn, Sylvia the elf learned that Freyja had been raised by a man who was a biological woman and who'd had a woman partner for about thirty years, and that Freyja had been around a few human men, although almost all of them were attached or married to human women. She was a virgin in every sense of the word, and because there were no women or men around, she simply didn't think about sex. Mating was something the animals around her did, and since she didn't have anyone to mate with, she put it out of her mind. Just like she didn't have anyone to go to the movies with. It was not a part of her world.

Whenever Freyja became restless or tense, she practised her magic. That always tired her out. She became very good at her magic.

The rape of Jo's sister had made her dad absolutely paranoid about men, and he made sure Freyja had very little contact with anyone of that gender. When she did, Jo was literally in the room the entire time. No one ever flirted with Freyja, not with Jo glowering at them. She was in her mid-forties when Jo died, and by then, Freyja was becoming really odd-looking, her abilities were growing, and the habit of solitude was no longer something that had to be enforced. She wandered the backwoods alone, burning off any excess energy with exercise and practising her magic.

The elf was, in turns, fascinated and appalled. "You mean you didn't even talk to men?"

"There were no men to talk to. Once every few years, I'd go to town to trade, and I always stayed with the Wallaces. They would take care of me, and as I became weirder, they were still kind but not in a sexual way, not at all. I guess, from what I've read, that it was like visiting my cousins if I had cousins." Freyja laughed. "I mean – I know what men are, I've seen them, and I read a lot, so I understand – in theory. But talk to a single guy? They weren't around. Kiss one? I've never kissed anyone romantically, male or female, much less had sex with anyone. The few people I've run into in my backwoods wanderings were either crazy or hurt and needed rescuing. Not anyone I wanted to be with, much less wanted to kiss!"

"You don't even want to be with a man?"

"Again, it's a matter of opportunity. After my dad died, I lived alone for over eighty years. Until two weeks ago, the first strange man I had talked to in decades was Bruce Scott, and he's old and happily married. This morning, I had a chat with Lord Chi and Lord Gary. They are literally the first single men I've ever been alone with." She gave a side-eye glance at Sylvia. "I wasn't impressed."

Sylvia laughed and laughed. "Oh gods! The first eligible men you meet are Lords Chi and Gary. AAAK!! It's a wonder you don't give up and go to women."

Freyja shrugged. "A woman would be fine, but I'm not attracted to them that way. When I'm in a room with people, I like to look at the men, so with that very tiny preference noted, I think I'm heterosexual. But who knows? I don't. So I don't worry about it."

Sylvia nodded. "Lord Freyja, you're not the only lord who has long-term dry spells. I think most of those who come here do. It's normal. But that makes it all the more important that you manage your pheromones – and *men's* pheromones – so you don't bond accidentally. That is a tragedy. I told you what happened with Lord Lester and Lena. A bad bond can kill you. It will certainly make you miserable."

"Anyway," she continued, "that's enough for today. You have a lot to think about, and I can see you're tired. Why don't you have a nap before dinner? Your mentor will tell you about your next class module."

"What mentor?"

After Sylvia promised to find out what was going on with Freyja's mentor, the lord took the elf's good advice and returned to her room for a long nap, so long she slept right through dinner.

There were no lords in the Breakfast room when she went in there, but a few elves were cleaning up a ravaged buffet. When they heard she had slept through dinner, they brought her some really good dishes. Freyja had never had lasagna before, and it was a treat; she ate the entire pan. That and some lovely greens and two nice slices of lemon cake, and she was set.

She was feeling so good that she walked off without the cane, and as she roamed the never-ending halls, she found she didn't need it at all. Freyja was on the mend.

Occasionally, she heard lords talking behind doors, and once she passed a laughing group of teenagers who nodded and smiled but walked by without another word. Then she heard music, a piano.

A door had an engraved brass sign on it that said "Music Room," and since it wasn't a private bedroom, she poked her head in and saw a lord playing a magnificent grand piano. He turned when she walked in, and for the first time that day, a lord looked at her, smiled, and waved her in.

"Hi! You must be Lord Freyja! I'm Lord Mordecai, but you can call me Dek. My bond-wife, Lord Althea, was the one who treated you when you got shot with that dart, so I know all about that."

"Pleased ta meecha! Thanks for all that. Please tell Lord Althea how grateful I am. I haven't seen her! I heard you playing from the hall. May I sit and listen?"

Mordecai nodded. "I'm just practising. I usually play the guitar now with my work, but I learned on the piano, and it's an old friend. I'll tell Althea. She saw you here when you were really sick, but when it looked like you were okay, she left you to the elves. They're very good. She only works with the sickest people. She's a Healer – a doctor."

"So what's your work? I didn't know lords had jobs."

Dec laughed. "Oh, all the blue coats have work! We stay busy. We do what we can to keep the Elf Nation going and the elves, red coats, and kids safe. I wake up elves that are still asleep, hibernating underground. Althea is a Healer, my brother Malachi is a Warrior Lord; there're lots of jobs."

Freyja stopped breathing. This is just what Jo said she should be doing to pay back. How did Dek wake up elves? So she asked him.

"I can't explain it, but I play them up. I wake them with my music, and then guide them up with my song. And that's all I can say." He was rather smug. "Only Lord Cadence and I are elf-wakers. It's a pretty rare ability, really. I'm not an Elemental, but I can do it. Caddy is the only Elemental who can."

"Oh! It must be a lot of fun."

"Yes, but it's tiring, and I like to keep practising, so if you don't mind, I'm sure your mentor will tell you all about the lords' jobs."

Freyja smiled and apologised for holding him up, and for the next hour she listened to him play and didn't interrupt. He was magnificent and, she wryly noted to herself, he knew it.

But as wonderful as his music was, it didn't stop her mind from racing. Dek woke up elves.

You go back to Canada, you protect the elves there, you wake more up.

We do what we can to keep the Elf Nation going and the elves, red coats, and kids safe.

They had hung a red coat in her closet, so she wasn't going to do either of those things if she stayed here. They would be keeping *her* safe, and Freyja simply didn't want or need that. She wasn't a china doll. Jo was right, as he usually was; she couldn't stay here, and her work would be in Canada. By the time Dek was done with his last son, she had made up her mind. She would leave as soon as she could.

When she got back to her room, she thought about what to do. Jo said to just ask an elf, and they would take her back home. But she knew by now that elves had different jobs, and porter elves and household elves weren't necessarily the same people.

If she asked how to go back to Canada, Freyja was sure the elves would ask why; they thought she was still sick and wouldn't want her to leave. They might keep her here. But if she wanted to go somewhere close by? So she asked the next housekeeper elf she saw in the hall how she'd go to London or Lowestoft, and the elf was very helpful. Just go to the porting station at the front of Aelfeham House; it looked like a circus tent. Can't miss it.

Freyja slept as late as she could, and when she rose, she took a good shower and then wrote a series of thank-you notes just like Lily had insisted she do whenever she visited the Wallaces. It was only polite.

Her kit was at Forty-mile; she'd ask the elf to take her there.

When she was brought to Aelfeham House, she was dressed in her sweater and ski pants, which had long since disappeared. Now she had nothing but a t-shirt, jeans, and the EN red uniform. Well, if she had to, she'd take the coat.

It was all very easy, really. She carb-loaded at lunch, going a bit late so that there were seats. A few people were eating, and they all seemed occupied with their own business. Gary walked up and sat down across from her and talked for a bit, but she couldn't make heads or tails out of what he was saying. Something about a computer game. He acted nervous and twitchy, and then Freyja suddenly realised *she* made him nervous, but he was trying to be nice and didn't know how; that made her feel sorry for him. So she smiled and nodded and let him blather on, and when she was done eating, she abruptly stood up. "Time for me to go, Gary. I have an appointment with destiny, I'm afraid." She grinned at him and winked. He looked stunned, but then just nodded and weakly smiled back.

Other than Gary, no one said anything to her, which made it all the easier to leave. No one would miss her. Then she just walked out the front door and across the lawn to the circus tent. Inside, she asked the first elf she saw to take her to Forty Mile in Canada. He paused, frowned, and asked if she was sure.

Freyja was firm. Forty Mile in Canada. He frowned again, and Freyja's stomach knotted up. If he wouldn't take her, then what could she do?

He was apologetic. "I'm sorry, Lord Freyja, but the closest I can get you is the port in front of the Scott's house. Forty-Mile is outside of our range."

Relieved, she nodded. "That's fine," and a minute later, there she was in front of the Scotts' in Dawson at six in the morning. As she looked at the house, a light went on in the kitchen. Miriam was up making coffee.

Freyja smiled, blinking back a tear. She was back where she belonged.

Miriam and Bruce were as ecstatic to see her as she was to see them. Although she had just eaten a huge lunch, Miriam insisted on making an equally huge breakfast for Freyja. And to Freyja's great relief, her clothes, her backpack, and the Remington were still all there, so she had her parka and her ski pants and boots all ready for her next leg.

Over breakfast, she told Bruce and Miriam her plans.

"I know this sounds weird, but I have a mission, and that's why I'm back." Freyja looked at Miriam and Bruce. "I've been having spirit dreams. It's why I left Alaska in the first place. Not because of any political thing."

"Spirit dreams! Weird, maybe, but not surprising. If anyone's going to have their life influenced by dreams, it would be lords and elves!" Miriam was very matter-of-fact about it. "So what do the dreams tell you to do?"

"Travel to Lethbridge and take care of elves and 'my people', which is you guys. I just gotta figure out the best route. I can't go by car or plane; I need to be on the ground, so I'm going to walk."

Bruce was looking at the map on his phone. Lethbridge? Where the hell was that?

"Jeez, Freyja, that's over eighteen hundred miles!"

Freyja nodded. "Yeah, about four months hiking, allowing for breaks. I should be there before the weather turns. I have all summer." Then she grinned at Bruce. "I'm going to live forever, Bruce. What's four months?"

He chuckled. What's four months indeed? "When do you plan to start?"

"Today, if you'll drive me to Forty-Mile to get my gear. I hope I can call some wolves in to help carry the stuff."

"Oh, you'll find some wolves," he said dryly. They'd taken over the entire town, causing a huge amount of publicity and bother. Half the townies loved them, and the other half were terrified of them. If the white wolves left with the lord, both sides would be happy.

Freyja looked up at him; the wolves must be causing problems. She sighed, then looked back down at her pancakes. She loved pancakes.

"When I started in Alaska, the Wallaces told me about the new laws, so all I was worried about was the local police and getting through the border. I don't have a passport. I didn't know about other people trying to find me, like the Elf Nation or those other guys who shot me with the darts. No one has ever told me who they were. My dreams told me to watch out for orcs. So this time I'm going to be a lot more careful. Can I trust the Mounties, Bruce?"

Bruce grimaced. "Of course you can trust *most* Mounties, but hey, we're people, too. There are always a few rotten eggs in any nest. Let me think about this. Why? Why do you need Mounties? As guards?"

Freyja sat back, finally stuffed to the gills. "I've been thinking about this. I'm going to need provisions every now and then. If I go into a town, that's a risk. I won't know who to trust, where to go, nothing. I'm not used to strangers; I found that out with my own people in England." She looked glum. "I'm pretty clueless, really, and being clueless means I stand out by asking stupid questions and not knowing how to act."

Miriam gave Freyja a sharp look. So Freyja didn't fit into lord society. That was disappointing, and she had a flash of anger. Who could not love Freyja?

"So I was wondering if Mounties could be trusted to leave caches for me. I have some money to pay them back. Soon I'll be too far away to ask you – that's the whole point – but there are Mounties everywhere. If you could, y'know, tell them what to get and where to put it, and I'll always be able to check the cache for traps. My magic and the wolves can help me with that."

"Let me think about that, too. So you still want to use your phone? What if the EN has it tapped?"

"Do you think they do? It's here in my backpack. I didn't have it on me when I was taken to England."

"I'm going to get you a burner phone; I know how to manage this. Drug dealers do it all the time. You'll get a new burner phone with each cache. I'll explain everything to you."

With that, they were done with breakfast. Freyja went to the front porch while Bruce got ready, and she turned to grin at Miriam. "Hey, Mir! Wanna see some real magic?"

She turned and howled, but it wasn't a human howl. Nor was it a wolf howl, but the howl of a siren, the drekavac, the glawackus. It was a howl that vibrated in the listener's bones and turned their spines into harp strings. The entire town heard it in their ears and through the soles of their feet and in the back of their teeth. The howl whipped around the town and out into the countryside, and it had words, but the humans couldn't understand them.

The wolves did, though. They understood, and they were waiting.

In unison every white wolf sprang up from the porches they sheltered on, from the convenience stores they sat in, begging for food from the people going in and out, from under bushes where they slept, and they ran to Freyja, a white tide that gathered on Fifth Street and ran to the edge of town as fast as they could go, stopping the early morning traffic and making the early risers run to their doors to watch.

Bruce ran out, and Freyja was waiting by his truck, a white sea of excited and happy wolves milling around her, all wanting a sniff and a pet.

"Well, Bo Peep, I see you found your sheep. Ready to go? We need to stop at a couple of places first, but I want you to sit in the truck. What are we going to do with these guys?"

Freyja smiled and turned to the wolves. In the language Bruce couldn't understand, she told them to meet her at Forty Mile; she'd be there soon. As one, they turned, and the alphas of each wolf clan led them in an easy ground-eating lope to the rendezvous point. As fast as they'd arrived, they left, melting into the surrounding forest.

A big hug for Miriam, and then Freyja and Bruce were gone.

Bruce drove to a gas station where he filled up and then went around to the back. When he returned to the truck, he tossed a box into Freyja's lap. "This is your burner phone. I know it's clean. It'll hook up to the internet, and you can use the stuff you got at Wallace's for recharging if you need to, but I expect you'll have a new phone before this one needs recharging. We'll see. But keep it turned off most of the time. Why don't we both agree that it'll be on at six am and six pm for ten minutes? If no news, then no news, but if there's anything to relay, we'll know someone will be at the other end. Either Miriam or me at my end."

That all sounded good to Freyja, and while they drove to Forty Mile, she set the phone up while Bruce talked her through it and by the time they pulled into the parking lot, she was confident that it worked and she could manage on her own. She'd have to set up any new phones by herself.

All the way up, Bruce looked for the wolves, hoping to see a flash of white in the trees, but he saw nothing. At Forty Mile, they stopped in the parking lot and went to look for Freyja's sled, and there it was, just as they'd left it days ago, not any worse for wear other than a dusting of leaves and dirt across the top of the bundles. Freyja quickly unloaded the sled, and when they both bent down to lift it into the back of the pickup, Freyja stopped and stood up.

"Bruce, just let me do this. It's heavy, and you make sure you get help before you unload it from the truck." She picked it up with one hand, her eyes glowing. She grinned at him when she was done. "Magic. It's handy. You should see me with a jam jar."

He laughed, and that was that. She wanted him gone, he could tell. There were still no wolves around, but he knew she had something planned. A hug, a wave, and he was back on the road. The sled wouldn't be sold as Freyja suggested. Bruce wouldn't part with it for the world.

He was back home by ten, having a cup of coffee and talking with Miriam about the cache thing.

Bruce's hunch was quite correct. Freyja had plans.

While she waited for the wolves to show up, she packed their individual panniers and then went out and shot a couple of deer for the wolves. There were always deer around, and with her ears she could hear an individual animal's heartbeat, never mind the noise of a herd. She really didn't want Bruce to see her do that and then be compromised if it somehow got back to anyone in officialdom that she was illegally hunting.

Then, that done, she sat in the parking lot and waited – and listened.

I wake up elves that are still asleep, hibernating underground, Mordecai said as he sat by the piano and practised. *I wake them with my music, and then guide them up with my song.* She could feel his magic as he played, and that gave her a hint of how he did it. Freyja knew she could put magic in her song; she'd been doing that since she was a kid. Her siren calls to the wolves were magically enhanced.

All of her life, Freyja lived in the woods. She knew every sound, every squeak and growl and murmur that living things made. She could hear heartbeats. Usually, she knew exactly what she was hearing, and because life was so noisy, she tuned most of it out, but occasionally she heard voices. Little voices, muffled voices that mumbled and sighed, voices that weren't much more than a buzz under her feet, and because at the time those voices made no sense to her, she'd ignored them.

But they were strong here at Forty-Mile, so for the first time she listened hard, trying to decipher what they were saying.

And having met elves, she now knew that the voices were elves talking in their sleep.

The wolves eventually showed up, a hard day's run for them, and Freyja told them about the dead deer. Once again, they were manically happy, spinning in circles in their joy and then feasting on the kill. While the rich food of Dawson City was nice, the deer were so much better. Even wolves get sick of hamburgers every day.

When the wolves were sated, she walked out to a small clearing where the voices of the elves seemed to be strongest, and she told the wolves to make a big circle and guard her; she was going to do some magic. They were fine with that and sat down to watch.

She listened again, this time her huge ears flicking around and taking in every sound. She was listening for humans because she wouldn't do her magic if humans were anywhere near her. Too dangerous. But it was clear that the closest humans lived miles away in Clinton Creek, and they were either asleep or gone to work, and no one was around.

Freyja began to sing. She sang to the elves sleeping below her feet. She sang just to see if they would awaken enough to sing back, to talk to her.

One did!

She sang louder, but she also sang stronger. Magically stronger. She sang a word poem, *I'm here, I'm waiting, it's time to wake up, Come to me!*

The elves stirred; she could feel them. She pushed. She woke up more. *It's time, Time to wake up, Time to taste the earth and come to this new world. I'm here! I'm waiting! Join me!*

Her body glowed, but she paid no attention to it, and she totally concentrated on the elves below her feet. How many? She didn't know. More than five, it seemed. Was that a clan, a family?

It didn't matter – she sang, and she pushed her magic to her voice and sang the elves up.

The wolves watched, and then they sang, too, because that's what wolves did. They were clan, and the alpha sang, so they all sang.

No human heard, but the elves did.

They seemed so close – Freyja could hear them. So close. She paused to catch her breath and gather her strength for one last push.

The ground exploded around her. Totally unexpectedly, but then she didn't know what to expect. No one said the elves came out of the ground in exploding eggs! She thought they would port up! But no; huge eggs popped out of the ground, and she ran to look at the first one. Inside, floating in a balloon-egg of fluid, was a perfect, naked elf. Through the semi-transparent sac, the elf's eyes met a stunned Freyja's, and instinctively she cut the sac with the bowie knife she always wore, lifted the wet, squirming elf free from the egg sac, and it ported away.

Then there were more eggs exploding around her, and to her left, she saw a wolf attack one egg. Horrified, Freyja ran to it, but the wolf wasn't eating the elf but freeing it the way a bitch frees a pup if it's still in the birthing sac.

Some of the elves freed themselves, and she turned and watched them port away. Then a couple stopped and clawed at their neighbour's sac, and they ported away, arm in arm. Freyja cut out two more, the wolves cut out four, and then it was over. She counted nineteen sacs left lying in the muddy ground. There were no elves left; they'd all ported somewhere.

Silence.

And Freyja dropped down to her knees in the mud and laughed and laughed and cried until she could cry and laugh no more.

It was done, and she'd figured it out just like Jo had said she would.

Caddy

Caddy was incandescent. Absolutely furious. Kyrylo didn't blame her; he was pretty ticked himself.

They had lost a lord.

Freyja just walked out, the first lord to leave Aelfeham House.

The thank-you note was perfectly polite. She had written a note to Lord Cadence as the representative of the Elf Nation, to the elves who had cared for her (Sylvia and Majorie and all the ones whose names she didn't know), and to Lord Althea for being her healer.

Dear Lord Cadence,

First, I want to thank you and everyone associated with the Elf Nation for the kind and generous hospitality you have shown me. You have done more than that, though. The RumLot Security and Elf Nation's efforts saved my life, and for that, I can only be forever in your debt.

But like any debtor or overstaying houseguest, it's time for me to go, and I go with the hopes that one day I can help you as you have helped me, if only in a small way.

I don't know who was actually involved in my rescue because no one has told me of the circumstances, so I can't thank them individually as they deserve, but I hope you will convey my deep gratitude. I know people are busy, too busy to deal with a new lord like myself, but maybe one day, if we meet again, you can tell me what happened. I really have no idea. No one talks to me.

I'm sorry I never met my mentor, but if you do find him or her, please convey my apologies. I'm sure they would have been as wonderful as the rest of the elves I met. It's a pity they were so busy.

Another apology I must offer is for taking the lovely red coat that was hanging in my wardrobe. It was the only coat I could find, and Canada is very cold now. I'll return it as soon as I am able. I understand from Lord Mordecai that the red uniform was for those lords in need of protection by "blue coats". It made me feel guilty to be another burden on the Elf Nation, a person not only in need of rescuing, but also needing continuing maintenance, and offering no contribution to the community. That's not a comfortable place for me to be in, a debtor, so please understand why I couldn't stay as a non-contributing dependent. That's just not me.

So again, many thanks for your wonderful hospitality, and I wish you and the entire Elf Nation every success in the future. I hope our paths cross again in happier circumstances. I'm sure it will.

Yours Truly,

Lord Freyja

"NO ONE TALKED TO HER!!" Caddy was so mad that she was sputtering. No lord, other than useless Gary and even more useless Chi, had talked to the new lord. She didn't know how she got there, who busted their butts fighting for her, nothing. Because once she got to England, she was essentially left to the elves, who didn't know squat.

No mentor.

No one stepped up to take Jack and Alizah's place because a new lord's integration wasn't their responsibility. They didn't step up because no one noticed Freyja was alone, and Jack and Alizah weren't around.

Freyja had slipped through the cracks, a victim of bureaucracy and complacency.

Reading between the lines, the old school teacher Caddy knew exactly what had happened. She'd taught in a rural school where new pupils were rare, and when one showed up, a real effort had to be made to integrate them into the class. Everyone had their cliques, best friends, and a routine that didn't need a new stranger to intrude on. So you assigned two "buddies" to bring the new guy into the fold; otherwise, the shy ones just sat in the corner and withered from neglect and homesickness.

Freyja was a shy one.

Caddy could have screamed. But this was her fault, too; she knew she needed to update the system, and now they'd lost a new lord – probably an Elemental! – who was, from all reports, mature, wise, and kind.

Every person Caddy called in just made the situation worse. The elves? They knew Freyja wasn't happy, and several had asked who her mentor was, but it was always "we'll fix this tomorrow".

Gary? He was beside himself. He had fallen madly in love with her, not bonded, thank the gods, but a real schoolboy crush. "She said she had a date with destiny! I didn't know that meant leaving! She winked at me, so I thought it was a joke! I thought she was flirting!" he wailed.

Mordecai? He was abashed that she'd left, but he was sure he hadn't put her off. They'd had a nice conversation, he thought. No, he had no idea why she was aimlessly wandering around Aelfeham House alone. No, he didn't ask her any questions; he did all the talking. Yes, he did say that bluecoats took care of red coats, but that wasn't insulting, was it?

No other bluecoat talked to her, not even to say hi. Not a one. Malachi shrugged it off, but Adem felt really bad over it. He knew what it was like to be ignored. Conary and Vrt didn't even know she was awake yet. And on and on it went.

Caddy was sitting at her desk talking to Norma about what lord would possibly be the best to bring forward as the "Lord Manager" when the elf looked at her phone and turned pale.

"Lord Cadence, I have some news," she gulped. The Primary leaned back and closed her eyes. What was it now? Every day, Norma called her Caddy. *Lord Cadence* meant something bad.

"Elves. Elves have just woken up in Canada. Seventeen just showed up in Safe Haven. A lord woke them up. Not one of our lords. An Elemental lord of great power."

Caddy's eyes flew open, and they were bright sparks of green fire.

"Well, isn't that just the perfect cherry on this Knickerbocker Glory?"

She put her head in her hands. "We have royally screwed this one up."

Freyja

By the time the Forty Mile clan's Warrior Elves showed up at the park to make sure their clan could leave the Safe Haven and live safely in their old lands, Freyja was long gone. It was a pretty big clan, and while she'd awakened seventeen of them, they set straight to work waking up their still sleeping brothers and sisters, building houses, and generally making themselves at home.

Freyja and the wolves marched south of Highway 9, and she found a place to stop, not to give the wolves a rest, but for herself. She was exhausted to the bone.

Her idea was to work her way down the west coast, just east of the mountains, but avoiding the towns. The further south she walked, the closer and more densely populated the countryside came, but "more" was a relative term. She'd still be able to hike through wilderness for a long, long time.

She didn't know how often she should look for elves to awaken. Every two days? Every ten miles? If she camped with the Forty Mile elves, humans would find her; she'd attract unwanted attention to herself, and that could be dangerous for the elves. Besides, the wolves would get in their way; there were just too many of them. So she walked for twenty miles, and when she was utterly exhausted, she made camp and slept for two days.

If she woke up elves there, where she camped, she'd be exhausted again, and she'd be moving on to Lethbridge at a ten-to-twenty-mile every two days pace. It'd take her years to get to Lethbridge, and in the meantime, humans and elf-hunters would figure out her next location by following her trail of bread crumbs. She decided to raise elves, walk as far away as she could to camp and sleep. Then she'd walk for two or three days, take a day to feed the wolves, and start the cycle again. That meant about eighty to a hundred miles between raisings. Freyja decided to try that for a while and see how it went.

If her goal was to wake up elves every hundred miles or so, that would put the next batch in the general vicinity of Stewart Crossing. Freyja hoped that after a few awakenings, she wouldn't be so wiped out. Dek seemed fine, and that's what he did for a living. Like anything else she learned to do magically, the first times were hard, then it became easier and easier. She was hopeful this new skill would be the same.

But for now, all she longed for was sleep. When they found a good spot, she made an igloo and crawled into her sleeping bag and slept for two days, guarded by the wolves who were happy for a little lay-down, too.

Bruce and Miriam

Bruce and Miriam came up with a plan. Bruce, who knew everyone, knew this guy, a First Nations guy named Nick Fortin, who was a Mountie. He was, Bruce said, one of the most straight-up guys he'd ever met, and he'd keep his mouth shut. He'd talk with him about getting a little group together who could set out the caches.

But he wouldn't do it on the phone. After poking around and talking to people after the entire lord incident, Bruce had a good idea that the local phones were tapped by the EN. Maybe he was just a paranoid old hoser, but there seemed to be some coincidences that pointed to that, and he wasn't going to take any chances. Instead, he simply sent a text to Nick saying he needed to talk about tribal stuff and to set a place. Nick chose White Horse, a six-hour drive, but hey, what else did he have to do with his life now? Bruce could drive there and back in a day if he had to, but in any case, he had loads of leave saved up, and he spent two of the days on this little project.

They met at McDonald's for lunch.

Nick listened to Bruce tell the entire saga of Freyja. He already knew quite a bit of the public info, and he also knew that she was shot at Bruce's house, so he knew, like every other Mountie in the north, that Mountie Scott was involved with a lord.

How could they not know? Everything was plastered on local, national, and international news. The helicopter incident when the lord fled Alaska couldn't be kept quiet. The bounty hunters chasing her were also now a matter of public record, as were their grisly deaths. Only two survived, and they were now cooling their heels in a Canadian jail for assault, attempted kidnapping, aiding and abetting, terrorism, cruelty to animals, and littering – you name it.

What Bruce didn't know was that Nick was a lord himself, and Nick didn't enlighten him either.

Nicholas Fortin, RCMP

At fifty-three, Nick was a very fit, very active, very large man. His friends called him The Thing, not because he was an orange superhero, but because he was large, broad-shouldered, very strong, and had a face only a mother could love. That, and because, like the comic book hero, he was also a really smart, really nice guy once you got past the ugly bit.

When he was a teenager, that time of life when his body odour changed, his hair started sprouting in surprising places, and the bullying typically started for young lords, Nick had the great fortune to be so much bigger and stronger than the local bullies and orcs that they left him alone. He minded his own business, and if someone got a bit aggressive, well, he got aggressive back. They didn't try a second time.

He was smart enough to go to junior college and get a two-year degree in computer repair, and with that piece of useless paper in hand, he joined the Army and eventually worked his way into the Canadian version of the SAS- Joint Task Force 2. By the time he made sergeant, he was married, had a kid, and life was looking pretty good. He was seriously looking into going back to school and moving up to the officer ranks. Yeah, he was gone a lot, but that was the downside of being in an elite unit. You constantly train, and none of that training was local. JTF2 was not a nine-to-five job.

One day, he was out on an Arctic exercise, and it was called off early for some reason. Something to do with their flight home being rearranged. He walked into the house a day early to a rather nasty surprise, and all of his meticulous plans for the future were thrown in the air and landed in the garbage.

Maybe if Tracy had taken a male lover, it wouldn't have been such a shock. But she hadn't; the naked person in bed with her was her best friend, Yvonne, and it seemed they had been lovers for years. Since before Tracy and Nick had met. It turned out he was just a meal ticket, a sperm donor, and she was a very good actress. It was humiliating.

It was not a dent that a few sessions with a marriage counsellor could buff away.

So that was the end of that marriage, and Nick not only left her, he left the Army so that he could have more regular hours that allowed him to spend more time with his son. He joined the Mounties and found that he loved that job even more than the Army.

He figured out that he was a lord when the first elves and lords showed up on the internet, since it explained the eye thing. He had the glowing eyes when he was angry (boy, did his eyes glow during the divorce!), but other than that rather inconvenient trait, absolutely nothing else lordlike. Not a speck of magic, no special abilities, no big ears, nothing.

According to Tracy, he was the world's worst lover, and according to the internet, he was the world's worst lord. That was humiliating, too.

Because his lord genes were so weak, and because his son needed him, he never contacted the EN. He preferred being a good every-other-weekend dad, an excellent Mountie, and he certainly loved his Mountie career. Maybe he would contact the EN when the Mounties finally kicked him out to the retirement pasture. Or not. He wasn't the type to be happy being the worst hoser in his new unit, and given the info on the internet, he would be.

Being a First Nations aboriginal, he was pretty familiar with normal racist nonsense, but as an everyday matter, his size and intelligence usually wiped that out; if anyone was rude, he wasn't too bothered. But the increasing bigotry against the lords was something that struck close to home. There was a massive difference between a white officer from Ottawa thinking a guy from the north was automatically a yokel and someone looking at his blue eyes and thinking he was a demon from hell. No one in this century was going to shoot him for being part of an Aboriginal tribe, but across the border in the US? Open season.

So when Bruce sat in McDonald's to talk to Nick about this woman lord returning to Canada after a kidnapping attempt to make her epic dream walk to Lethbridge, Nick could see all sorts of problems, but he also had a lot of sympathy for her. It was a romantic, wacky, totally illogical quest from what he could see. Why not just take a flight to Lethbridge? She could be there in a few hours. Why not drive? But no, Bruce said she "had to touch the ground."

Bright blue eyes or not, he was a full-blooded native from a culture that took dreams seriously. When your own dreams were shattered, you knew their power.

And wolves – that was another issue. She had a pack of wolves with her, her spirit animals. A super pack of white dire wolves, like *that* mess was going to blend into the background. She might as well be leading a circus parade with clowns and elephants.

Lord Freyja was walking down the spine of North America on a dreamquest, and she needed someone to put caches of food out for her and probably for her wolves, too, if they weren't going to help themselves to the locals' cattle and household pets. It was about the stupidest operation ever. Nothing but a slow-moving disaster from what he could see.

Nick looked at Bruce and took a sip of his coffee, and made his decision.

"I'm in."

Bruce and Nick

Bruce was relieved. Nick knew how to do things that Bruce didn't, like how to really manage a covert operation with complicated logistics. Wasn't that what special ops was all about?

And while Nick was only ten years younger than Bruce, physically, he was in his forties. Bruce had to admit that he'd had his own come-to-Jesus moment when the bounty hunters showed up and pointed guns at Miriam. He wasn't a kid anymore. And while Nick's single status might not be much of an advantage in his personal life, he didn't have a wife at home to worry about.

Every time Bruce left the house, now he worried about Miriam and the chance that some elf groupie or bounty hunter would show up on his porch when she was there alone. He showed her again how to use the pistol they kept in the house, just in case, but she, in turn, worried about having a loaded weapon in the house with kids. But there was no helping it; the Scotts were well-known in elf-fantatic circles now.

He asked Nick how many trustworthy guys they needed to recruit, and Nick shook his head.

"We don't need to recruit anyone. You stay up north and man the phones and be the buffer between the world and me. If I need help, I'll call you, and we'll deal with any problems as they come up. But the best thing to do is just keep this as close to the vest as possible. Just you and me. She thinks she'll be done in late summer? I'll take a couple of months off on medical leave. I have plenty saved up, and I'll just make something up. Some mental health issues that I don't have to go get medical tests for, like stress." He grinned. "I'm having an anxiety attack just thinking about this."

He took a bite of his hamburger and chewed thoughtfully. "The big problem I can see is money. I have some savings and a good line of credit, but it's not unlimited. Staying in hotels, gas, supplies, food for a lord, and food for those wolves – that's all going to cost. How many wolves need to be fed? How often? Can you and Miriam figure that out?"

Bruce nodded. He hadn't thought about the money thing. He'd sic Miriam on that. She was good at budgeting.

"What do you think it will cost?"

"Oh, I don't know, about five grand a month? I can manage about forty grand, I think, so we can do it, but I'd really rather not drain my pension. I'm sure it'll all work out in the end, but we need to be prepared. I don't want to go to the ATM for an emergency and have my card declined when I need to buy some ammo. I have no idea what a side of beef costs that'll feed the wolves."

Bruce nodded. He gave Nick a couple of the burner phones, and with a handshake, Bruce started his six-hour drive back to Dawson. Nick sat in the McDonald's for a long time and made notes on a little paper pad he kept in his pocket. He was old school that way. He'd worked around computers too much to trust them.

When he returned to his jeep, he unhooked the sat-nav and the automatic hookups to the internet that allowed the Jeep people to monitor the health of his vehicle. He didn't trust them either, and there was no point in using burner phones if his SUV could be tracked.

Freyja

When Freyja emerged from the igloo after her two-day sleep, the wilderness was calm and unchanging, but out in the busy world, people were moving.

Caddy and Kyrylo shoved the entire Freyja mess onto Lord James and General Jameson's laps. They, in turn, sent Maksym and Darnya back to Dawson City to trace Freyja's movements from there. Wendell and new Ranger trainee Lord Ritchie were sent to Lethbridge, ready to move at a minute's notice to any border site to intercept her if she tried crossing into the US. All the elf clans along the US border were put on alert.

Nick drove back to his apartment, threw a couple of weeks' worth of clothes into a gym bag, and then armed up. Camping supplies, Mountie uniforms, his laptop – all the stuff he'd take on a military exercise – went in the back seat of his 4x4, and he was ready. Then he thought about the wolves and went out and bought a cow, which was a bit harder than he thought it would be. But after a few calls to some ranchers he knew, he found a dairy cow that was days away from the dog food factory, and all thousand pounds of Bessie were thrown on his trailer, and he was done. Bear bait, he told the rancher, and he managed to keep a straight face. Thank god it was still cold out, and he didn't have to try to fit Bessie in his kitchenette freezer.

With those chores completed, he headed back to White Horse to wait for a call from Bruce.

The wolves were hungry, and a hungry wolf was a cranky wolf, so Freyja walked out and shot a couple of deer. She could just let them do what came naturally and stalk and hunt their own dinner, but the pack was floating around thirty now, and if they started running, who knew where they'd end up and who would see them. It was better if she just took care of them and kept them from roaming.

While they fed, she ate her own cold breakfast, and when everyone was done eating, she wouldn't let them sleep; instead, she loaded up the unfortunates with the panniers, and they started on their way. The Rand McNally said she would be near Stewart Crossing on Hwy 2 when they hit the hundred-mile mark from Forty Mile. There was a scattering of tiny villages and settlements to wind through, and then she'd have some pretty clear (of humankind) terrain as she worked her way south. Somewhere around Stewart Crossing, she'd feed the wolves again, and if she felt safe, she'd see about waking more elves. That was the plan, at least.

Freyja walked all day, only stopping to pee or eat or both. The weather was pretty good, and the terrain varied enough to be interesting. Sometimes she sang to the wolves, and then a couple of ravens started to follow them, which was fine. The inky birds knew the wolves meant dead things to eat, and Freyja always found it entertaining to talk to them. They told her where the people were, and between her own good ears and their eyes, the odd person and house were easy to avoid.

At five, she started to look for a place to stop for the night, and by six, she was sitting next to a tiny, smokeless fire and talking to Bruce on the burner phone. When they were driving to Forty Mile and she was setting up the phone, Bruce had told her not to use any words that might trigger an AI program to eavesdrop on their conversations, so no words that referenced the Elf Nation or herself, like "elf," "lord," "Lethbridge," or "wolf".

He told her a Mountie named Nick Fortin was going to trail her all the way to the end, dropping off caches wherever she wanted them. Nick had a cow on the back of his trailer, and he was waiting in White Horse. When she was ready, she should just let him know where to drop off the cow.

Startled, Freyja didn't quite know what to say. "A cow? Won't it wander off?"

Bruce didn't laugh. He didn't know if you could laugh at a lord. "No, it's dead. But Nick might need help unloading it. It's a whole knackered dairy cow, and it's pretty heavy, but it will be enough for your picnic. Is there anything else you need?"

She said no thank-you, not at the moment, she wished Miriam well, and they hung up. A whole cow! She didn't know if she could lift a whole cow off a trailer. Maybe they could dump it. A cow! Well, she didn't have to worry about hunting for the pack at the next stop. A cow should be enough for her "picnic" guests.

An hour later, she got a text.

Nick – "Testing."

When she sent a "*thumbs up*", the message didn't show her name, but "Lupina". It made Freyja smile. Someone had a sense of humour to call her the female wolf. A bitch? Sometimes she felt like one. She was certainly causing a lot of people a lot of problems, catering to her whims.

Then she simply typed in *"Stewart's Crossing. 2 days?"*

It took a day and a half to get to Stewart's Crossing, which was not much more than a gas station and a couple of buildings. When she was a few miles out, she stopped and texted.

Lupina – "I'm here. You?"

Nick – "NE on Silver Trl. Power line cut."

She asked the ravens to go look for the trailer with the dead cow, which they were happy to do. Dead cows were a treat! They almost didn't want to come back because the smell of the cow was so alluring. But being smart birds, they knew the male lord wouldn't let them pick at the cow until the female lord had eaten her fill.

Crossing the highway was easy; it was very deserted, and she found the shaved area where the utility lines crossed the forest. Off in the distance, she saw the ravens circling. Using them as her guide, Freyja and the wolves headed right for them.

And there he was.

Nick and Freyja

Nick sat on the roof rack of the Jeep even though the cow was beginning to reek, and from there he used his binoculars to search the piney woods. He was well off the highway, and according to the satellite photos on his laptop, there wasn't a single building on this side of the highway for miles, so he wasn't expecting any accidental encounters.

The nights were cold, but yesterday the temperature rose above freezing, and nature was starting to do her work, breaking down the raw, unbutchered carcass. Overhead, the crows were already beginning to circle, lured by the smell of death. He sure hoped the lord came soon before the thing exploded.

And there she was.

Freyja was wearing her parka with the hood up, which would have been odd to a native Alaskan at this temperature, but the ski mask was gone. She wore oversized, mirrored sunglasses, and she was in jeans and hiking boots, not ski pants and snow boots. She had a rifle slung across her back, and loping alongside her were six wolves with packs on. Six! Nick grimaced. He didn't need a whole cow for six overgrown huskies!

She stopped about fifty feet in front of him and just waited, saying nothing.

He jumped off the roof, thought for a moment, and then he grinned and waved. "Hi, Lupina!"

And she smiled back. "Hi, Nick!" And that's what she wanted; she needed to make sure she was talking to him and not just any random hoser sitting on a Jeep Rubicon and towing a dead cow into the middle of fucking nowhere. The lord didn't want any mistaken identity mix-ups between Nick and other dead-cow-hauling idiots.

She wouldn't come too close, probably because the cow stank, but at twenty feet away, she bent over to take the panniers off the wolves.

"Can I help?"

"No thanks. Better stay where you are. These guys don't know you yet, and they're hungry." Then she took off the parka. "Man, I'm hot!" That left her in a t-shirt and jeans.

And Nick didn't say anything because she certainly was. Probably the hottest woman he had ever seen, bar none.

He had never seen a lord of either gender before, and certainly not a full lord and the internet drawings didn't begin to describe what he saw in front of him. Her face looked like she was around thirty, but her hair was stark white, and her ears flared up into foxlike points well above the top of her head. When she smiled, her green eyes snapped and glittered, and he could see them glow even from twenty feet away.

When the wolves were free of their packs, she circled the Jeep, giving Nick a wide berth. He didn't try to get closer and stayed where he was because obviously she wasn't going to allow that, and he didn't want to spook her. Freyja stood looking at the cow and then turned to Nick and grinned, her emerald eyes twinkling.

"So, Mr Nick, how is this Holy Cow going to get off the trailer? Do you have a plan, or should I try something?"

"No, no real plan. The rancher put it on there with a forklift. I thought maybe the wolves could jump up there and eat what they could, and it would be lighter to pull off after they're done. But six wolves won't make much of a dent in old Bessie. She's pretty big." He looked at the cow. "Another way would be to unhitch the trailer and put the Jeep in front and use the winch."

Freyja looked at the cow. "The other wolves are in the brush, guarding us. When I call them, they'll come. But I have an idea. Can you unlock the tailgate?"

He did, and then she simply looked at the trailer; her eyes glowed, and out of nowhere an ice ramp formed along with a thin sheet of ice on the bed of the trailer.

"If you can push the cow from the back, there's just enough of a slope that it might just slide down on the slick ice. If that doesn't work, you can try the winch."

Nick jumped up on the back of the trailer and wedged himself in with his boots on the cow's ass and prayed that the thing wasn't so rotten that he'd lose his boots in its butt. Then he leg pressed just like when he went to the gym. It took a minute, but then the cow gave way so suddenly he almost fell, and the entire carcass slid down the ice ramp, hitting the ground with a disgusting splat. Dancing with impatient energy, the waiting wolves whined and yipped. Dinner!

He jumped off the trailer, fired the Jeep up, and pulled it well away. When he turned to walk back, he could see two dozen white wolves emerging from the brush, obviously waiting for the lord's signal. She said something in some language, and Nick thought she said, "All yours, boys and girls." But whatever she said, it was all the wolves needed to hear, and they attacked the cow with gleeful ferocity. Nick couldn't see the cow anymore; it was covered in a heaving mass of white fur.

Smiling, she turned and walked away from the wolves but still gave Nick a wide berth.

"Hey, Lord Freyja, I have supplies for you, too. I'll put them here, and you can come get them when I'm gone." Nick piled up some grocery bags, and he showed her where her new phone was. "When you have the new phone set up, I have the number, and I'll send a text to make sure it works. When we're good to go with the phones, just take the old phone, remove the SIM card, and throw everything in your campfire. Make sure that the SIM card is burned up and everything is buried. I'm going to try to give you a fresh phone every other cache. I think that's safe, but you tell me if you want one every time we meet. I'll be staying in a motel in Carmacks, waiting for your next leg."

Freyja nodded, one eye on the wolves who were noisily devouring the cow. "Thanks, Nick. You have no idea how much your help means to me, and I won't forget any of it. I'll text you as soon as I can."

With that, Nick stood by the open door of his Jeep and for a minute watched the wolves, too. "Are you going to be okay out here, Lord Freyja?"

"Just Freyja, Nick. I only use the lord thing with the EN people. Yeah, I'll be fine. I'm better off out here than I am with humans. Always have been." A slight shadow passed over her face, but she quickly smiled. "Bye! Don't worry. I'll be fine!"

And dismissed, he got in the 4x4 and left for Carmacks, where his room was waiting. At least the Jeep drove a lot better without a thousand pounds of dead cow in the back. Smelled better, too.

Darnya, Maksym, and the Scotts

"I could live here."

"Really? In Dawson?"

"Yeah, I really could. It's not too hot, it's a gorgeous country, and I like the people."

Darnya smiled and shook her head. She didn't think Maksym could settle down anywhere, but she had to admit that it was nice sitting on the porch swing and gently rocking while they waited for Bruce Scott to come home from work.

Mrs Scott wouldn't talk to them at all, and she wouldn't let them in the house, and Darnya couldn't blame her. But she wasn't a hostile woman, just a cautious one, and she told the two they could sit on the porch swing while they waited for Bruce to come home around five thirty. She'd call and tell him they were waiting. She even brought out some cold Cokes for them to sip on.

Mountie Scott arrived home right on time, waving to the RumLot Security pros as he drove in. Miriam came out, and they both pulled up a chair across from the porch swing and drank coffee. Darnya noticed that they weren't invited into the house, and there were no cookies or snacks offered either. They were treated with elaborate courtesy and exactly as if they were selling insurance.

Mountie Scott was a perfectly affable, chatty man who asked a lot of questions and offered absolutely nothing in return.

Maksym poured on the charm, and he talked about RumLot Security and how some of what they did for the EN paralleled the RCMP's mission and how clever Scott was to figure out where the lord was going to cross over into Canada and get Lord Freyja to trust him. Maksym was sure Mountie Scott had a good idea where the lord was heading. What were his guesses?

Scott didn't fall for any of it. Neither did Miriam.

Then they tried the "she is a lord and needs to be with her own people" tack, and that didn't go down well at all.

"If her own people had treated her a bit friendlier, she might be in England now," said Miriam tartly. "At least she'd be communicating with you. From what you're saying, she's not doing that. Why do you think that is?"

Darnya looked embarrassed. "I don't know what happened, but it seems that the ball was dropped at our end. But it was all unintentional, and the EN would love to have her come back and give them another chance to get to know each other. As you can see, no one is being held hostage; lords can come and go as they please. If she came back for a week or so, she could easily come back here whenever she wanted to."

"When she calls you up, will you tell her that?" Maksym asked Miriam, figuring she was the softer touch.

"*IF* she calls me up, I'll pass on the message. But she doesn't call me, and I have no idea where she is." Miriam looked Maksym right in the eye because what she said was true. Freyja didn't call Miriam (she called Bruce), and Miriam had no idea where Freyja was (Bruce did).

"Every lord is precious to the Elf Nation, and it's our job at RumLot Security to keep them safe. Not every lord is as talented as Lord Freyja, and they all have many serious enemies. Even Lord Freyja, as strong as she is, was overwhelmed by those bounty hunters. If we had known she was here, we would have had guards around the house, and the outcome would have been different, I think. For her own safety, she really needs to reconsider her relationship with us. We want her to be comfortable, and we want her to roam; we're not a prison, but we just want to keep her alive in a dangerous world. I hope, as her friends, you'll talk to her about the risks she's taking." Maksym stood up and smiled at the Scotts. And then they stood up, and the meeting was over.

Bruce watched the RumLot agents walk back to their car, and he could see by the set of Maksym's shoulders that he was pissed, and Bruce had to make sure he wasn't smiling. The guy was very slick, but Bruce had been doing essentially the same thing Maksym and Darnya did for almost forty years. There was a little bit of professional satisfaction in that he hadn't said anything he shouldn't have, and he smiled at Miriam. Neither had she.

As he walked into the house, his phone buzzed. It was his daughter. "Dad, did you know elves are living at Forty Mile now? Real elves. Settlers."

Bruce shook his head. Freyja, it seems, had been busy after he left. He was very sure any elves out there weren't imported by the EN. They had their own agenda where new elf clans settled in Canada, and not a single location was north of Winnipeg. The

EN might want to make sure lords are safe and happy, but they also want to make sure lords and elves are under their control.

The two RumLot agents visited today because Freyja was not under their control, and she was bringing in elves where *she* wanted them to be, not where the EN wanted them.

Bruce wondered how new elves in the north were going to be viewed by his government in Ottawa.

Freyja was shaking things up.

The next morning, Bruce and Miriam drove to Forty Mile to see what they could see. When he turned onto the side road leading to the parking lot, there was a traffic jam of cars sitting in the road waiting for free spaces in the parking lot, and the Scotts ended up pulling off onto the berm and walking in. It appeared others had heard, too.

Off on a little field to the side of the museum was a tiny farmer's market. There must have been fifty humans walking around, and more were wandering in as Bruce watched. The elves had put up four stalls selling jam, honey, tea towels, beef jerky, and, of all weird things, The Rum Lot Christmas ornaments. The goods all said "Made in Lowestoft by the Dogger Bank Clan". A small sign informed the browsers that, "Coming Soon! Authentic Forty Mile Clan products will be available in the coming weeks!". Elves showed people how to find their website on their phones (www.rumlot.com, it was easy!) and how to download books. Miriam wondered how the elves knew about the internet, but they sure did!

A stall selling cakes, coffee, and sandwiches was doing a booming business, and stunned, frankly dazed, humans were buying everything as fast as it could be set out. About ten elves were working the stalls, talking with visitors, and having selfies taken, and four very dangerous-looking elves with swords walked around, watching everything and refusing to talk to the humans or have their pictures taken. If anyone looked like guards or warriors, those guys did.

The elves didn't look like the European elves, and Miriam pointed that out to Bruce. These were Five Nations elves, Little People of their own legends, and they were dressed in beautiful Aboriginal clothes, just like they would have been before the first Vikings set foot in Canada.

Everyone was having a grand time.

As soon as the Scotts walked into the market area, the elves noticed them, and an old woman ran up, the clan leader, and introduced herself to the Scotts as Belinda Four Feathers.

"Mountie Bruce and Mrs Mountie Miriam!! Welcome! We are so happy to – " And she burst into sobs, and Miriam had to bend down to hug her. People stopped to stare, and some of the elves started to cry, too.

"We are so grateful, so happy to be awake and back in our home again." She wiped her eyes and tried to pull herself back together. "You two took care of our wonderful Lord Freyja and brought her here to bring us back. We'll never forget that. Never. We've been waiting so long. Dreaming of home –" She started to cry again, and now there wasn't a dry eye in the house, including the humans.

All Bruce could choke out was "Welcome back. We've missed you."

Conary and Caddy

The Canadian Ambassador Zang to the UK was very courteous and very, it seemed, conflicted. On the one hand, the Canadians emphasised that they were thrilled – absolutely thrilled – that more elves were being raised in Canada. No problem. Please continue.

But on the other hand, didn't the Canadians and the EN have a working agreement about *where* they were being raised, and shouldn't the EN have told the Canadian government of changes in plans and protocols? It would only have been polite. The Canadian government was always helpful and would have been happy to provide security as they had in the past. Was the EN unhappy with them?

Lord Conary spent the entire morning smoothing ruffled feathers and promising more cooperation without promising anything firm, which is what a good diplomat does. Lord Cadence even showed up halfway through the meeting, and the Ambassador was sure she had been called in as an emergency backup and fellow feather-smoother. She was a bit off, and he could tell she was thinking as she was talking. Then she just came clean.

"To be absolutely honest, Ambassador Yang, we are surprised, too. The elves at Forty Mile were brought there by Lord Freyja, whom I know you are familiar with in her adventures fleeing from Alaska." She waved her hand vaguely. "It was a bit of a free-lance job."

Yang leaned back and, with great self-discipline, resisted giving his aide a side-eye glance. Well, that explained a lot.

"Oh! So now there is a third elf-raiser with the EN! That's wonderful! The Canadian Government will be very happy to know this. Will she come back to Canada to raise more? Maybe we can set up a schedule? From our perspective, we would like to be able to welcome the elves properly and integrate them with the humans of the area and control any orcs or bad actors. Security, you know."

The aide jumped in. "I'm sure Lord Cadence knows that when elves came to Ottawa, we set up a Department of Elf Affairs equal to our Aboriginal efforts. We have systems ready to help them."

Caddy nodded and glanced over to Conary, which Ambassador Zang noted.

"We'll definitely work on that. Security is of utmost importance; we can all agree on that."

With promises of tighter cooperation, continued friendship, and assurances that the EN was absolutely happy with their relationship with Canada, Ambassador Zang left.

As she was leaving, Caddy got a text on her phone. Newly awakened elves were porting into the Safe Haven. From a place called Stewart Crossing. Freyja had woken up more elves.

When the Ambassador settled in his seat in the limo, he looked over to Linda, his aide. "Freyja is a rogue lord. Cadence had no idea she was going to bring elves to Forty Mile. I betcha she doesn't know where Lord Freyja is. Notice she didn't offer to talk to her or introduce her or anything."

Linda nodded, frantically typing notes on her tablet.

"So do you think Lord Freyja is trying to set up an alternative to the EN? Her own power base? Who are these elves going to be loyal to?"

Zang looked out the window. "That's what we have to find out. The last thing we want is for Canada to be a battleground between warring lords. Cadence and Kyrylo are the leaders of all the lords that we know of. But with Russia threatening war now in Europe, they have their plates full. A new lord might be taking advantage of the chaos to jockey for power. We have our own threats from the US. Canada needs to thread the needle and get *all* lord factions on board."

"Do you want me to arrange a meeting in Ottawa? No phone conferencing, I think. Too important. I can set up a port."

Zang nodded. He could port directly to Ottawa from London, and the PM and senior military and intelligence people could be there within an hour. Boy, having elves on your side was certainly a God-send in so many ways, great and small. The Canadians would make sure that didn't change.

The Intel Team

"Thirty elves! Thirty! How did she manage that by herself?" Caddy was incredulous. "Are there other lords helping her? Humans? And why Steward Crossing? It's in the middle of bloody nowhere! There's not even a human town there! Just a couple of houses and a gas station."

The conference room was packed with RumLot intel as well as a human Canadian regional expert and General Lord James, the senior military man under Warlord Kyrylo. General Jameson walked in about fifteen minutes after the meeting was called, porting in from Ottawa.

Kyrylo looked at the map on the screen. "All I can think of is that it was her next stop south. There is no military or logistical reason for the place. James, what do you think?"

James agreed. "If I were going to raise elves, there are better places. I'd put them up against the Alaskan border if nothing else."

The intel elves reported no increased car activity in the area based on geo-location satellite traffic. All reasonably new cars were hooked up to the internet now for sat-nav purposes, so they were easy to track. But if Freyja was driving something vintage, over thirty years old, she was probably off the grid.

James ordered the elves – unnecessarily, but that's what generals did – to blanket the area for phone intercepts and to get the AI to filter all of the CCTV, too. He looked at the map again.

"About a hundred miles from Dawson – let's cover for a hundred and fifty in all directions. How far can she go in a day?"

Kyrylo turned to the intel elves, and they huddled.

"On foot? On horse? By car? It all depends. Those wolves have disappeared from Dawson, but some were reported back in Alaska. Are they with her again? Will they slow her down? Can she drive herself?" The elves looked at Caddy, who rolled her eyes. She sure as hell didn't know if Freyja could drive. Neither did she know Freyja's relationship with her pack. No one had talked to her.

"We'll do our best with intercepts, but here's the problem. It's wilderness, and wilderness isn't wired. There is no need for cameras and CCTV and all that if you have a cabin in the middle of nowhere; a lot don't even lock their doors, and many of the people who live in the backwoods are there because they're paranoid about modern life and big government. Not all – but a lot of them. CCTV is only on government sites, big businesses (like McDonald's, Loblaws, or Walmart) and places with something to steal, like petrol stations. That leaves private phones, and if they're stuck in someone's pocket, they're not taking pics of random people or cars driving by."

Kyrylo nodded. "We know she was in the Steward Crossing area twelve hours ago. All we can do is get someone down there and at least have a look. Maybe she camped; maybe someone saw her or noticed some weird activity. Every clue will help us track her. In the meantime, let's see if we can figure out her route. We only have two points on the map, but a third will be a direction of travel. Is she going down the highway? Will she go overland, and if she does, east or west of the highway? I'm assuming she's an accomplished woodsman and can go anywhere, but we don't know her experience in the woods." He looked at Caddy.

"No, we don't know how she was brought up; all we know is that she lived in a cabin with her dad in Alaska. That doesn't mean she ever learned to be alone in the woods. We don't know if she had friends in Alaska other than the Wallaces. We don't know if she had ever been to Canada at all. She might have a summer place in Stewart Crossing for all we know." She looked up at the ceiling, clearly frustrated.

"No one talked to her."

Gary

General Jameson had a problem. Twice, Lord Gary had ported to Ottawa to offer to help find Lord Freyja. The first time Jameson had looked at the lord kindly and told him that everything was under control and that he was not needed. Then an elf hustled him back to Aelfeham House so fast that the only thing left in Jameson's office was the lingering odour of an unwashed lord and a sense of bemusement. The second time, Jameson was not so kind and scared the lord half out of his smelly pants. He told the lord to get his rank ass back to Aelfeham House and forget about looking for Lord Freyja and not to bother him again.

The next day, Lord Gary showed up at Lethbridge. This time, he had taken a bath and was now dressed in motorcycle leathers, demanding a Harley and provisions, and a port for all of that kit to Dawson City. He was going to look for Lord Freyja by himself.

To his great surprise, the elves said there were no motorcycles or provisions or anything else going to be provided. He had used up his elf credit with the leathers and was actually in their debt, and the Bank of Elf was closed to him.

"What do you mean I've used up my trading credit!" He was incensed. Didn't elves give lords everything they asked for?

The elf was patient. "It's like the survival game you play online. You work for credit, bargaining chips, trade – you call it what you want – and that gives you supplies, transportation, all that sort of thing. We elves also keep a book of accounts, Lord Gary. Always have. Lords like Conary or Berke, the blue coats, have almost unlimited credit with us elves because they do so much for us. They keep us safe. Lord Althea is our healer and has saved so many of us. Even Lord Grace weaves for us. What's your contribution? You eat elf food, you sleep in elf housing, and we pay for your game time. We work hard for you. What do you do for us?"

Gary was stunned. He could play and win the survival game online, but in the game of life, he was a loser. He created nothing and provided no benefit in return for the support the elves gave him. It was a stark lesson, and when he was honest with himself, he knew they were right and fair. He actually got much more benefit from elves than they got from him, and now he had reached the limit of what they would do for him.

If he had asked, the elf would have told him that in Before Times, a Lord Gary would have simply been chased off and left to starve. A parasite lord was cut off totally from elf support, but in this new world, with so few lords, elves weren't so profligate. Even the most useless parasite lords were clothed, fed, and housed. But there were limits.

He was assigned a very basic room in Lethbridge in the human workers' dorm and a pass to the mess hall. There was no computer for him to play on. He was fed, he was housed, and that was it.

Gary lay on the bed in the darkened room and gamed out his options.

What were his victory conditions? To meet up with Freyja and bond with her. She was the ultimate prize. Gorgeous, strong, she would always have credits with the elves, if only from the Scent she would make when they finally bonded. Just the thought of Freyja climaxing under him –

He was madly in love, so much that it was a physical ache, and when he dreamed of her naked and in bed with him, the ache was unbearable.

On Freyja's part, Gary was realistic enough to know she was madly in tolerance with him, which was miles better than any other woman he had ever been with. She talked to him; she seemed to like him. She had winked at him once, which was flirting. If they had more time together, he was sure she would fall in love with him.

If she bonded with him, she'd have to.

What were the obstacles? Well, foremost, she was magically stronger than he was. She was a full-on lord. With those magnificent ears and white hair, there was no doubt about that. He had read online all about the helicopter at the border and her freezing those two bounty hunters. Some of the lords in the Breakfast Room gossiped that she was an Elemental, and Gary felt her power, too.

At forty-five, he was ageing into his abilities, but even with training, he was only able to move a few pencils, and he had no idea what his ultimate speciality would be. With his pale blue eyes, probably not much of anything. But who knows? The elves always said that what was important wasn't so much the ability as the cleverness in how a lord used his ability. Gary had a good opinion of his intelligence and thought he was smart enough to maximise his ability, whatever it turned out to be.

Gary remembered the day Malachi had thrown him out of the Breakfast Room because his man-scent was so strong he made the women gag. While it had been embarrassing for a couple of days, after a while, the entire incident made him strut a bit. His smell was macho, virile. Women couldn't help their reaction to it.

Freyja wouldn't be able to resist his pheromones either.

He had to get close to Freyja without alarming her and get her to breathe in his scent. A kiss, really, that would be enough. She didn't even have to want to kiss him back, just breathe. The sex class taught him that if he was horny enough to make a strong man-scent and she was at all receptive, she wouldn't be able to help herself. By all the stars, Freyja made him horny, so that was not going to be a problem.

In Before Times, what Gary was planning was called bond-rape.

He would never dream of raping her "for real," but forcing her to a lifetime bond against her better judgment or will? He didn't see anything wrong with that. She would come around, and they had a forever lifetime to work on it. He loved her with all his heart and only wanted what was best for both of them, whether she wanted it or not.

But first, he had to find her. Lethbridge was the starting point, and now he was in the game.

Freyja

Thirty elves. It just about wiped her out. It was only by accident that she found that baby still in the little sac, and if she had let the poor thing drown, she would have never forgiven herself. That's when she also learned that the mom or dad elf would port back to rescue it. She didn't know she needed to throw it in the air, and the very idea would have appalled her. But when she yelled, "Hey, does anyone know who this kid's mom is?" a tearful, hysterical, naked elf instantly ported back and held her arms out for the baby.

Freyja grinned in teary-eyed relief and said, "Welcome to the world! Take good care of your baby!" and the elf ported out without a word.

But in the end, between her, the wolves, and the elves who were strong enough to help free their clan members, they managed. She sang the elves awake first thing in the morning, made sure they were all gone, and then she and the wolves marched the rest of the day. The wolves were fine, but by the time Freyja made her igloo and rolled into her sleeping bag, she was staggering with exhaustion. It was a good thing she was in the wilderness and had the wolves to guard her; she had nothing left to defend herself with.

When she woke the next day, she was still tired, but it was manageable. She made herself a huge breakfast, and refuelling helped out a lot. She had planned to sleep that day, but the ravens told her that back in Stewart Crossing, some humans had shown up at the place where the elves had entered the world. The elves, it seemed, could talk with the elves in the UK, and they told the EN where to go.

They had drones, which meant they were looking for something or someone, and Freyja had a good idea who.

She couldn't tell Bruce because his phone was only on at six in the morning and six at night, but she could text Nick on the old phone, so she did.

Lupina – *"No time to mess w/ phone. Later tonight. Moving on. Tell our mutual friend our neighbours now have drones!"*

Nick – *"Okay. Be careful."*

So Freyja gulped down the last of her breakfast and broke camp. She walked for about ten miles and then stopped for lunch, protein bars, and hunks of cheese. Yesterday, she would have told you that she was going down towards Carmacks, but the drones changed her mind.

Instead of taking the obvious, easier route, she decided to go cross-country and head to Faro. She sent Nick a text.

Lupina – *"Straight line to Faro. Four days?"*

Nick – "Food?"

Lupina – "Will make do. Fluffy can catch mice."

Nick – "Text!"

Lupina – "*happy face*"

And so that's what she did. If she weren't worried about being chased, the hike to Faro would have been a joy. The wolves were in good humour, and she was hiking down a long valley fold in the mountains that ran as straight as an arrow to Faro, crossing over some fantastic salmon country, criss-crossed with clear streams and abundant wildlife. It was as nature intended the world to be. Freyja sang as she walked, and while she could have used a little more food, generally she was healthy and happy, and at night she slept well.

The ravens still followed her, deciding that the wolves and this odd new creature guaranteed a steady supply of carrion. Besides, she talked to them, and it was interesting.

In the meantime, Nick worried. The internet said lords ate a tremendous amount of food because of their energy requirements when they did magic. Freyja was bringing elves to the world, and that surely took a toll on her. What could be more magical than that?

Then, to add to his worries, a new couple had just checked into the hotel in Carmacks, and he was dead sure in his wizened old heart they were Elf Nation agents. They sure weren't what they claimed to be at the reception desk, nature photographers. That drone he saw them assemble in the parking lot was very, very sophisticated. The guy had a definite accent, Slavic of some kind, and she looked like a professional gymnast, all lithe muscle, if Olga Korbut bit off the heads of snakes for breakfast.

Miriam had sourced a load of hogs with First Nations people in Little Salmon, and thank the stars the farmer was holding them "until they could be picked up for the butcher," so at least Nick didn't have to think about hauling dead meat in the trailer for a while. Freyja would shoot deer for the wolves, but she needed something other than deer meat for herself. Nick looked at the terrain maps and wondered how far into the backwoods he could get his Jeep. But shit, if she could walk it, so could he.

When she texted that her next phone was set up, he was ready.

> *Nick – "Testing"*

> *Lupina – "I'm here!"*

> *Nick – "All okay?"*

> *Lupina – "Yep. No prob. Very quiet here."*

> *Nick – "I'm going hiking. Look for me."*

> *Lupina – "No need! I'm fine!"*

> *Nick – "I'm bringing cake."*

There was a long pause.

> *Lupina – "I like cake."*

Nick grinned. That's what Miriam said.

> *Nick – "What kind?"*

> *Lupina – "Chocolate. Pound. Walnut. Carrot. Vanilla. Coffee. Cheese. Red Velvet."*

Nick – "It will be a surprise. Enough talking. Sleep well. Text me tomorrow."

Wendell, Richie, and Gary

When Rangers Bunn and Cowen checked into the dorm at the RumLot Security Outpost in Lethbridge, Alberta, Lord Gary was already there. Jameson had told Wendell that Lord Gary was, in his words, "a whack-job who was obsessed with finding Lord Freyja" and to be careful. He was an EN lord, of course, and that meant kid-glove handling by the RumLot Security humans, but he needed to be kept on a firm leash.

Lord Richard Cowen was worthy of his own pair of kid gloves. He was a new Ranger and a lord in his own right, the son of General Lord James Cowen, and was shadowing Wendell on his first real assignment. He was, by all accounts, quite a swordsman. Jameson wasn't talking about the one made of steel, useful for cutting off orc heads, but the one used in bedrooms, useful to most females. He already had a reputation, and he was only twenty-one.

Jameson wanted the lord to keep his sword sheathed and not blab about RumLot business to any pretty locals in Lethbridge. This was a business trip.

Both Richie and Gary were unripe lords and had no useful abilities when it came to magic, but they both had full lord stink and would attract any orcs who were passing by. Richie could fight and defend himself, or he would never have earned the rank of Ranger, but Gary was a redcoat who could only move a couple of teaspoons if he busted a gut. Victor joked that Gary couldn't defend himself against a pack of geriatric butterflies.

Since Wendell expected to babysit both lords, he told Richie before they left the UK that they would be hanging out with

Gary. Maybe he knew something about Lord Freyja that he was holding back. Why did he think he could find her? In any case, they would be polite and keep an eye on him. The last thing they needed was to spend time chasing after Gary if he went a-roaming.

Wendell and Richie strutted into the packed cafeteria on the RumLot Security compound in full Danger-Ranger black, complete with swords, knee boots, and lemon-squeezer campaign hats with ostrich plumes. The room was packed with a full artillery company of the Canadian Army training with the RumLot Security soldiers, and there was a little murmur when the Rangers walked in.

Alone in the back, Gary sat in cargo shorts and a t-shirt, and he noticed the stares the two men attracted, especially from the female soldiers, but he just put his head back down and worked on his meat loaf.

Then the Rangers came to his table!

Wendell introduced himself and Richie, and then, without waiting to be invited, just pulled out a chair and started chatting about the weather, what everyone at Aelfeham House was doing, general stuff. Richie didn't say much, just looked at Gary quizzically, and that started to get Gary's goat.

Richie, whom he didn't know at all other than by name, was meltingly handsome. Anyone would have to admit it. And he knew he was meltingly handsome, *and* a Ranger, *and* a pretty charming guy from a top-ranked EN family. Gary didn't need a Big Man On Campus to rub his nose into his own inadequacies, and Richie's rather bemused expression was grating.

Finally, he couldn't help himself. "Whatcha lookin' at?"

Richie had the grace to look embarrassed. "Sorry, bro, I didn't mean to stare. But why aren't you in uniform? I mean, look at this place! There are loads of women here. Lonely, away from home, very healthy, fit women. And they do like a uniform." He smiled and winked. "Don't you want a little side action? The human ladies love a lord, y'know."

"Rich." Wendell's voice was a warning.

Gary was gobsmacked and didn't know whether Lord Richard was making fun of him or being, as he said, a "bro" making guy talk. He must be making fun of him.

"The women aren't interested in redcoats." Gary looked down at his dinner and frowned.

"Oh, not true! Not true at all. Maybe some in Aelfeham House are a bit snobby, but out here in the real world? Hell no, a redcoat is a chick magnet." Richie looked at Gary and grinned. "I bet you ten Canadian loonies you could have a bird in your bed tonight if you had your uniform on. And cleaned up a bit. Women like well-groomed men, and mate, you're looking a little rough today."

Gary looked aghast at Wendell, who just shrugged.

"Don't pay any attention to him. Dell-boy's weenie is locked in a safe-deposit box, and only LeeAnne has the key. When're you two getting hitched?"

"September."

"Hmmm, maybe you should have a bit of fun, too, before you lose all control over your life."

"No thanks. I'm good. My Danger Ranger days are over."

Richie hooted at that. "Shit, they never started." He turned to Gary. "Dell here met LeeAnne when she was fekkin sixteen! That's a bit young even for me. Anyway, why don't we go out for a drink tonight? We don't have anything on tap in the morning. There must be a bar or something in this town where the girls hang out." He looked at Wendell, who was rolling his eyes. "Hey, Dell-boy, am I legal in Alberta?"

"Yeah, the age is 18 to get a drink here. You're twenty-one, you idiot; probably legal everywhere."

"If you tag along, you can be the designated tight-ass, and Gary and I can go cruisin'!" Rich turned to Gary, "But if you get too wasted, the bet's off. Even the lord bit won't work if you're barfin' on the chicks."

Gary just stared at Richie. Never in his life had any guy ever, ever, invited him to go with the guys for a night out to pick up girls. Never.

Richie just grinned. "I'll give you an hour. Shower, shave, and put on your clean knickers; someone might see you nekkid, my boy. Let's go see if we can find some fun ladies. There must be one or two around here. There always is."

Gary stood up and looked at the Rangers.

"Really?"

"Sure, it'll be fun. We'll wait here for you."

After Gary left, Richie turned to Wendell, who was trying very hard not to bust out laughing.

"I feel like Henry Higgins, I do."

Gary and Alma

Alma shook him awake.

"Hey, sweetie, I have to go to work. Do you need a lift to the Compound?"

Gary smiled weakly at her, nodded, and dressed as fast as he could, apologising for making her late for work. What did she do again?

"I'm a kindergarten teacher, and no, I'm not late, not yet. But, hon, you have to get a movin'." She tilted her head and looked at him. "Do you want my number?"

Gary stared at her. This woman wanted to see him again. Again! As in "more than once". He smiled shyly and nodded. "I'd love to have your number. I'm not allowed to give mine out, but I can set up a WhatsApp."

Alma frowned. Not *allowed* to give out his number? That was a new one.

"Not allowed, or don't want to?"

"Not allowed, for real. I really am a lord, and the EN takes security seriously. They pay for the phone; I have to follow their rules."

Alma nodded, mollified that she wasn't being jerked around. "And you're not married, right?"

Gary shook his head. No, not married.

"Okay then. Let's go before I really am late." And they both left Alma's apartment, each quite happy. She knew this guy really was a lord because last night his eyes were glowing all over the place, and when he came, his skin glowed, too. It was super sexy, and while he wasn't great in bed, he was certainly keen. He said she was beautiful. Yeah, this was probably one of those three-day things, but for her, it was one for the memory book. She had fucked a lord.

Gary, for his part, had a non-virtual sexual encounter with a real, live woman. And he owed Richie ten dollars.

Freyja and Nick

On Freyja's third day on the trail to Faro, the ravens flew back and told her a man was walking up the valley, towards her and the pack. He was, they said, one of her kind.

The way they put it made Freyja chuckle. "What do you mean, one of my kind? Are you surprised he's not a bird? What did you expect?"

The raven would have looked puzzled if he were capable of facial expressions. "*Your* kind. Not a human kind. The talking-to-us kind."

Surprised, she asked if Nick had talked to the ravens. "No, he didn't try to. He listened to us, though. He watched us."

Freyja looked thoughtfully at the ravens. Then she turned to the wolves and asked them. "Is Nick, the man who brought you the cow, human or like me?"

The wolves thought this was a ridiculous question. "Like you, of course! Don't be silly."

So Bruce had found another lord to help her. Was he with the EN? Was this all an elaborate stage play to keep her under observation while she worked through her quest?

It would really piss her off if Nick were a spy or fake, but he didn't feel fake. She could tell when someone was lying or hiding something, and he always was very matter-of-fact with her. Very honest. If she asked him outright if he was really with the EN, she would know if he was lying.

When he texted her and asked if she was okay, he meant it. He was concerned. She could feel that.

That night she texted him.

Lupina – "You're not far."

Nick – "How do you know?"

Lupina – "I have spies."

Nick grinned. The wolves must be watching him.

Nick – "I'm sure you do."

Lupina – "I'll meet you for breakfast. Is there a creek near you? A place to wash?"

Nick – "The river is too fast now. I'm near a pond."

Lupina – "Wash good and I'll wash good and we'll have breakfast. I can't eat with smelly bodies around. It's a quirk."

Nick – "Cold!"

Lupina – "And?"

Nick – "And I'll wash."

Lupina – "Nick, have you ever been to Europe?"

He stared at that one. What was going on? Was someone from the EN around?

Nick – "No. Went to the US once. I like Canada better."

Freyja was relieved. He wasn't lying; Nick had never been to Europe, and that meant he had never been to Aelfeham House. If Nick was a lord, he was either a lone wolf or part of some other group. She would find out tomorrow.

Lupina – "Going to sleep. Sleep well!"

Nick – "You, too. G'night."

In the morning, Nick crawled out of his sleeping bag and jumped into the pond. Jesus, it was cold! A quick scrub with some swiped hotel soap and –

"Hi Nick!"

He'd never ducked so fast in his life. It didn't matter anyway because the water was so damn cold his dick and balls were seeking warmth halfway up his spleen.

Freyja laughed and laughed, squatting on the bank of the pond with two wolves sitting with her. She looked like a river nymph, only in jeans.

"I didn't see anything! I promise! Your modesty is preserved!"

"Good, because everything I have is shrivelled up like a little raisin. It's COLD!" He grinned back at her and watched her laugh; it was hard not to laugh too.

"Your eyes are glowing."

He stopped smiling. Shit. She'd figured it out.

"It's okay; don't be mad at me. I'm a freak of nature, too!" Freyja sighed. "That's why you had to take a bath today. I did this morning, too. It's the pheromone issue. I think we're okay to have breakfast now, but we have to be careful."

"Pheromone?"

"Yeah, it's a lord thing. I'll explain at breakfast. I'll back off now so you can get out." She smiled and winked. "I promise not to peek."

True to her word, she was waiting back at his camp, and she didn't peek, not once. Nick unpacked the dried eggs, a big bag of shredded cheese and dried ham bits, and made a huge mess of scrambled omelette on the campfire. While he cooked, Freyja told him all about her sex ed class with Sylvia and what she'd seen at Aelfeham House.

He didn't say much, just listened until she was completely done, and then it was his turn.

"I've known I'm a lord for a few years now. I've had the glowing eye thing for as long as I can remember, but it wasn't until the European elves and lords emerged and got on the internet that I found out what it meant. I figure I'm a better Mountie than I'd ever be a lord, so I decided to stay as a Mountie and give the EN a pass." He shrugged. "I can always change my mind, but if I didn't like the lord business and I leave my job, I don't think I could get it back. The RCMP is going to kick me out when I turn sixty-five anyway."

He looked at Freyja. "But these pheromones – it's like when dogs go in heat?"

"Sylvia says it's a permanent bond that can't be broken without a lot of trauma. Usually, the lord will die. It's more than heat, although lords *do* go into musth like the moose do when the woman is fertile. But with bonding, we change physically to match our bond-partner, and that can't be unchanged. A dog, they'll go into a mating frenzy with the right smell, but when it's done and if the female is pregnant, the male isn't crazy any more. They can mate with others.

Sylvia said that it keeps the very small population of lords from fighting with each other over mates. If I got mad at my husband for fooling around, I could do a lot of damage, maybe not to him but to everyone else. So we're one and done. No divorces, no widows, no second chances. Not for ninety-nine per cent of bonds, she says."

"So you're willing to talk to me face-to-face if I keep the BO away."

Freyja nodded. "I don't want either of us to be doomed to a lifetime of grief with an accidental mistake. My mother got pregnant out of wedlock, and it was not on purpose – she was raped. Then she couldn't handle that and committed suicide the day after I was born. Sex accidents, rape, they're deadly."

Nick looked at her for a long time. "I'm sorry about your mom, but she didn't know you."

"My mother killed herself for a lot of reasons. I was just one of them. I was brought up in love, and I think I had a good childhood. I was adopted by my mother's twin, and we lived in the backwoods. I was a kid with glowing eyes who could talk to animals, and he was a man with a woman's body. He lived as a man but couldn't live in the real world. So we lived together in our own world away from people.

I was forty-three when he died, and until about two months ago, I never had much to do with people at all. I'm an old bitch and happy to be by myself." She grinned. "I never had to worry about smells and hormones and stuff like that."

"I'm pretty old, too. I'm fifty-three."

"I was born in 1910, Nick," she said softly.

"Whhhee…" he whistled. "You *are* an old bitch! But still beautiful and with all of your own teeth, I see."

Freyja laughed. "Of course, I have all of my own teeth! I keep them in a jar." Nick grinned back; he loved to hear her laugh. "Well, let me pack up, and we'll move on. What do you say we agree that if one of us gets too stinky, we just tell the other. No embarrassment, no hiding. Just say 'Nick, you smell like a pig,' and I'll deal with it. No accidents."

Freyja nodded, happy with that, and they broke camp.

Maksym and Darnya

Everyone, the intel elves, Jameson, Rashid, James, Kyrylo – everyone from top to bottom was absolutely sure Freyja was working her way down Hwy 2 to Carmacks. It was the next logical place if she was going to wake up elves every hundred miles or so. After all, that's what Caddy did when she was setting up the UK to be Fortress Elf Nation.

If it took her X days to go between Forty Mile and Steward Crossing, then it should take X days to go to the next stop off, Carmacks.

So when the day passed and no elves were raised, then another day and then another, worry started to grip the Elf Nation cadre. Was Freyja sick? Hurt? Lost in the forest? Captured by bounty hunters or taking a well-deserved holiday? No one knew.

Maybe, one small voice mentioned in one of the many meetings they had to discuss Lord Freyja, *maybe* the lord had sensed that people were gathering in Carmacks and decided to skip the place. Where would she go then?

If she went down Hwy 2 to catch Hwy 1, she'd pass through more towns. She'd need to reprovision soon, and more towns meant more opportunities for the lord or her helpers to find a grocery store. Other routes were through the wilderness. Every possible route ended up in Watson Lake, where she would finally leave the Yukon and enter British Columbia.

The team sent Darnya and Maksym down Hwy 2. They were in Whitehorse when word got out that a new crop of elves was now awake on Hwy 4. It appeared that Lord Freyja was not bothered by the wilderness and didn't miss shopping in a Walmart.

By the time Darnya and Maksym snaked up the tiny road through the mountains to Ross River, Lord Freyja was long gone, evaporating like a dream into the vast wilderness just like her white wolves.

Maksym was starting to take this chase personally. Darnya could only roll her eyes at him; the woman was obviously clever, and she simply would be a hard nut to crack, but they would find her sooner or later, she was sure. In the meantime, she and Maksym were having a very nice busman's holiday. They had given up the pretence of separate hotel rooms and were starting to bicker like an old married couple. She cut his hair for him, and he gave her foot massages.

Darnya drew the line at doing his laundry, though. Some boundaries just weren't made to be crossed.

Tim Snelling

When Tim Snelling enlisted in the US Army at age eighteen, he went in as an E-nothing grunt, Army MOS 11-B, Infantryman. It was either join the Army or go to jail, according to the judge who sentenced him for jacking that car. The judge took a long look at him and said that one day she hoped Tim would thank her for giving him the option, and Tim thought to himself, No way, whore. You're lucky I don't fuckin' kill you, but Tim was not stupid enough to go to a fed pen to pay for the satisfaction of getting even with a judge for giving him a crap choice. He chose the Army.

The irony was that two years later, he wrote a thank-you letter to the judge. She was right.

He liked the Army. He liked the discipline, the pay, the three hots and a cot, the men in his unit – most things about it. He was in a man's world in the infantry, and that was cool, too. Two years later, when his first re-up came around, he knew how to negotiate his next contract and applied for and was sent to sniper school in Georgia.

Being a sniper suited Tim to the ground. For one thing, he was really, really good at it. For another, it was bad-ass, and he liked the respect he saw in the eyes of civilians when he told them what he did. But mostly, he liked that a good sniper worked alone and killed. By the time he made sergeant, he was one of the top snipers in the army, and he had some good combat experience in the Russian War. He was supposed to be training Ukrainians, but hell, you can't train someone in an office, can you? He would go out with them and demonstrate his skills on Russians. That got him in trouble a couple of times, but it also got him noticed. When his next enlistment cycle came up, he left the Army and was hired by a major defence contractor who managed things off the books for the CIA.

That's how he ended up working for the CIA. They gave him some very interesting training, and when President Meecham was elected, Tim was working all over the world. He'd get an assignment, study the target, plan the hits, plan his escape routes, and then do the job. He was very, very efficient. He only did a couple of jobs a year; after the first few, they reserved him for the most interesting, most sensitive ones. Otherwise, he trained and learned new things like bomb making, disguises – the whole super spy enchilada.

Being in the same post for months at a time meant he was able to meet people and nest a bit; one guy Tim met took him to his church, and he found God there. God, he learned, must be pleased with Tim's work because he was so good and successful at it. It never occurred to Tim that Satan rewarded his minions, too. The preacher never mentioned that. He said God rewarded those who worshipped him with money, women, success – everything. Just as the preacher said, a few weeks after he joined the Church, he met Angel at Bible Study, and three months later, they were married.

He never told Angel what he did. She knew he travelled and worked as a government contractor, and that was all she needed to know. Angel was docile, compliant, and godly. She was just the perfect woman for partnering with Tim and following God's orders to be fruitful and have a proper family, because she became pregnant the week they were married, and she had twins.

He was sure they were his because he'd kill Angel if she fooled around when he was gone. Besides, they had his purple eyes. So she gloried in her role as a supportive wife, mother, household manager, and someone to screw, and Tim had his role as defender of the republic, absolute leader of the family, and breadwinner. They were both very happy.

When the demons rose from Hell, Tim totally supported President Meechum's efforts to keep them out of the US, as did his church. It was a no-brainer, really. Democracy was good, but only when the right people were in charge, and if a few democratic principles had to be set aside to make sure the entire country was kept pure, that was fine. It was like being in the Army. You didn't get to do or say whatever you wanted there either.

At the beginning of President Meechum's second and forever term, Tim was assigned to a very, very special group of operatives who worked directly under Meechum, and sometimes he wondered if the CIA even knew about his new chain of command. His job was to go find lords inside the US and kill them, a pretty straightforward assignment.

The problem was that they couldn't find any. Not one. They were surprised at first, especially when eight documented demons now living in Europe had come from the US, but two theories emerged. One was that the eight were all that existed as adults, and any lord children were being hidden by demon sympathisers, and the other was that Satan was helping all the adults and children hide. Tim was sure Satan was involved, which made the demon hunting all the more difficult and important.

Now there was another demon showing up on the radar. An escapee from Alaska. A proven killer who froze people on sight. A demon who could look at a helicopter and freeze up its rotors and make it crash. A woman who lived with familiars, wolves.

A demon witch who raised imps.

Tim was sent outside of the US for the first time in years, to Canada. His job was very straightforward – find her and kill her.

He looked forward to it. It was what he was made to do.

Nick and Freyja

During their hike to the car, Freyja stopped to feed the wolves. When Nick heard her talk to them, the language she used teased his brain. He could almost make sense of it, and when they talked back to her, to his astonishment, he understood. They told her where the deer were, and when they flushed out a small herd, she raised her ancient Remington Repeater, fired six shots as fast as the old gun would allow, and six deer fell like rocks.

The lord was a damn good shot.

As they waited for the wolves to have their feed, Freyja taught Nick a few words in what he learnt was Elvish.

"I didn't know it was Elvish, I thought it was just animal talk, but when I got to Aelfeham House, I found out what it was. I'd been speaking to animals since I was a baby; who else did I have to talk to? But in Aelfeham House, they all spoke Elvish. The difference is that animals use very, very simple language, and the elves' version is more detailed. But it's a language that we know in our bones. You'll catch up fast once you start using it."

She started speaking Elvish to him, and like she said, he picked it up quickly.

When Freyja and Nick reached the Jeep, she continued on foot towards Ross River, and he drove back to Little Salmon and finally picked up the pigs. The pig farmer wondered what the holdup was, and he had to give him another twenty for the extra feed.

Back-tracking to Freyja, he caught up to her in the wilderness near Pelly River, and there she fed the wolves again, and Nick stayed with her when she woke up a clan of elves.

It was the most extraordinary thing he had ever seen in his life, and while he experienced it again and again as they worked their way south, the first time was seared in his soul forever.

Freyja found a place she said had elves, and early in the morning, she prepared herself to raise them. She said she wanted to be at least ten miles away by dark because once the elves were raised, the EN would know where she was, and Freyja didn't want to mess with the EN now; they would just get in the way and bring more attention to her.

He couldn't see any difference between that particular meadow and all the others in the Pelly River valley, but she did.

"I can feel them sleeping here; they're deep, but they're there. It's like a vibration, a buzz. They want out, to waken. They're ready."

He couldn't feel it at all. "This is your special magic, Freyja, not mine. Maybe not anyone else's."

She nodded, but no smile. This was work. The wolves arranged themselves in a huge circle, guarding Freyja, and Nick could see they were tense but excited. They yipped happily to each other, and while some sat quietly, others spun in tight, excited circles, getting rid of nervous energy. He could hear them talk. "A whelping! Freyja's whelping again! Fun!!"

Earlier, she'd told Nick to get his Bowie knife out and what to expect. Freyja would sing, and her voice would guide the elves to the surface. The eggs would pop out of the ground, he would run around and slit the sacs of those who were too weak to do it themselves, and once free of their sacs, they'd pop away. The wolves would help. It should take about half an hour, maybe forty-five minutes, depending on how many eggs there are. Not hard, she said, just tiring.

Freyja began to sing, and her eyes glowed laser bright. The song was otherworldly, a siren's song, and while he understood the words in his head, it was the song he felt in his bones that woke and guided the elves. He could feel it pulling the elves; he could feel the magic creating a rope, a guide, a command, and once he felt that, he felt the elves under his feet moving towards them.

Her voice soared and echoed across the valley, chasing impossible octaves, and all the while it commanded, cajoled, *"Come to me. It's time to wake, it's time to taste your clan lands, it's time. Come to me…"*

Freyja's entire body glowed, and in the wolves' circle, she was a bright beacon of light, a flaming pillar. Nick could feel the incredible energy she was using, and he could feel her tiring, but the song was unrelenting. No elf, no human, no lord was going to resist her call.

There was a pause as she listened, and Nick felt the ground rumble under his feet, and she sang again, this time a joyful, welcoming, lilting song.

Nick felt another rumble, and then the ground exploded around him, huge eggs like boulders flinging out of the ground like cannonballs. Suddenly, the wolves leapt forward and, like Freyja did the first time, Nick was jolted out of his frozen shock by the

fear that the wolves were going to attack the eggs, but they didn't.
They slashed at the eggs with their teeth and claws, freeing the
elves like they would free a whelped pup from a birth sac.

He jumped forward, the instinct to assist a new birth
overtaking any other thought, and he bent down over his first egg
and through the semi-transparent shell he saw an old man staring
back, his hands pressed against the rubbery shell. Nick slashed, the
elf was free, and the old man grinned and nodded his head in
thanks, and *poof* in a shower of sparks, he was gone.

Nick ran to the next egg, freed a young woman who
looked at him, terrified, as she cowered in the soupy egg. He lifted
her out, and in his haste to move her, he threw her, and she ported
out, leaving another shower of sparks. Speeding from egg to egg,
faster and faster, he was a whirlwind, and while he didn't notice it,
his eyes and hands glowed as he worked.

Freyja freed some elves, but she was much slower, and
when Nick looked up, her own glow was fading away, and she was
swaying.

"Freyja! Are you okay? Sit down; we'll get this!"

She waved, staggered to the next egg, and Nick shook
his head and just worked faster, frantically slashing and freeing
elves.

The next egg, her last one, had a young woman in it. The
naked woman was already punching her way out when the lord, all
in full glow with eyes like green stars, knelt by her and widened
the hole. "Thank you," the elf whispered, and as the two women
looked at each other, Freyja had to smile. They were both equally
exhausted and swaying like metronomes.

"What do you command? What can I do?" She was so, so tired, but this Lord Freyja had awakened her, and if she wanted porting or feeding, the elf would do her best.

Freyja laughed and shook her head. "I don't want anything. Go join the Elf Nation and live your best life. That will make me happy." And the elf ported out.

Between the wolves, Nick and Freyja, and the elves who came back to free their kin, they freed forty-six elves, and then it was over. Freyja stood up, listened, and then yelled to Nick, "Done! We've got them all!" He ran to her and in a wild moment of exultation –

He kissed her. Freyja bonded. He didn't. And that was that.

Nick didn't notice the flash of heat that came off her from the bonding, and to be honest, Freyja didn't either. She'd expected to be wracked with a tidal wave of hormones and emotions after raising the elves; this was not her first time. She was exhausted from the energy drain from using so much magic, and Nick backed off the minute he realised what he had done, and any extra flush right after her full flame up wasn't anything to remark on on an already remarkable day.

But he couldn't stay apart more than a second, and Nick laughed and grabbed Freyja in his arms, spinning her around, his tornado of joy unrestrained. "Look at what you did, you beautiful woman! Whoooo-hooo! Magic. You're magic!"

She laughed and returned his hug, and it took a minute to get their emotions under control, but like all extremely good things, the joy ended too quickly, and they settled down.

"I don't know how you manage to hike another ten miles after all this. The Jeep is just a couple of miles from here. If you can walk that far – shit, I'll carry you if you need me to – we can drive a good thirty away, and the wolves can catch up. Can't you call them or something? Bruce told me they found you in Dawson when you told them to stay away."

Freyja thought about it. She dreaded another forced march, and she didn't want to stay in the meadow's whelping circle now. The EN would find this spot within minutes now that there were elves here. It was really an easy decision.

A half hour later, they were in the Jeep, the wolves' panniers stowed in the back, and Freyja told the wolves her direction of travel and that they were to meet up in a day or two. She also, very sternly, told them not to eat any farm animals they came across or any humans, for that matter.

Freyja crawled into the Jeep and immediately fell asleep, and Nick drove to Watson Lake, where he had a motel room waiting.

Caddy

Caddy was told about the emergence of the Pelly Lakes Clan just minutes after it happened. When the clan leader had passed through the Safe Haven New Elf Reception Station, cleaned up, and rested, she immediately ported to meet with the Primary in Ukraine, as all new clan leaders did now. Caddy warmly welcomed her as she always did, and when the elf told her of her clan's extraordinary experience, Caddy learned something new.

One very important bit of information was that there were two lords. There was a male lord with Freyja, which suddenly put a whole new twist on things and explained why she'd gone back to Canada. Was this a bond-man, an uncle, a cousin, a brother, or a friend? They didn't know. No one had asked Freyja about her present family. All the elves knew (from Sylvia) was that when Freyja was at Aelfeham House, she was still an unbonded virgin, and her father was dead.

And the other important thing was that Freyja had talked to the clan leader herself. The clan leader knew their clan owed the lord and had asked what she wanted. Freyja had replied,

"I don't want anything. Go join the Elf Nation and live your best life. That will make me happy."

That news changed everything. Freyja was not working against the EN. She was not setting up her own power base. She had a lord-man with her, relationship unknown, and he was surely her reason for returning, although the reason for her journey south was still a mystery.

As Caddy wryly told Kyrylo later, "I bet he knows why. He probably talks to her."

The temperature of the Rogue Lord meetings went down, and the emphasis changed from wondering how to catch her to wondering how to keep both lords safe as they roamed.

_____

Bruce and Commissioner Threader

Bruce's boss told him to come to a meeting at HQ, ASAP, PDQ, and every other acronym he could muster. It was a big deal, he said. Don't be late.

It was a bit insulting, really. Bruce was never late to meetings, but his boss was in a right tizzy that was for sure. The Mountie had a sneaking suspicion it was about Lord Freyja. He was pretty sure his boss wasn't worried about the menu for Bruce's retirement party.

So that morning, he dressed in his good work stuff, the blue serge uniform, made sure his peak hat was as perfect as it could be, and went off to face whatever music was going to be played for him.

"I'll either come home a hero or fired – no in between," he told Miriam as he walked out.

The conference room was packed to the walls. Boss, boss's secretary, transcriptionist, and, for god's sake, the top guy of the RCMP and the top guy from the government's EN Relations Division. *And* their manicured and suited hangers-on. Bruce bet he was the only person in the room with a ten-dollar haircut.

Bruce was shown his seat and offered a coffee, which was a good sign. No one offered coffee to someone they were about to fire.

The RCMP Commissioner, a wiry Mountie named Threader, started off.

"Mountie Scott, first of all, we don't want you to think you're in any trouble." He paused, and the unsaid "yet" hung in the air.

"The Elf Nation, as you know, was part of a rescue of a lord, Lord Freyja, who originally fled from Alaska. She was hurt and taken to their place in the UK for recovery. For some reason, we don't know why, she decided not to stay with them, and she came back here, where it appears she stopped at your house. Is any of this untrue?"

Bruce said no, it was all true as far as he knew.

"It's obvious to everyone that she's not with you now because she's waking up elf clans up and down the Yukon, outside of the Elf Nation sphere of influence, and it appears without their permission or help."

He stopped and looked directly at Bruce.

"Mountie Scott, we want to help her if it's in Canada's interest. Even if she's outside of the Elf Nation's control, she's still working for Canada. She's been a huge asset so far, but we don't know the endgame. Is she heading to the US to set up elves there? Is she setting up her own Elf Nation? Is she planning on taking over Canada? The world? We don't know." He leaned forward. "But you do."

Bruce considered this. Commissioner Threader didn't ask any questions he hadn't asked himself. None of these questions so far would tell anyone where Freyja was.

"Sir, in my opinion, she is waking up elves because that's the right thing to do if you have the ability. I don't think she's anti-Elf Nation, but during her time there, she didn't fit in. I think, basically, she felt useless, maybe unwanted. But she also has a quest, a dream, that she has to fulfil. If you're First Nation like I am, you understand the power of dreams. She had a powerful dream, and her dream told her to do exactly what she's doing now. I don't think we Canadians have anything to fear. She's not going to set up her own Elf Nation or take over Canada or anything like that. She's not power hungry. She's pretty shy, really."

The room murmured and shuffled. The Commissioner looked at the men in grey suits. One nodded.

"That's good to hear. Are you going to tell us where she is now?"

"No, Sir."

"Didn't think so, but, eh, thought I'd ask." The Commissioner tented his fingers and leaned back. "So I assume you're managing this operation on your own, freelance."

"Yes and no, Sir. I'm managing but not alone. I can't tell you anything else."

Threader gave Bruce a long, serious look. "Any operation that is as quiet as yours has been must be very small. That makes it brittle. If one or two key people go down, the thing falls apart."

"Yes, Sir. And a big operation has too many moving parts, too many people with mouths and their own agendas. Lord Freyja has enemies; the bounty hunters were a surprise to her, but she has learned the value of not letting everyone know her business."

Threader nodded. No one that he knew of had cracked Scott's group, electronically or from hum-int. It was a tight operation, and they wanted to keep it that way. So far, they'd been successful.

"Any operation has expenses. I suppose you can send us a bill. For costs, food, gas, that sort of thing."

Bruce was taken aback. The RCMP was usually not so free with its money.

"The Mounties will pay her expenses?"

Commissioner Threader grinned and pointed to the suits. "Hell, no! They will. We can help in other ways. Clear roads, intel, that sort of thing. If you're running this thing on your own, and

Lord Freyja has no income that we know of, where's the money coming from?"

"Our pensions, Sir. Savings. About six grand a month."

Threader winced. "Well, I have to admire your commitment. Okay, this is what I want from you. *Want*, because I can't order civilians to do anything, and what your group is doing is not illegal. But if we're going to pay, we need some cooperation. I'll assign you full-time to this operation; all other work duties are suspended. I expect a status report twice a week and every time something notable happens – confidential – directly to me. I'll pass on what needs to be passed. You'll put in an expense report once a week and keep the accountants happy. *Any* conversation – *any* contact with the Elf Nation – must go through the embassy and government. No free-lance diplomacy. If you need help, you ask for it. Got all that?"

"Yes, Sir." Bruce cleared his throat. This was a lot more than he'd expected. He'd expected to be told to hand over the entire operation or be fired. He and Miriam were prepared to walk. Maybe he'd keep that pension after all.

"Thank you, all of you. She's trying to do the right thing. Her dream told her to wake elves, and keep her people safe, and we're her people. She's very powerful, I think, and she's on our side."

"We got the power part, Scott. Not many people can bring down a helicopter by frowning at it. It's good to know she's on our side. That makes all of us sleep a bit better. God help us if she wasn't. And Scott? Do try not to kill too many people. That last mess in Dawson created a ton of paperwork. I'm still dealing with it."

"Yes, Sir. I'll pass that on."

And that was the end of the meeting. Bruce left, a bit unnerved by the Commissioner and the silent men who watched and listened. He wondered how long their private meeting would last because he knew, as sure as he knew the sun was going to rise, that what he said was going to be parsed and chewed down to the last syllable.

Bruce was right. After he left, the meeting lasted for hours. If Scott was telling the truth, and they all felt he was, as far as the Mountie knew, Lord Freyja was working to do what the EN wasn't, and that was putting all of her efforts into waking up Canadian elves.

While the EN, from their point of view, had invested a lot into Canadian security, to the Canadians facing a huge and now hostile neighbour to the south, as far as they were concerned, there could never be too much magical help. While several lords had fled to Canada, none had stayed, not even the one who was living in the mountains, their own Lord Ratna. Lord Freyja, it appeared, agreed with the Canadian government, and not only that, she was pretty powerful stuff. Even Lord Kyrylo couldn't raise elves.

Ottawa felt that it had won the lord lottery, but that didn't mean it was turning its back on the EN. They would have to find a balance between the interests of Canada, their Lord Freyja, and the EN. That's where the diplomats earned their penny.

That night, Miriam prepared a bill and sent it to the Commissioner. It charged the Canadian government for all expenses so far under headings of "Consultation" and a general "Travel, Food, and Lodging" category. "Consultation" was the biggest expense; it was for the wolves' food, but Miriam didn't think that needed to be discussed. As vague as it was, it was paid in three days directly to the Scotts' bank account, just as if Bruce had gone to Toronto for a convention.

Three days for reimbursement. That was freakin' magic right there.

Tony

The one thing about covert operations was that they cost money. In any bureaucracy, even the most secret ones, someone in accounting was tracking the money. In today's accounting world, everything is done on computers, and computers (and accountants) demand that every line item have its own code and fit in a certain little box. Was this restaurant receipt for lunch or for dinner? Was the hotel government-approved, and if there was a rebate on the invoice, where did that five per cent go? Even James Bond had to submit an expense report, and Q still had to send purchase orders through proper channels.

So when Mountie Bruce Scott suddenly had a very large reimbursement sent to his bank account from the Office of the Intelligence Commissioner, an AI program at the RumLot Security offices in Lowestoft was watching for just that sort of thing. It had access to the computer systems of normal retail banks, and one of the accounts it watched was Mountie Bruce Scott's joint checking account. The large deposit from the OIC was flagged as unusual, and an alert was emailed to Tony, the elf in charge of Elf Nation financial operations.

Tony then asked the elves to send him a copy of the Scotts' bank statement. That took about half an hour to produce (they were busy), and after looking over the outgoings for the last year, Tony saw an anomaly. Miriam Scott was suddenly buying an amazing amount of meat. Not nice meat either. Old cows, pigs, even a horse, and all from First Nations farmers and ranchers. A thousand here, two thousand there, and that was real money for an older couple to spend on groceries.

You'd have to be as hungry as a wolf to eat that much meat.

So Tony sent the report to Lord James.

James thought those meat purchases were interesting, too, and asked Maksym to check on them. One payment was to a pig farmer on the Little Salmon/Carmacks First Nation's reservation, not too far from where he was staying.

The farmer wasn't there, but his daughter was and happily gave Macksym a copy of the invoice for the old pigs, "so he could send it to the accountants," but the paperwork didn't say who'd picked up the pigs. Was that the same person who'd purchased them? Maksym was concerned that the right person was reimbursed. Oh, no, she said. The man who picked up the pigs was a really nice guy staying at the motel in Carmacks. The very same motel that Maksym and Darnya had stayed at. At the same time. But the girl didn't know his name.

The motel in Carmacks wasn't helpful; their client records were confidential. What if that guy was having a sexy but illicit weekend with someone? Since Maksym didn't have a warrant and the hotel guest register was kept in an old-fashioned black ledger, Maksym drew a dead end. He'd have to break in that night to get at it.

When he went out to the car, Darnya was lying back in the seat, napping, which ticked her partner off until she grinned at him and showed him her phone. When they were testing the drone in the parking lot, she had filmed it on her phone and had accidentally taken video of all of the cars parked there that day, all ten of them. Make, models, and license plates were all on the video. She had already uploaded it to Ukraine and (fingers crossed) their guy was in his room then and not enjoying the wonders of downtown Carmacks.

The elves were pretty quick, and the report landed in Lord James's inbox within the hour. All of the cars and trucks at the motel seemed perfectly normal, but one was of interest. It was a green Jeep owned by a man named Nick Fortins, who (surprise, surprise) was a Mountie. His HR file at RCMP HQ was quickly accessed. Ex-Canadian Army special forces. One adult child who was his beneficiary. Divorced. Who was on temporary medical leave for anxiety attacks.

James hooted. Anxiety attacks! He would remember that one.

The 4x4 had a sat nav and direct internet access to the Jeep maintenance computers, but it was disabled. The Mountie had a phone, but it was offline, and the last geo-location ping was in Toronto. No odd activity in his bank accounts. Not even a credit card entry to pay for the motel, and yet they knew he was there.

The man certainly knew how to cover his tracks, but there were always cracks, and it was usually a human who made them. The girl at the pig farm remembered that the man who picked up the pigs was staying at the motel, and that was all the crack they needed. James now had a name, a license plate, and a car description to work with, which was a sight more info than he'd had a day ago.

The report was sent to the Rangers and to the agents.

Nick and Freyja

She only woke up long enough to walk into the motel room, and then she flopped on one of the double beds, and that's where she stayed for two days.

Nick took her shoes, coat, and jeans off, talking to the comatose Freyja the entire time because the last thing he wanted was for her to wake up and think she was being raped or something. That would certainly put a damper on their relationship! But the t-shirt stayed on when he discovered she wasn't wearing a bra. Then, as fast as he could, he shoved her under the sheets and tucked her in. She never woke up.

Goddamn, she smelled good, but mindful of her worries about bonding and pheromones, Nick cracked a window and put the room's HVAC fan on high and hoped that would be enough.

Every time he got woozy from her perfume or found himself staring at her too much, he would go take a walk or get something to eat and clear his head. In the meantime, he did some texting with Miriam about the next meat purchase and talked a long time to Bruce (WHOOO-hoo! Money came in!) about the suits from Ottawa.

He started spending a lot of time on the elf-fan sites. Most were crap, but a couple had real news and info on them, and one in particular was interesting. It had a page for each known lord and links to mainstream news reports, along with artists' renderings of the lords. There was even a page about Freyja as the newest lord, along with a report on the helicopter incident, the bounty hunters, and the wolves. There was something there for everyone. Adventure! Animals! Magical power! Beauty! (Although Nick thought the drawing of her was pretty lame, she looked like an anime doll.) She was very popular, according to the comments at the bottom of the page and had her own fan club. But there were creepy comments, too, from men. If those were the comments the AI filters let through, Nick would hate to see the unedited ones.

He stayed busy while she slept, washing their clothes in the motel laundromat, bringing sacks of take-out to the room to eat, and researching the next leg's motel and food options.

He wasn't used to sleeping in the same room with someone else any more. Tracy was a noisy sleeper, and if she had an allergy attack, she snored like a longshoreman. But they'd divorced fifteen years ago, and since then, there had been a couple of casual girlfriends, but he never stayed the night, which is one reason they stayed casual. He was worried about his eyes and their reaction to them.

It was fifteen years since he served in the army, and, oddly, he could still sleep in extremely loud places, like on a transport prop plane. But a metre away from a woman who quietly sighed and snuffled in her sleep? Insomnia. Every noise Freyja made woke him up.

When she finally woke up, Nick was fast asleep and didn't hear her go to the bathroom and take a shower. When she came out, she poked him in the shoulder like he was a sleeping bear, and he just about jumped out of his skin, which made her laugh and laugh.

Freyja found her backpack with the laundered clothes and was fresh and clean from the skin out, but she didn't seem too worried about his stinky ass. She sat on the bed cross-legged and combed out her long, wet hair. Breakfast, it seemed, was more of a worry than his studly pheromones.

"When I'm out of the shower, we'll go get something to eat. There's a restaurant down the street. We can walk there."

Freyja frowned and looked down at a knot she was untangling.

"What's the matter?"

She sighed. "I've never eaten in a restaurant. Not sure how to do it, and I don't want to draw attention to myself."

Now it was Nick's turn to laugh. "Oh, babe, no worries. We'll pretend we're time-travelling from the fifties, and I'll order for you. It'll make me feel superior and in charge. Once we've done it a couple of times, you'll see what to do, and you won't need me." He looked at her. "You just need to cover your ears. Mine aren't going to bother anyone, but you – That's where all the attention is going to go. Do you have a ski cap or something? It's getting too hot for the parka."

She smiled and nodded. Nick, Freyja thought, I'll always need you – but she pushed that thought out of her mind. Where had that come from? Instead, she worked on her hair while he showered and shaved. Nick hadn't shaved in a week, and while he had almost no body hair, being a full-blooded First Nation, he had a few chin whiskers, and they needed to go. He might not be pretty, but he liked being neat.

The restaurant was a typical country place with Formica-topped tables, and each table was festooned with the ubiquitous bottle of ketchup in a handy metal rack along with the salt and pepper shakers. The place was fairly busy, but then breakfast always was when you're located at the entrance to an RV park. It was shoulder season, and the park's rates were still cheap.

Elderly adventure campers from the RV park made up half the clientele, and the other half were locals – construction workers, ranchers, hunting guides, all the people who served the tourists.

Freyja had a ski cap pulled over her head and two long braids, and between the two, her ears were covered. Jeans, a t-shirt, a jeans jacket, hiking boots, and she was in full Yukon summer uniform. Aside from the fact that she filled out her outfit in more interesting ways than the other women in the restaurant, she blended in just fine.

Nick found a booth, handed her a menu, and with that, the lord's first experience with eating out began. She had a great time choosing, and when Nick told the waitress the lady wanted three full breakfast platters, the waitress didn't even blink. Some people were weird, and if the lady didn't finish all the food, she certainly didn't care. Just pay the bill and leave a tip.

They were doing fine until the orcs walked in. Freyja was working on her third and last Yukon Maple Leaf Early Morning Pancake Platter when the three men made their grand entrance. They were brothers and, from the sour look on the waitress's face, a familiar sight.

They made a lot of noise as they strutted through the centre aisle of the restaurant, yelling at the waitress to bring them coffee, they were fuckin' hungover, eh, and jus' starvin' and...

One stopped and looked right at Freyja. Then at Nick. Then back to Freyja.

"Boy, you're wa-ay too ugly to have a piece of ass like this." He bent over and leaned on the table, his brothers laughing at him and trying to get him to move on. "Sweetheart, why don't you come and sit with us. We can..."

Was it Nick's ability coming into play? How did he move so fast? One minute, he was sitting in the booth, and Freyja didn't know how he did it, but a second later, he had the guy by the collar, and he was halfway to the door. Two seconds later, the jerk was flying halfway across the parking lot. Nick spun and faced the two brothers who were coming at him with purple blood in their eyes and flashed his Mountie badge, shoving it right into the nearest orc's nose.

"Royal Canadian Mounted Police. Mountie to you two hosers. I'm on vacation, but if you want me to go back on duty, you just keep doing what you're doing. I'd leave now if I were you."

The two brothers looked at each other, took the measure of the huge Mountie, mumbled something about not being hungry, and edged out the door, avoiding Nick like he had scabies or something. When the door slammed shut, the stunned customers laughed and clapped, and the incident was over.

Until the tires on the orcs' truck blew up. That made everyone run to the window.

Nick walked back to Freyja and saw her eyes glowing. But before anyone else noticed, her head was bent over her pancakes, and she resumed working on them.

"Looks like those guys are having a bad day." She didn't look up as he sat down, but he could see a little smile. "They must have overfilled their tires."

"Looks like those guys are having a bad life. Sorry you had to put up with that. Don't let it put you off going out with me." He grinned and leaned back. "But now I can say my dates get dinner *and* a show, even at breakfast."

Freyja laughed, and for Nick, all was right with the world. They finished breakfast and walked back to the hotel, ready to go on to their next leg and look for the wolves.

On the way back to the motel, Nick found that Freyja could heat as well as freeze. Either way, it was all the same amount of effort to make atoms move, creating friction, or make them quiet, creating cold. It was just easier to make things cold in cold weather and hot in hot weather, and it was warming up now. She had made the ground under the orc's truck heat up, melting the tires.

Amazing. The possibilities of what a lord could do with that magic were endless.

Gary

Wendell looked at the report during lunch. He was in McDonald's, chewing on his second Filet o' Fish, and told Richie that HQ had identified the guy Lord Freyja was with. It looked like she was getting help from some Mounties, but they had a name of one and his car ID'd, and that was a good break. They had something to track now.

Gary heard the news, too, when he was with the two Rangers at McD's because he followed them everywhere.

Richie started calling him Barnacle, which he immediately shortened to Barney, and while the lord was a bit wet, Wendell didn't mind him tagging along. He was supposed to watch him, and if Barney was glued to them like a limpet, that just made his job easier. Aside from the fact that he was always skint when they went out (which was really annoying), Gary didn't cause any problems.

Freyja was with a man, but Gary wasn't worried about that. She couldn't bond to a human, and that meant she was still open to him. Finding her was the only obstacle, and if the EN now had a fix on the people protecting him, it was only a matter of time before they found the lord herself. Gary was pretty sure that these two Rangers would be sent up to help with any new EN contacts with Freyja; that's what Rangers did.

Lord Richie, now that one thought he was a real stud, and Gary could see him making a move on her. He made a move on anything vertical with an X chromosome who winked back, and although he wasn't looking for a bond-wife, he was good-looking, very confident, and would definitely get in the way. Gary was already gaming ways to neutralise him. The lord was still totally unripe, but he was a Ranger, and he knew how to fight, and Gary had no doubts that Richie could pound him into talc if it came to one-on-one combat.

Wendell was a legendary Ranger and even more formidable than Richie, but he was human and madly in love with someone named LeeAnne, so he was just an obstacle, not a potential rival. Gary had no intentions of getting into a fight with Wendell if he could help it.

He thought about getting a gun, a pistol of some sort, but he didn't have enough money. What he did have was Alma. Alma seemed to be getting rather fond of Gary, which was a constant surprise. They had sex every time they went out, which was another constant surprise. She taught him a lot, it was fun, and she seemed to like him in the sack if he did what she told him to do. Until Alma Gary had never once thought about making a woman happy in bed; his previous encounters were so frantic that all he thought about was getting his own rocks off, and since the women never came back for seconds, keeping them happy wasn't part of the game plan.

Not one of the games he played online worried about keeping a woman happy, in bed or out. Women were to be destroyed if they were with the bad guys and rescued if they were one of the compliant good ones, and the reward was typically a virtual blow job. When he left the virtual woman, a new half-naked, boobaliscous babe would show up. That's the way games were designed, and Gary honestly thought his video games were modelled on real life. Every time he discovered they weren't, reality was a disappointment.

Alma had a car, which she let Gary drive when they went out "because he missed driving a car," and when he talked to her about the risks of being a lord, she bought a pistol for her apartment, just in case a bounty hunter or religious fanatic broke in while he was there.

Alma, her apartment, money, car, and the pistol were all part of the cache he was accumulating. When the Game of Freyja moved to the top level, he'd be ready.

Freyja and Nick

After Watson Lake, Freyja and Nick left Yukon Territory and drove into British Columbia. At least Nick drove. Freyja walked with the wolves.

The rhythm established between Pelly Lakes and Watson Lake seemed to work out. Freyja would walk south with the wolves, avoiding any human settlements and staying in the wilderness areas. In the meantime, Nick drove the 80 to 100 miles to the next town with a motel, checked in, arranged the next carcasses for the wolves, and drove back when Freyja found a good feeding spot. They'd feed the wolves, and Freyja would find a secluded camping spot near a place where she sensed elves. The next morning, they'd meet at the camp, break camp, raise elves, and Nick would drive them back to the hotel where Freyja would sleep like the dead for a day and a half, minimum, but usually two days.

She walked roughly parallel with Hwy 97, and this time both the Canadians and the EN figured out her route. Unfortunately, so did the elf hunters and paparazzi. The human fans and stalkers were slow because not all of the elves emerged near human towns, and it was humans who told the world about the newest elf settlement. But eventually they connected the dots, and to Nick's great annoyance, finding a motel started to get tricky. The little towns generally weren't stuffed with tourist lodging, and some of the motels and guest houses were really nice, while others were, to put it bluntly, dives. Nick told Bruce in one phone call that he felt like Joseph taking a very sleepy Mary to some particularly mouldy mangers.

He didn't tell Bruce why he was suddenly getting so prissy about his sleeping arrangements, but one depressing place had the windows nailed shut, and he had a hard time that night dealing with her pheromones. It was getting too risky to nap in the Jeep if he needed some clean air. Strangers were poking around, and he wouldn't leave her alone in her comatose state.

The towns were getting closer and closer, and the farms and ranches were taking over the wilderness. They were roughly halfway to Lethbridge when they had to finally call the Mounties in for help. As they headed southeast, the rivers, lakes, and streams became further and further apart, and then Freyja had a day when she had to sneak the wolves onto a ranch and use their stock pond. The wolves were dehydrated, and so was she.

Freyja had always lived in a place where water was never more than fifteen minutes away, and even then, it rained or snowed all the time. It never occurred to her that she and the wolves were using up a lot of water in their long hikes, and as spring changed into summer, it was getting hotter, making both woman and beast use up more water.

Nick pointed out they were just at the start of June, and it was going to get hotter still. He wanted to talk to Bruce about getting the Mounties to bring in mobile water points; he called them water buffaloes. Yeah, there was a risk they could be used by bad guys as bait if they found out about them, but Nick thought he could manage to keep them secret. Same with the meat for the wolves.

His idea was that wolf provisions could be helicopter-dropped, and the pilots wouldn't be told the exact coordinates until they were in the air. That would give Freyja and him at least a couple of hours of safe time to feed or water the wolves before they bugged out, even if the copter pilot was a traitor and told a bad guy where they were. Freyja had already brought down one copter, and the pilots knew it, so Nick thought the pilots would be very careful around the lords. That was his opinion, but Nick wasn't going to arrange anything without Freyja's agreement; this was her show.

Freyja readily agreed. For one thing, she trusted Nick. For another, what choice did she have? She had thirty wild wolves following her around in a much more heavily populated area than they were used to, and you didn't let wolves get cranky. They get snappy.

Of course, bringing in the Mounties meant there was a risk that the good guys like the Elf Nation would find out what was going on, too, but Nick was pretty sure they had figured their route out already and had decided to back off. He thought he had spotted the "nature photographers" tailing them at Muncho Lake, and he deliberately slowed down so that they would get too close and feel like they had to veer off to avoid being spotted, and that's exactly what they did, confirming his suspicions.

So one hot day in June found Nick and Freyja sitting at the edge of a clearing, uncomfortably close to Edmonton, the first big city they'll have to circle, waiting for a meat drop. They sat in the shade, Nick watching the sky with his binoculars, the ravens slowly circling overhead. Freyja had the wolves patrolling a wide area, looking for intruders, and they weren't happy about it at all. Today was a meat day; it was hot, they were hungry, and they would much rather be sitting in the shade next to Freyja and nagging her.

It was warm, and the spring meadow flowers were fading, and the grasses and fireweed were starting to dominate the field. Freyja sat on a motel towel and fiddled with a stem of hairgrass, bored. She looked over at Nick, suddenly jumped to her knees and examined his ear.

"*What* are you doing? Do I have fleas?"

"No, no – don't look at me. Keep looking at the sky." She edged closer. "Nick, I think your ears are pointing." Freyja was about three inches away now, and he could feel her breath on his ear. "Yep, there's definitely a point going on here," and she touched it, making him jump, and he batted her hand away.

"Hey!" He turned, and her face was only inches away. "That's personal! No touching!"

Did Freyja look disappointed? If she was, it was such a brief flash, a micro-expression, he wasn't sure he'd seen it. She shrugged and smiled, and moved back to her old seat. "Sorry, got carried away, but I think you're ripening as the elves say. In the last weeks, I've noticed more white in your hair, and now your ears are pointing. You're fifty-three. Right on time from what I was told."

"So when did your ears point? You've made it sound like you had lord ears all your life."

"I did. I was born with ear points, and by the time I was fifteen or so, I was pretty weird looking. I could talk with animals, and I had a very loud singing voice, and I did both singing and talking a lot. Not much else to do. I could move things, little things, in my late teens. The big magic came in my mid-twenties. I was pretty much as I am now by my forties. But in my one and only conversation with an elf, Sylvia said I was even weird at being weird. Most lords ripen at fifty to sixty."

She looked at him, appraising, as if she were judging a bull at the county fair. "I think you should try moving things now. Have you even tried?"

"No, never crossed my mind. I wouldn't know where to start. I don't think I have any magic in me."

Freyja chuckled and patted Nick's knee. Damn, she was awfully touchy-feely lately! He shifted uncomfortably. If she didn't stop it, and if she didn't back off, he was going to have to take a walk. She pulled her hand back and looked at the meadow again.

"I think you have more magic in you than you think. I think you've been using it and not realising it. I don't realise I'm doing things that average humans can't do. It's part of who I am, and it's so natural it's unconscious."

Nick chuckled. She was grasping at straws. Freyja even had one in her hand! "Like what? What do you think I'm doing that's magic!"

"I think you can move really, really fast. I've seen you moving around at the elf whelping, and I think you're moving magically fast. Tomorrow morning, if we raise a new batch, pay attention to your speed and – " she paused " – your inner self. You'll feel it. I also think you can move air. Sometimes, if I'm sweaty, I feel a breeze blowing, taking my stink away in the opposite direction of all the other wind, so you don't get caught in my pheromones. I don't think you realise you can do that."

He thought about that for a minute, and just as he was going to say something, Freyja's ears swivelled, and she jumped up. "They're coming!"

Nick leapt up and ran to the centre of the meadow, waving his arms. As agreed, Freyja stayed hidden in the trees, watching the helicopter, ready to defend him if she saw anything threatening. Just inside the treeline, the wolves hid, too.

The H145 had a sling hanging from underneath, and at first glance, anyone looking would think it was hauling a bladder of water, like it would for a forest fire. But on the second glance, they'd notice a hoof poking out. The helicopter hovered over the meadow, dropping down until the cows were about fifty feet up, and then a helmeted man came to the door. Nick gave a thumbs up, the man returned it, and the next minute the sling collapsed and two cow carcasses dropped like wet sandbags and gave a sickening thump and a bounce as they hit the ground. They were dead when they were loaded onto the copter; they were even deader now.

As soon as the cows hit the ground, the wolves shot out from the undergrowth, and by the time the copter turned back, the cows were covered in a snapping, snarling feeding frenzy. Nick waved and walked back to Freyja, obviously pleased with how the delivery went.

"Well, the puppies are happy! Ready to go?"

Freyja nodded and thought about reminding the wolves to meet them at the whelping site in the morning, but then shrugged. They weren't paying any attention to her. She sighed. Neither was Nick.

Driving to the motel, Freyja seemed to be in a down mood, and that wasn't normal for her. She was even a bit snappy when Nick asked what she wanted to do for lunch. He snuck a glance at her, she was looking out the window, her ski cap down low over her ears, her mouth glum.

He knew better than to ask what was wrong because the answer would be "nothing," and she'd get moodier. That's what women did. They had been on this quest, whatever it was, for months now, and she was probably tired. Tired of hotels, of camping out and of fast food, and tired of being exhausted. She probably missed her cabin. Nick wouldn't mind a few days back at his own apartment either.

This was work; she was constantly on guard for bad guys, she worried about the wolves, and Nick knew she worried about him. Maybe they should take a few days off. But doing what? Go to a movie? Then, as they drove down the arrow-straight highway, he saw a billboard advertising a powwow, and today was the second day of a three-day event. The festival wasn't far, only a half hour away, and he always liked a good powwow. It would be an easy diversion, something to break up the routine, and there was no reason they couldn't take an extra day if they needed to. It wasn't like they were on a schedule.

He asked Freyja if she was up for going; she thought about it for a minute, smiled, and perked up. That was all the affirmation Nick needed.

After checking into the motel, they cleaned up and were back on the road within an hour. The closer they got to the fairgrounds, the more excited Freyja became about it, and she peppered Nick with questions until he had to laugh and tell her to calm down.

"Look, I know you've never been to a powwow before, but it's pretty straightforward. It's a bunch of different tribes getting together, showing off, and having a good time. There'll be singing, dancing, drums, maybe some contests, crafty things, and definitely a lot of food. Past that, who knows? Everyone is different. I hope you're not disappointed; don't expect the moon."

"I've never been to anything before! I've read about festivals and fairs and circuses and all that, but I've never been to one. I can't be disappointed; it'll be the best one I've ever been to!"

Nick remembered that she had never been to a restaurant until he took her out to breakfast, and it hit him how cloistered her life had been. Here was a woman of unimaginable power and well over a hundred and twenty years old, and the common experiences that were normal to modern humans, like shopping at Walmart or going to a movie, were as foreign to her as if they were on Mars.

They followed the signs and parked in a dusty field, and immediately Nick wondered if he was doing the right thing. The place was packed, and just leaving the parking lot was an exercise in crowd management, but Freyja was fascinated. There were loads of people in regular clothes, but at least half were decked out in a huge variety of First Nations regalia representing every tribe, in every combination, and in every colour. Much of the clothing was a hundred per cent authentic, and the wearers looked like they'd just walked out of a pre-Columbian Aboriginal camp, while others – let's just say they used their imaginations.

Nick paid an entrance donation, and they were in, walking around and taking in the sights and smells. It was hot, dusty, loud, very crowded, and a feast for the eyes. When Nick grabbed Freyja's hand to keep her close in the crowd, she clung on for dear life, and when the crowd thinned as they left the entrance area, she kept a firm grip on him. They walked around hand-in-hand, he thought wistfully, just like they were dating.

They spent all afternoon wandering around, looking at the craft displays and market stalls, eating everything that was offered for sale, and together they sat and watched the dances and contests. Nick explained what was going on, even if some of the events were a bit mysterious. How the Powwow Princess was chosen – he couldn't answer that one. The horse events? They watched but never could figure out who won.

It was still light out at eight, but by then they had been at the festival for almost seven hours, and Nick started to steer Freyja back to the car. The dancing was still going strong, but some of the young people on the sidelines were getting rowdy.

They both decided to use the port-a-potties before the drive back, and Freyja was standing in a very long line waiting for her turn at the women's toilets when an angry shriek made her jump. Four burly security bouncers were frog-marching two young men to the gate, and a young woman followed the parade, screaming at the guards, her purple eyes glinting on her red, furious face, pushing and slapping at the guards, who weren't letting go of the men. Her companions both looked the worse for wear, with one developing a black eye, and both had cuts and scrapes on their faces.

"You can't kick us out! We weren't doing anything!" Screaming Lady was in the middle of a full-blown high-velocity temper tantrum, stamping her feet and flailing her arms, and in her fury, she knocked over an ancient granny standing in line, to the shock of the waiting women and children.

Jumping forward, Freyja knelt and asked the old lady if she was all right, as did others, and the old woman moaned, the breath knocked out of her. The screamer didn't care or even look down; she just yelled louder.

"My father's a judge! You can't do this! Who cares if they didn't take their hats off for your fuckin' procession." As fast as a spider snatches a fly, she grabbed the pompom on Freyja's ski hat and jerked the cap off and shook it at the guards. "Look at this bitch! She has her fuckin' hat on! Kick her out, too!"

Freyja was looking right into the grandmother's eyes when her hat was stolen, and the old woman told her family later, "She was kind to me, worried I was okay and helping me up, but when that hat was pulled from her head, Oh *my*! The lord's eyes got very wide, like glowing moons, and they flashed so bright I couldn't see them. She was spittin' mad, and you could see it. Her ears popped up like two pieces of toast out of a toaster!"

Freyja stood up and slowly and deliberately turned to the screamer.

"Give me back my hat."

The woman had her back to the lord and was holding the hat by the pompom and shaking it at the bouncers like a dustrag. The bouncers, though, weren't looking at the hat; they were staring open-mouthed at Freyja. Despite suddenly finding a very angry, glow-eyed lord standing in front of them, they still kept a tight grip on the men they were evicting.

"GIVE ME BACK MY HAT!!"

"Bitch, shut the fuck up. I'll give you back the hat when I'm good and –" And she turned. But she never finished the sentence because she flew into Freyja's stiff-armed grip and found herself with a furious, green-eyed lord holding her by the neck, her feet swinging three inches off the ground. When you're hanging by your neck by the viselike grip of a glowing-eyed lord, it really doesn't matter if you're three inches or three feet off the ground; it's damned uncomfortable.

"Are you good and ready now?"

The terrified screamer couldn't scream any more with the lord's steel grip cutting off her breathing. She could barely nod, but she managed.

"Give me back my hat." And the orc did. Freyja dropped her, and the woman fell to her knees, gasping for air and clutching her neck. The still furious and glowing lord jammed the ski cap back on her head.

"Now, apologise to this woman you knocked down. Damned rude of you."

"I'm sorry." Clawing at her throat, the screamer could barely croak now, and screaming was no longer an option. Then she looked at Freyja. "Please don't kill me."

"You're a fucking idiot. If I wanted to kill you, you'd be dead. Now take your fellow fucking idiots and go home. Don't stop, don't talk, drive home – very slowly. If I find you so much as had a fender bender, I'll come looking for you. It won't be pretty. Do you understand?"

"Yes," she whispered.

"And don't you ever go to another powwow anywhere. Ever. You three are banned for life."

Freyja looked at the bouncers. "Let the idiots go." They released them, but the men stood frozen.

"Shoo!"

And all three ran off to the parking lot as if all the demons from hell were after them, which is what it probably felt like. The women in line and the bouncers stared at Freyja; she smiled apologetically, shrugged, and turned to walk to the parking lot, looking for Nick.
Just as she passed the men's toilet area, he walked out.

"You okay?"

"Yeah, but the line is too long, and I still have to pee. I'll just wait till we're home."

He smiled and took her hand without thinking, and they walked to the jeep, just another couple in the crowd.

The next morning, as they ate breakfast before going out to raise elves, Nick was scrolling through elf sites on his phone and suddenly looked up.

"You didn't tell me you had trouble at the powwow!"

Freyja shrugged. "Idiots. Knocked an old woman over and stole my hat! Really rude people." She bit into her Egg McMuffin. "Are you going to eat that last hash brown?"

He looked at his phone again and then back to Freyja. "No, you can have it." He sighed. "We're going to have to buy you another hat. Pink ski hats with pom-poms are now your new signature."

"Well, let's go wake up some elves and get to our next motel, and we can worry about my headwear later." She frowned at the mess of McDonald's bags, and if Nick had looked, he would have seen her lower lip tremble. Nick had bought that hat for her and said she looked cute in it, but now he just looked irritated at the powwow thing. He didn't say anything more, but she could tell he was off. He was mad at her.

The elf whelping went fine, but Freyja only pulled up ten of them, a much smaller haul than what they were used to dealing with. Just like after the others, Nick drove her to the next motel, and she immediately went to sleep.

Freyja was wrong, though. Nick wasn't mad at her; he was mad at himself. His only job was to keep her safe, and the one time she was alone, some stupid person came along and exposed her ears and caused an incident. She didn't read the elf fan and news sites, but he sure did, and dust-ups like that were hot topics online. There were at least fifteen witnesses, and everyone had something to contribute to the story. And the worst part was that now people out in the "real world" were looking for her. She was known to be in the Edmonton area, and Edmonton was a huge town compared to what Freyja was used to. Bypassing the place was going to take a lot of effort under the best of times, and they didn't need every hoser in Alberta looking for her.

Nick was also sure by now that the EN was tracking them, and he really didn't want any confrontations with them either. He checked the Jeep's tires every day and always looked underneath for oil leaks or any issues, so he spotted the tracker the day it was put on. It wasn't even dusty. So someone knew his jeep and wanted to keep tabs on him. He took it off and put it on another green SUV in the parking lot. Let them follow that guy for a while.

Taking care of Freyja had become a point of pride for him, and he didn't want some condescending RumLot officer to come and tell him to run along, go home and play Mountie again; he was no longer needed.

But what if she went off with them? That was the big question, the unsaid fear. The further south they went, the more densely populated Alberta became, with the risks of running into orcs and worse and the risks that came with being close to the US border. If she returned to the EN, they had the vast resources to keep her as safe as the Queen of England.

Once they got to the border, then what? Would it be "Thanks, Nick, nice to know you, see you later?"

He watched her sleep. In every motel, he reserved a room with two double beds, and for a couple of months now, she would come back from waking up the elves and pass out in the bed next to him. Never once did she give him any indication that she wanted any different arrangement. Oh, sometimes out in the wilderness, she would pat him on the arm or sit next to him by the campfire, but while she had stopped being so paranoid about bonding, she never made a move on him. They were buddies, nothing more.

It drove him crazy. But then he didn't blame her. She was gorgeous; he was not. She was a hugely powerful lord; he was not. Nick could go on and on. The indisputable point was that Freyja was out of his league, not interested in him, and he knew it.

Gary

Wendell knew exactly where Freyja was staying. He never told Gary where because that was purely on a "need to know" basis. And from the Ranger's point of view, Lord Freyja's location was not any of Gary's business.

But the Ranger knew, and it was on his phone. The EN was following her as she moved south and had put a tracking device on Freyja's driver's car. Wendell could track the car, and he obsessively checked the car's location. Gary watched him do it.

Gary watched the elf fan sites, too, and he could see her direction of travel and had a very good idea where she would go next. But a "good idea" was not a definite pinpoint location, and he'd need that to find her and bond with her. He needed to catch her alone and surprise her. Gary had no illusions that if he walked up and said, "Hi, Freyja, let's get naked and bond", that she wouldn't do anything other than laugh and then probably turn him into an ice cube.

Of course, after the bond, she would dote on him, and they'd get naked whenever they wanted, but that was dessert. First, he had to prepare the main course, and it wasn't going to be easy. He began to study Wendell's habits with his phone. If he could get the phone off of him while it was still open, so he didn't have to worry about the security locks and passwords – just for a few minutes – he might have a chance.

If he could tease out Freyja's exact location, then it was a relatively simple matter of getting to Alma's apartment, stealing the pistol and the money she stashed in the mayonnaise jar in the kitchen, and jacking her car. Gary had gamed it out a hundred times in his head, and he knew exactly what to do in every possible scenario. That was part of the fun, really – figuring all this out.

There were times when he was with Alma that he wondered if he really wanted Freyja at all. Alma was so easy. She thought he was hot stuff.

Too easy, really. The game had become more important than the victory conditions, and there was no gameplay with Alma. Freyja was the prey and the prize.

Nick and Freyja

North of Edmonton, they sat together and looked at the old *Rand-McNally* and the map app on Nick's phone and planned their route. Freyja told Nick her dream had her standing in front of a road sign with Lethbridge on it, and when she made it there, her immediate quest would be over. So Nick had the location of his execution, if not a date.

They had the choice of skirting Edmonton to the west and going down the mountain roads, but that meant doing their best to avoid the cities of Banff and Calgary while dealing with the tight mountain roads, all the while herding thirty wolves. Or they could circle Edmonton to the east and go straight south through the open plains and use 36 as their guide. They decided on the eastern route because, while it was drier and they'd need more water from the RCMP guys, it was more manoeuvrable and easier to hike through.

Nick looked at all the different routes until he was sick of maps and despised the name Lethbridge, even though he had no idea what the town was like. Other than the new RumLot Security outpost on the internet, it looked like any other small Canadian prairie town, but it wasn't the town that filled him with dread. It was the EN outpost.

When they got to Lethbridge, something would happen, and Nick couldn't see any good outcomes. Freyja would be finished with her quest and finished with him.

He became very quiet. Occasionally, he would look up and see Freyja looking at him sadly, and that just made him quieter.

It was at the motel in Royal Park where everything came to a head. Freyja had raised up elves in Elk Island National Park just east of Edmonton, and it was a good haul, over thirty of them. Nick drove her to the motel so she could sleep just as their routine dictated, and just like at the other small motels they had visited, she curled up on one bed and passed out and he lay on the other planning the next food drop for the wolves, checking out the water situation, their own supplies, and scrolling for news for problems on the route.

The next big milestone was reaching 36, which would be a pretty straight, due south shot through the ranches and farms of the Great Plains and on to the US-Canadian border. It was 320 miles from Royal Park to Lethbridge, about four more elf whelpings. They'd be done in three or four weeks.

She didn't sleep for two days this time, just one, and Nick knew she had woken up because he couldn't sleep either; he could never sleep when she was making noise. It was the middle of the night, and Freyja was crying.

They were tiny muffled sobs, and it was pitch black in the room when he looked at her bed; all he could see was a mound of blankets. Upset, he sat up and thought for a second about turning on the light, but he was only in boxers and a t-shirt. But hang all modesty, he had to say something.

"Freyja, what's wrong?" He got back the one-word answer he was expecting.

"Nothing."

"Now, babe, don't tell me that. Something's bad wrong. What is it?"

There was a shudder and a gulp, and Nick could tell she was trying to get herself together. It was a knife in his gut to hear her cry, so he shifted from his bed to hers and sat next to the lump and gave it a pat and a little shake.

"Babe, you gotta talk to me."

Then it all came out in a rush.

"I don't know what to *do*! I love you so much, and you don't love me, and there's *nothing* I can do to change th –" She started to sob big gulping sobs, and Nick could almost hear the shatter of her heart breaking in them.

He was stunned to silence. Freyja loved him? Loved him so much she was broken-hearted over him?

"But Freyja, I do love you!" And his voice cracked.

"No, not the way I mean it!" the lump said. "Not like a friend or your sister. Not *like* love." She gulped again, and Nick could feel her shudder under the blanket. "I don't know how – I've never been around men. I don't know how to flirt or seduce or anything. When I tried flirting with you –" And her voice turned into a wail. "You left to go check the air in the tires!"

Nick stared at the lump. He opened his mouth to say –

But he didn't know what to say. He was horrified that she was saying she was in love with him and he was breaking her heart, and then horror warred with the dawning elation that Freyja loved him, which was its own miracle.

"Baby, I love you with all my heart, the way you say, but I can't get any closer to you without bonding. When I walk away, it's because you're –" And he sighed. "It's because if I don't get some fresh air, I'm afraid I'm going to grab you and kiss you, and if I do that, I don't know if I can stop. Look, you were very clear that an accidental bonding is a tragedy, and I'm just not going to do that to you. I don't want to bond with you and then moon after you for the rest of my life after you run off with some Elf Nation Elemental lord who's your equal. I don't want you to accidentally bond to me and spend the rest of eternity thinking you could've done better."

The lump stopped shaking and went very quiet. Then Nick saw two glowing balls of green light as Freyja sat up.

"You love me?"

"With every fibre of my being, babe. You have no idea. Obviously, you have no idea. I don't know what I'm going to do when this quest thing is over and you don't need me any more. That's why I can't bond with you or sleep with you or anything like that. It's bad enough now, but it'll kill me if you leave me, and I was bonded to you. I'll be like that Lord Lena you told me about."

The eyes got closer, and Nick felt her hand on the side of his face, and she leaned in.

"Bond with me! Do it now!"

Her lips were so close he could feel them on his cheek, and her heady perfume filled his head, making him dizzy. "Freyja, I don't know how to b –" And she kissed him.

And just as he'd said, once he started kissing her, he couldn't stop, and to his inexpressible joy, Freyja didn't want him to stop. He kissed and stroked and played with every inch of her until she glowed, and then, when she was a panting, sweaty, moaning mess and thought she couldn't take any more, he rolled on top of her, and she discovered that, yes, there was more.

Nick

Freyja loved him.

Nick just couldn't get over it. He woke up in the morning, and she was still in bed with him, so he had to touch her to make sure she was real. Every time he touched her, there was that same sense of wonder. Freyja loved him as much as he loved her.

After months of trying to avoid an accidental bonding and mooning over her from afar, he could be with her all he wanted, touch her all he wanted, talk and laugh with her about anything, and the miracle was that she wanted him, too.

The grey pall that hung over both of them for the last couple of weeks simply blew away in the morning breeze. They talked about "the end game", but just decided to see what would happen and not worry about the future. Nick was pretty sure the RCMP would reassign him to Freyja duty when his medical leave was used up, the way they had with Bruce, so they wouldn't starve. Not that a lord could ever starve, but he knew they'd need an income if they wanted to live in the modern world, and that meant offering something of value to the Canadian government. He thought vaguely about buying a place in the northern wilderness and building a cabin for her like Freyja's old place in Alaska.

She said she had bonded with him at his first elf raising when he kissed her. Nick had no idea, although he noticed that afterwards she didn't care about the pheromone thing as much. And she touched him when she couldn't help herself, but the touches were so light, so non-intrusive that he never thought of them as flirting or sexual. Was a pat on the arm a flirt? To Freyja, it was practically an assault; to Nick, it was just an occasional gesture between two friends.

It took two days before Nick had his bonding moment. Amazingly, during sex and making out during the day, he never bonded. It was in the morning when he had gone through the Taco Bell drive-thru and brought back their breakfast burritos that it happened. He bent over to kiss her ear as he handed her the bag, and boom! A sudden wave of heat, he flushed bright red, and it was done. He knew it as soon as it happened.

Nick could never see a Taco Bell without being reminded of that first moment of perfect connection with Freyja.

When Freyja wailed that she didn't know how to flirt or seduce or that she had never been around men, she wasn't kidding. Nick learned just what that meant, and she was very forthcoming about her upbringing because, rightfully, she didn't see any reason to be embarrassed over it.

Her dad wasn't physically a male, but he acted and lived as a male. She never once saw him naked, and in her rare visits to the town when he went there to trade, she was never alone with a man or boy. The occasional trappers she glimpsed in the woods were always chased off by Jo. Freyja didn't realise until she was much older that the rape of Jo's sister and his own vulnerability to rape made him paranoid about men in general. Freyja wasn't taught to hate men – Joe didn't hate men, he thought of himself as a man – but the male gender was dangerous, like bears, and needed to be kept at arm's length and treated with a healthy caution.

When Freyja was fourteen, Jo met a new woman in town, Lily, and fell madly in love with her. Lily loved Jo, too, and if two humans could bond, they did. Lily was rich, educated, independent, fearless, and what she called her "Sapphic nature" led her to leave her very wealthy family in New York and head off for an extended bout of adventure tourism, which was fashionable for some independently-minded, well-off Edwardian women. She wandered up to Alaska to visit the exotics who lived in the Territory and wrote stories about the wilderness and the Klondike that she sent back to eastern newspapers. Somehow, she met Jo, whom she hired as her outback guide. That lasted about three days, and then they became lovers and Lily settled in town where Jo would visit her.

He never took Freyja with him, which made Freyja sad and jealous, but what could she do? She felt left out, but she didn't know that Jo and Lily were having an affair and that a fourteen-year-old, bright-eyed, inquisitive freak-of-nature watching them was a buzz-kill. By that time, Freyja was perfectly safe being alone in the cabin; her magic was still very faint and limited to moving a cup across the table, but it was the animals who protected her. Wolves, bears, cougars – no wandering native or miner would get past the invisible cordon of teeth and claws that surrounded Freyja.

Lily didn't like Freyja. The girl unnerved her, but worse, Jo wouldn't move into town with Lily while Freyja was around, and Lily wouldn't move to the cabin with its utter isolation from humanity, to be stuck inside all winter with a glow-eyed weirdo.

On one of Lily's early, rare visits to the cabin, Freyja heard them arguing. Lily was trying to convince Jo to move into town, and when he said no, she lost her temper. Lily had no maternal instincts at all, and she didn't understand why Jo "was clinging on to that freak of nature; she's not even your real kid! She'll be fine here with her animals, and you'll be happier with me. You know that!" Freyja never forgot the agony she heard in both their voices and that she was the cause of it.

So they were at an impasse. Both the girl and the woman claimed Jo, and he loved them both dearly, but neither could live with the other. So he commuted. He and Lily bought a motorcycle, a 1920 Rex with a sidecar, and the forty miles between the cabin and town went from a two-day walk or a one-day mush to only two hours at most. It was a workable commute, and he visited Lily at least once a month, often more when the weather allowed.

For her part, Jo's more frequent visits made Lily feel guilty about the long periods Freyja was left alone, and she insisted that Jo take back books and magazines to keep the girl occupied in the cabin. Eventually, there was even a wind-up Victrola, and Freyja learned about the human world from the wide range of literature and music that Lily sent. Not a single book discussed sex or showed a man naked, not even the art books. Especially the art books. They were missing pages.

So until Freyja kissed Nick, she'd had no idea what a man's penis looked like or anything about erections, so she found Nick's hydraulic body part endlessly fascinating. Oh, she knew how the wolves and other animals mated, but she thought Nick's body was just perfect, and she told him so.

"I mean, you don't get hooked on me! The wolves can't release right away, and sometimes the male gets stuck on the bitch, and they have to walk around like that for ages!"

Nick laughed. "That would be really inconvenient. No late-night runs for pizza, that's for sure."

"Yeah, I don't think you could steer the Jeep if we were still hooked together. And best of all, no barbs on your dick! Not like the cougars; they say it hurts. And you can mount from all directions! The moose and deer can only do it one way, and sometimes they fall off." She was lying in bed, her head on his stomach, examining the member in question. "Yours is perfect. It works just right."

He laughed until he cried. No woman had ever said he was perfect because he didn't have barbs on his penis and managed not to fall off during sex. Freyja set a low bar.

The next day, they were back to their routine with Nick driving Freyja out to meet the wolves and walk with them on the next leg of their journey. The terrain had changed from heavy forests to open grasslands, and now, instead of islands of humanity lost in a sea of trees, the ground that Freyja walked over was exactly reversed. Freyja travelled through open grasslands with scrubby trees when there were trees at all, and almost all of the land seemed to be fenced. The fences weren't a problem; Freyja and the wolves easily hopped over them. It was what the fences meant that was concerning. Fences meant people claimed that land, and they lived nearby. Fences meant civilisation.

The wolves blended into the prairie – most of the time. They weren't as clean as they used to be, and the dust and blood that stained their coats when they fed on the carcasses didn't wash away with snow and streams, dying the stark white fur a dirty tan that allowed them to be almost invisible as they loped through the beige midsummer prairie grass. Freyja, on the other hand, was exposed. While she tried to hug the verges and trees that the farmers had planted as windbreaks, there were many times when she had no choice but to walk across the huge, empty fields and pastures.

Ranchers, farmers, and motorists on the endless web of roads noticed the tall woman with thirty wolves running alongside her. Elf fans in particular were tracking where the elves were emerging and settling, and making educated guesses about where the next group would emerge. Nick watched them speculate online, and then Freyja would make a change and try to throw them off. It added miles to her trek as she erratically meandered back and forth on both sides of Hwy 36 as she walked south.

It was just getting too difficult to find a place with elves *and* keep the actual awakening private and secure. Freyja and Nick wondered if they should wake the elves at night instead of in the morning, when there were fewer people about, and they decided to change their routine.

Freyja took a jog to the west of 36 and walked almost sixteen miles west to a provincial park on the Battle River, where she hoped to find some privacy and get the wolves fed. The extra miles she put in weren't worth the effort.

Nick arranged a carcass drop for that afternoon, and as he drove up to the park, he was disgusted to run into a goddamn festival! Dammit, this wasn't posted on the park's online events schedule!

As he got closer to the mass of cars, trucks, vans, and people, he slowed down to a crawl, and he could see that it wasn't a festival. It was just a bunch of random cars and pick-ups parked on the side of a road leading up to a small picnic area. There were traffic cones and "Do NOT Enter" signs.

Nick saw a barely organised ant's nest of picnickers, people in lawn chairs with telescopes on tripods, and photographers setting up cameras with huge telephoto lenses. Pulled off to one side, there was a hamburger truck open for business, complete with a couple of folding tables to sit at, and someone played music on a boombox. The road was blocked with construction barrels.

When Nick stopped and parked in front of the barrels, an officious man in a hi-viz vest and a hard hat immediately ran up and waved.

"Hey! You can't come through here! The road is closed! Only authorised people can pass through!"

Nick wasn't fooled. He'd been a Mountie way too long to be snookered by random civilians in hi-viz vests giving orders. Clipboards did not intimidate him.

"And who are you? Where's your permit, eh?"

The man stopped, momentarily taken aback. No one had ever challenged him before. "The permit? Oh, yes, the permit. It's back in the office." The man was lying, and Nick knew it.

"Where's the office? Please take me to whoever's in charge here."

"Listen, I don't have to prove anything to you, I —" Nick showed him his badge, and the man immediately deflated. The big guy with the mirrored sunglasses was an RCMP officer. Shit.

Picnickers walked up to see what was going on, and Nick was soon surrounded by a scrum of sullen people who wanted him gone; three were dressed as fairies, complete with wings. Half of them, male and female, were wearing pink ski hats with pom-poms.

"What's your name, sir?"

The man's name was Harry, and Harry was the president of the Edmonton branch of an elf fan club, the Elves of the Alberta Region Society, or EARS for short. They had good information that Lord Freyja was walking this way; she was spotted some hours ago turning off 36 and going west, and this seemed a good place to wait for her.

Nick raised an eyebrow. "So you're stalking a *lord*? Don't you think that's a bit dangerous? What if you scare her? Aren't you afraid of being zapped?"

"No, sir! We're here to protect her! We'll stay a respectful distance away, block the road so she has safe passage, and we'll chase away random hikers and tourists! We love elves! And this might be the only time we'll get to see an actual lord." He paused. "She's an elf-raiser, you know. Even for lords, she's a really big deal."

An elderly woman piped up. "She's been raising elf colonies all over Canada! We think she might bring one here! "

"But what if you scare her away? Have you thought of that? People are trying to kill lords —" But before they could answer, a voice yelled, "*She's here!*"

Everyone ran to their equipment, and Nick was immediately forgotten. He wandered over and stood behind Harry to see what they were looking at. Off in the distance, Freyja crested a hill – a fierce Valkyrie Bo-Peep in ragged shorts, hiking boots, Nick's worse-for-wear Mountie hat, her rifle slung across her back, and her demonic sheep-in-wolf-clothing loping around her.

Harry looked back at Nick and then turned to squint through his telescope, "See, we're right! There she is!"

"Freyja," Nick whispered. She froze in her tracks; the wolves immediately followed her lead and turned to look at her. She dropped and disappeared into the grass. Then the club heard a whistle, a high, piercing shriek, and the wolves melted into the grass and brush, disappearing as fast as they'd appeared.

The crowd moaned. They had scared her. Harry looked like he was going to stroke out.

Nick's phone rang. "Hey, Freyja." Harry whiplashed around.

"Nah, I don't see anyone here who's a problem. A bunch of elf-fanatics having a meet-up. They think they're going to protect you by blocking off the road."

Nick listened. "Okay, I'll ask." He turned to Harry. "Lord Freyja says she doesn't need any protection, thank you. But she would like to know if you're selling any baked goods. Do you have cake?"

No one said anything, then one of the older fairies raised her hand. "I have a pan of Nanaimo bars. She can have those. No charge." She ran off to get them, and Nick turned to Harry. "Are you watching where she dropped? She'll be moving." Harry nodded, and the club members all turned back to their cameras and telescopes to see if they could catch sight of her.

Nick walked back to the Jeep and watched the club members intently scanning the hill; he almost didn't notice the first wolf brushing up against him. However, when the middle-aged fairy trotted up with the bars, she couldn't miss them. Lined up across the road, watching the club members' rear ends as they all intently watched the hill, was a line of not-so-white-anymore wolves.

"Whatever you do," Nick's voice was low and deliberate, "don't drop the bars." He put his index finger to his mouth, shhhh, and reached out with the other hand, and she passed over the shaking pan.

Then, without looking back, he swung the pan around behind him. The fairy-lady looked, gasped, and there was Lord Freyja. She grabbed the bars, mouthed thank you, and disappeared into the brush as silently as a ghost, followed by the wolves.

Nick grinned at the fairy lady and whispered, "Let's give Lord Freyja a minute." Then he yelled to the crowd. "Have you spotted her yet?"

Harry looked disgusted. "No, no sign of her or the wolves."

"Well, I have to go. She's probably long gone now. But I think you guys should move those barrels. Obstructing a road is against the law if there's no public safety need for it."

Tim

Tim was patient, which was the number one characteristic of a good sniper and a good hit man. He knew he had no chance of intercepting the demon as she wandered through the Canadian wilderness. For one thing, his woodcraft skills were pretty basic, and hunting her in the vast forests and mountains was a fool's errand.

As any good hunter knew, the alternative to tracking down your prey was waiting for it to come to you. You set up a blind on a known trail, and you waited. As the demon walked, she was noticed, and her direction of travel became more and more obvious.

The intelligence people in the US were watching as closely as they could; they intercepted communications, they had satellites, they analysed, and the technological expertise the US had was formidable.

Tim learned all about the habits of the EN, elf raising – everything he could – and found that the EN and the Canadians had a system when they raised elves. They would take a local military unit and use them for outer perimeter guards. The unit would be called up a few days before the Devil's Orgy, and a day before, they would be given the exact location. The guards didn't know where they were going until they were on their way. It was a pretty good system.

When Tim looked at the direction of travel and cross-matched that with available Canadian Army units, it was easy to figure out who would be called up in each place. The demon hadn't called any up, but she would. The EN had done it before when they needed them. As she moved to more populated areas, she'd need privacy for her rituals, and the CA would provide that.

It was just a matter of finding a godly member of the CA to tip them off when they got a call-up. After that, Tim could figure out the best place to intercept her. He'd just wait for her to come to him.

The special unit sent people to godly churches on the demon's expected route and looked for active duty military personnel who attended them. It didn't take long to recruit some willing eyes. Not everyone in Canada was happy with living in Satan's Back Yard.

Nick and Freyja

The feeding was uneventful; dead cows fell out of the sky the way cows do, and a care package from Bruce with burner phones joined them.

Nick was sure some elf-groupies were hiding in the hills, watching them with their long-range telescopes and cameras. Freyja could feel their eyes on them, and while it was a bit creepy, she just shrugged. Those guys were harmless, but what they signalled was not. Nick, Freyja, and the wolves had lost their anonymity and ability to hide in the terrain as they moved south.

Raising elves with so many strangers, however benign, running around simply could not be done. Sooner or later, the wolves would catch and kill some onlooker who looked threatening, and then it would be open season on them, and Freyja knew it. It was one thing for the wolves to protect Freyja and kill a known assassin or kidnapper; it was quite another to maul an elf-fanatic grandma dressed as a fairy. That would not go down well.

It meant, Nick said when they got back in the Jeep, that they either had to move at night or get help from the RCMP and the Canadian government. They had to assume their cover, such as it was, was totally blown.

The elf sites had articles about perverts and kidnappers trying to capture elves when they emerged from their eggs, and Nick told her of rumours of that happening in Scotland. As they moved closer to the US border, the risk of running into religious fanatics who thought elves and lords were Satanic would only get worse.

She sighed. "Oh, well, we both knew we'd get to this point. The RCMP doesn't seem to be tired of us yet, thank goodness. Maybe we can have a meet-up with them. Why don't you and Bruce set something up, and we'll see what they are willing to do? We can take a few days off while we plan, and in the meantime, I can walk around and look for some good sites."

Freyja looked out of the window as they drove back to the hotel, chewing on her lip, thinking.
"I'm not worried about the pack if we take some days off. The river's there, so they have water. They know how to avoid traps and hunters; I've taught them that. And if they're fed regularly, they'll just sleep and play. They won't go hunting for fun."

She looked over at Nick. "Now it's you and me that's the worry. You say the EN has tried to track us. I think they just want to *keep track* of us, not try anything bad. They know more than anyone the power of lords, and they depend on elves, so they don't want to piss them off. It's the *Elf* Nation, after all, not the *Lord* Nation. If the EN wants to help, on our terms, I wouldn't have a problem with that.

Nick, if our cover is blown and we have people we don't know watching us, maybe it's time to come out of the shadows. Hiding from the real world only works if they don't know where we are. If they know where we are and we choose to stay hidden, they are trapping us like a rabbit in a burrow. I don't think we need to go looking for trouble, and we need to be careful of orcs and religious fanatics. But those elf people? I wouldn't mind talking to them, getting them on our side. They might be useful, especially with info."

Nick thought about that. "I agree about the EN. I think if they wanted to do anything to stop us, we would have already heard something from the Canadian government. They're tied into each other, and Ottawa would cut us loose before they'd lose the EN. So I think the EN is quietly on our side. But the elf people? They're undisciplined and amateurs. They could be as much of a pain as a help. They'll tell the world what they know. What if they decided to capture us for our own good? What if they tell the bad guys where we are? A hundred bucks for a tip off to a newspaper is a lot of money to some people."

For Freyja, who wasn't used to people running around trying to guide her life, it was a toss-up, so she thought it was better if she controlled them instead of allowing them to control her.

"Yeah, they'll tell the world everything they find out about us, so we make sure they know what we want them to know. And guide them to do what we want them to do." She looked out of the window again. "I wonder if they're still at that picnic place."

Nick smiled at Freyja and then made a U-turn. "Let's go see."

The EARS Club

When the green jeep pulled up, Harry and most of the club were still at the picnic area having their regular monthly meeting, social, and barbecue. Amber, the middle-aged fairy who'd made the Nanaimo bars and who was also interim secretary while Eddy was having his knee replaced, was reading the minutes of the last meeting.

Amber saw the jeep pull up, and her voice faded away as Freyja and Nick stepped out and walked up to the circle of EARS members sitting on folding camp chairs and blankets.

"Hey! I just wanted to bring back the pan! The bars were really good! Thank you!" Freyja recognised Amber and walked up with the pan. She didn't have her hat on, and her ears were in full glory, towering above her thick white braided hair. Freyja was kissing six feet tall, and with her ears, she certainly broke that height marker. She grinned at Amber and winked.

"I bet you thought I'd run off with the pan."

That broke the ice, and everyone started talking at once.

Freyja was mobbed for selfies, but Nick hovered in the background, chatting with people as they came up and doing his best aw-shucks ma'am Mountie thing. No one bothered with him when there was a fully ripened Lord to talk to and take pics with, and that was the way he and Freyja wanted it. If he could still get around in the human world for a bit longer without people knowing he was a lord, too, it would be helpful, and they had decided on the ride back to the picnic area that they would string that one out as long as possible.

They were invited to the barbecue, which was gratefully accepted, and Freyja sat and chatted with everyone and signed their lord log books. Every single club member had a logbook that tracked their elf and lord sightings, and Freyja was amused to see what they held. A few proud fans had three or four lords in their book. One had been to Lowestoft and had ten sightings with Freyja making the eleventh. But she was the only lord who had *signed* the Canadian's books, and a couple of the fans were in tears when she did that.

Nick asked them *not* to follow Lord Freyja around because it attracted bad guys and made his job harder, and to *not* post their lord tracking data, and they all solemnly agreed not to do either any more. The Mountie knew that they wouldn't hold to their promises, but he'd made his point, and all he could do was ask.

They weren't halfway to the motel when the first geo-located Instagram post of a fuzzy Freyja eating potato salad was uploaded, and by the time Freyja walked into their room, they were all over the internet.

Bruce

When Bruce sent up a special report to Commissioner Threader requesting help, he was told there was no problem with the Canadian government providing security for an elf raising. Just give him two days to get everyone on board, and they would set up a meeting in Red Deer and plan this out. Bruce said if they wanted to invite the EN to be part of this, that was fine, but this wasn't an EN operation.

The Canadian government was quite happy with that turn of events. Ever since the first meeting with Lord Cadence, they had been the junior to the EN's senior, and now they were in the lead.

Did it mean much in practical terms? No, but pecking order is a thing, and this was, after all, about Canadian elves on Canadian soil.

Caddy, Kyrylo, and Conary

Caddy, Kyrylo, and Conary looked at the top-secret message from the Canadian embassy, and Conary had to smile to himself. The Canadians weren't asking for help with Lord Freyja's elf raising; they were inviting the EN to participate, a subtle but important difference. He thought his mother was more irritated than anyone else. Kyrylo didn't even note the wording; to him, it was all practical, logistical concerns, and since they didn't need to move any military resources from Europe, he was fine with whatever they decided.

For Caddy's part, while it stung to be "invited" with anything to do with her elves (and they were all *her* elves, as far as she was concerned), she wasn't going to let an opportunity pass to bring Freyja and this unknown lord, Nicholas, back into the fold. She told Conary to give the Canadians whatever help they asked for (probably nothing) and that General Jameson would attend their meeting at Red Deer along with Lords Mordecai and Malachi. She was going to request (and the way she said "request" made Conary chuckle) that Mordecai and Malachi both go to the awakening as observers. She wanted both lords to see how Freyja did it and if they could learn anything from her. How she managed to raise fifty or more elves at a time (with just one lord to help!) was worth learning.

The Canadian elves never once mentioned the wolves helping the elves out of the egg sacs. When Caddy or another lord asked them if any humans were around to help, they said no, which was the truth. And when they were asked if there were any other lords, they'd all just look sincerely into Caddy's eyes and say "No, just Lord Nicholas," which was also the truth.

Elves, bless their hearts, are very literal.

Nick

While Freyja was in the shower, Nick called Bruce and got that ball rolling, and then they took a nap where they actually napped. By the time they woke up to get ready for dinner, Bruce could tell them about the results (all positive) from Threader and the meeting in Red Deer in two days. There would be reps from the RCMP and the Army there, probably generals, a rep from the Elf Relations Department, and the EN was invited to send some people, so expect them, too.

"Everyone," Bruce said, "wants their fingers in this pie. If you think this is going to be hashed out around a dinner table, think again. It could be, but in the end, I can see a huge fucking [Miriam shouted, *Bruce, watch your mouth!!*] Broadway production."

Nick nodded. To be expected, he guessed. "Hey, if Threader will be there with a bunch of brass, I guess I need to wear my blues. And I don't have a campaign Stetson any more. I gave it to Freyja to wear out in the sun, and it's a mess now."

"Guess you'll have to have one overnighted to you, eh? With your big head, you won't find one in stock in Edmonton." Bruce chuckled. "Everyone sacrifices in their own way."

"Yeah – well – it was a good hat, too. It was broke in." Just at that moment, Freyja emerged from the bathroom, drying her hair and wearing her jeans and a t-shirt. The t-shirt had a hole in it, and Nick was suddenly aware of how ragged she looked. Every bit of clothing she had was now aerated with holes and snags from her marches through the forests and fields. Nick frowned. His beautiful Freyja wasn't going to a meeting with bigwigs looking like a homeless tramp. Not going to happen.

He said goodbye to Bruce and then went online and ordered a new campaign hat just to have one. He had one set of all of his uniforms, boots, and peaked hat packed in the back seat of the Jeep just in case he ever had to go full-on Mountie, so he was covered. What to do about Freyja? He'd have to think about it. He worried that if he mentioned it to her, she'd have a meltdown. She was insecure about her "freak of nature" looks as it was, and nothing he ever said made her think of herself as anything other than a scary oddball. Nick supposed he had the long-gone Lily to thank for that.

After his own shower, Nick went to the Jeep and checked that the suitcase that held his blue and red uniforms was still where he'd stowed it at the very beginning of this journey, and there it was – untouched. While he was out, he checked the tires and looked under the chassis for anything amiss – and spotted another tracker. Tutting to himself, he pulled it off and stuck it in his pocket. Like the other one, it was brand new and had not a speck of road dust on it. The people tracking them were probably staying at the motel, too, and had recognised the plates.

As he walked back to the room, he noticed that, unlike that morning, the motel parking lot was pretty full of rental cars. Yeah, it was summer tourist season, but was Stettler, Alberta, a bucket-list destination in the Lonely Planet guidebooks? Nick didn't think so.

Back in the room, Nick told Freyja about the tracker and the curious number of rental cars. They were across from a hospital, so that accounted for a lot of the cars, and those would belong to families visiting sick relatives. But rental cars were easy to pick out; they had stickers on the bumpers with the company logos on them, and Nick counted four. That seemed to be a lot to him. He asked if she would mind going to the motel restaurant for dinner to see what sort of people were eating there, and she agreed.

The restaurant was pretty full, and while Nick and Freyja waited for the hostess to seat them, Nick noticed that most of the room was studiously ignoring them. It was as if they didn't want to be seen looking at the new diners. But how anyone could ignore Freyja even without her ears on show and wearing a drab sun-bleached t-shirt and cutoffs, Nick couldn't fathom. Unless, of course, they didn't want to be *seen* looking.

Then he saw them – the Carmack nature photographers with the drone. A big guy with curly dark brown hair and a little blonde woman, the gymnast who bit off snake's heads for breakfast. *Those* photographers.

"Freyja, stick with me." He walked to their table, stopped, smiled, and put the tracker down between them.

"I think you lost this."

Maksym looked up. There weren't many people bigger than he was, but Lord Nicholas certainly was. All he could do was grin and shove the tracker into his pocket. "Thanks! I wondered where that went!" Darnya put her head in her hands.

"No problem. I'm sure you'd find it sooner or later. Enjoy your dinner!"

"We had steaks. Highly recommended!"

Nick nodded, Freyja smiled and waved, and they moved on to their own table where they ordered steaks, too. Maksym was right; the steaks were excellent.

Darnya and Maksym

"Well, we know they're here. He knows we know they're here. He knows we know he knows we know they're here. There's no point in being silly about it." Darnya was philosophical. "We might as well go up, introduce ourselves, and trade addresses for Christmas cards."

Maksym was glum. He took it as a personal affront that he (and Darnya) were discovered.

Yeah, the guy was a Mountie and had had some long-ago tech training, but as far as Maksym was concerned, he was James Bond and Lord Nicholas was a beat cop, and the two amateurs had evaded the pros for months.

A dozen RumLot security soldiers were staying at the hotel, pretending they were going to a farm equipment auction in Red Deer and had booked the wrong hotel. It was a good cover, which allowed them to move en masse to a new location as needed, as long as no real rancher wanted to chat about the virtues of a John Deere over a Massey Ferguson over breakfast coffee. Their cover had to be considered compromised, too.

They knew the first tracker hadn't done its job, and there were frequent debates as to whether Maksym had stuck it on the wrong green UTE or if it was discovered and moved. Maksym insisted that he put it on the correct Jeep. He had memorised the license plates for fuck's sake! They tracked that damn tourist family all over British Columbia for two days before they realised the tracker was on the wrong car.

Then they lost the lords altogether. The Ukrainian intel elves were going crazy, and while Rashid Hadid in Lowestoft didn't laugh in their faces, there was a certain amount of satisfaction in his smile. He was still being teased for losing Lord Cadence when she went a-roaming.

As soon as they told General Jameson their cover was blown, he said to hold tight, stuff was happening at the diplomatic level, and as soon as they could, he or Lord James would be back with further instructions. In the meantime, keep Lord Freyja and Lord Nicholas under surveillance and a weather eye open for any bad guys.

So Darnya and Maksym just sat in their room, playing cards or surfing the internet, only leaving to eat or take their shift with the soldiers watching the parking lot and impatiently waiting for General Jameson to get back to them.

Nick and Freyja

Over the months of travelling together, Freyja and Nick talked a lot, and one of the recurring topics was Freyja's experience in the UK with the Elf Nation. She was a fearless and confident Magical Viking Warrior Maid when it came to all things that Magical Viking Warrior Maids were good at, but when it came to everything else, she was painfully shy. Nick could see that her time at Aelfeham House had simply reinforced her opinion of herself as a socially inept freak of nature. She simply didn't see or accept that her beauty and magic, or even her height, could be intimidating, even to other lords. What she'd experienced as a cool reception, she took as proof that she really didn't measure up to whatever invisible standards the EN lords lived by.

The last thing she needed was to walk into a meeting with a bunch of brass-assed men and women to discuss security arrangements and be treated as an ignorant side piece. As a person classed as "aboriginal" in Canada, Nick knew what it was like to walk into a room and be automatically discounted because of what he looked like. He demanded better for Freyja.

There were no clothes to be had in Stettler that Freyja could wear to meet a general or the Commissioner. Nick wasn't an expert on high-class women's gear, not at all, but while waiting for Freyja to be finished in the bathroom, he scrolled through the photographs of Stettler clothing shops on the internet, and even he could see that the women of Stettler either wore jeans or little party dresses that showed a lot of boob and leg. Freyja had a damn good set of her own and fantastic legs, but that's not what a lady wore to a business meeting, and the more Nick thought about it, the more irritated he got.

How the shit did they dress themselves?

Red Deer, though, was bigger and had more shops and a real mall. Edmonton was a big city, but hours away, so Red Deer it would have to be. They'd be going there anyway for this meeting, so moving to a motel there wouldn't be a problem. So, very abruptly, he yelled through the door for Freyja to get a move on; they were going to break camp and head out to Red Deer right after breakfast. When she asked why, he just grinned and said it was a surprise.

Since Miriam handled all of their hotel reservations, he called up Bruce and told him to see if they could move on a day early, and that was that.

When they walked into the motel restaurant for breakfast, two of the tables were taken up by very fit young men and women who carefully didn't look at the lords. There wasn't a chubby or grandma, or kid in the bunch. Nick had spent a lot of time in the Canadian special forces and had long ago learned that you can just look at an ex-SAS or American Green Beret and pick them out in a crowd. This crowd had more than its fair share of ex-military.

"Freyja," he whispered, "I'm going to have a little fun. I'm going to clear this room."

She scrunched her face. "You're not going to fart, are you?"

"No! I'm shocked you'd even suggest such a thing! But watch those two tables." Nick leaned back and pushed away his plate and then, rather loudly, said, "Babe, you ready to go? If we're going to get to THE HOLIDAY INN at RED DEER by lunchtime, we need to get our butts in gear."

Freyja looked at Nick and then nodded. "Just a minute; I want to finish up these pancakes."

By the time her pancakes were gone, the occupants of the two tables were gone, too.

Freyja looked at the empty restaurant and then at Nick, "So what was the point of that?"

"Oh, no point. I just want to jerk their chains. Make them earn their Elf Nation money. I'm not even sure if we're staying at the Holiday Inn; Miriam hasn't texted me yet."

As they pulled out of the motel parking lot, they passed the blonde gymnast pulling a suitcase to her car, and Freyja waved bye to her as they drove by. "Later gator!"

Darnya waved back.

She hoped the new tracker worked, but when she looked at her phone to see if they were indeed going west on Hwy 12 to Red Deer, the tracker showed they were still in the motel parking lot.

The tracker said they were sitting in her own car.

Maksym was going to be so-oooo pissed.

Nick and Freyja

The drive to Red Deer only took an hour, but when they got there, Nick didn't take Freyja straight to their next motel, throw her on the bed, and make her a very happy woman, which is what she half expected. Instead, he took her to the mall.

He seemed to know exactly where he wanted to go, so he didn't let her stop and look around, and oh, she really wanted to. That would have made her a very happy woman, too.

Freyja had never been to a mall. She'd read about them in newspapers, but photos in the paper didn't do justice to the sensory overload of a mall. Up until she had met Nick, she had never been to any modern retail store, just Wally's Emporium, and their trip to Walmart was an eye-opener. This mall place was even bigger and certainly a lot prettier. It even smelled good.

But Nick was on a mission, and he said that when they were done, she could spend all afternoon looking around. They'd even eat in the food court. But first, business.

Business turned out to be a women's clothing shop. Unlike Walmart, this store had wood floors, soft lighting, with a selection of clothes carefully displayed like works of art on dark wood shelves and wrought iron racks. A woman was refolding sweaters on a shelf, and another was working behind a counter, but as soon as Nick walked in, the sweater folder walked up and asked if she could help him.

"Hey, nice ta meetcha. The lady here, the love of my life, and I are going to a big meeting with some very important people, and I have a suit to wear, but she doesn't have anything. So she needs outfitting from the skin out. Can you do that?"

Freyja turned to Nick, shocked. "Nick, I –"

"Babe, you can't go talk to generals, commissioners, and such in cut-offs; they won't take you seriously, believe me. You get whatever you need. No worries. That's what credit cards are for, and besides, I'll get reimbursed. So have fun."

The woman turned out to be the manager, and she wasn't going to let this free-spending mountain of good luck pass her by. "Sweetheart, we can set you up for anything. Like the gentleman says, no worries! A lot of people lose their luggage and need clothes!"

She tilted her head and stood back to take a good look at Freyja; this one was going to be fun to dress. "My name is Nell, darling. Now, you need something nice to wear to a meeting – trousers or a skirt?"

And with that question, Nick sat down in the dead man's chair and played on his phone for the next hour. He only glanced up when he heard a gasp in the fitting room when Nell insisted Freyja take off her hat so that a dress could be dropped over her head. Then Nell simply moved into super high gear. Oh, god, she was dressing a *lord*! When that got out, she'd be mobbed, and it would set her shop up for a year.

Every ten minutes, Nell would pop her head out and snap instructions to the other woman (Beth, it turned out) like a drill instructor and duck back in. Then Beth was sent out somewhere to buy underwear (Darling, you simply have to wear a bra with this blouse, the guys can see your nips!), and when she came back, Nell fitted Freyja up with proper underwear, dressed her like a doll, and, with a flourish, presented the entire package to Nick. Freyja was gorgeous; the clothes were perfect, and when Nell said she had another outfit to show off, Nick just shook his head; he didn't need to see anything more. Freyja was looking a bit frazzled and overwhelmed, and he had promised her time in the mall. They would take all of the outfits with all the extras. Freyja walked out wearing new chinos, sandals, and a t-shirt that fit her and didn't have holes in it.

Nell's shop ended up with a $1,974 sale and a selfie with a lord. Freyja was happy with her clothes, and Nick was even happier. When this idiotic meeting finally happened, Freyja would look good, feel good, and be given the respect she deserved.

The day ended with a grand tour of the mall, where they had lunch in the food court, and Nick stopped off at a travel shop and bought a bunch of luggage trackers. When Freyja asked what they were for, he just shrugged and smiled to himself. "Varmints."

Maksym and Darnya

Miriam did end up getting a reservation at the Holiday Inn after all. When Nick walked into the office to check in, he stood in line behind two of the RumLot guys and the gymnast. As each got their room keys, they'd pass by Nick, who would grin, wave, and hold the door open so they could get their bags out. When it was Darnya's turn to leave, she got the door treatment and a "Nice to see you again!"

"Likewise," she said, smiling at the lord. "Maybe we'll see you at dinner?"

Nick smiled. "Who knows? We do seem to keep running into each other." And he walked up to the counter and checked in.

When Darnya gave Maksym his room key, he was filthy but quite pleased with himself. When he'd put the trackers on the Jeep the first two times, he had just reached under the chassis and found a good hunk of iron, and the magnets on them did the rest. This time, he crawled under the Jeep (and at 6' 2" it was a tight squeeze) and slammed the damn thing on the transmission. Then, just to be clever, he put another one on the passenger side just like he had before. "That way," he said to Darnya, "he'll find the easy one and think he's done, but the other one will still be there. I don't know why I didn't think of that before."

He and Darnya went for Italian that night at a place called Forno's. Just as they were tucking into the appetisers, Lord Nicholas and Lord Freyja walked in. He was wearing "business casual" and was totally forgettable, but she wore a floaty summer dress, sandals, a straw hat, and a beautiful smile. Someone had been shopping, Darnya thought, and she had to admire the dress. Tall women could carry off flower patterns that drowned short women like Darnya, and she sighed.

The host guided the lords to their table, and as soon as Freyja was seated, Nick turned and strolled over to Maksym and Darnya. As he walked across the restaurant, Freyja could only think that the man was swaggering.

"Hey! Hello again!"

Maksym smiled, fully expecting what was next. "Hi! Good to see you again! Good weather for driving today!"

Nick nodded. "Yes, it was! But I'm not going to chat long. I see you're waiting for your dinner." He placed a tracker on the table. "I found this one; you seem to be losing them. Are the magnets going?"

Before Maksym could say anything, Nick put the other one on the table. "This one, too! The problem with these modern cars is that so much is plastic and aluminium. Not a lot of steel. It's a pity, don't you think? Anyway, have a nice dinner. I think Freyja will go for lasagna tonight, but I'm still thinking about it. G'night!"

And he turned and left, leaving Maksym to stare at the trackers. Darnya picked one up. "At least he didn't put it back on our car." She was thoughtful. "I wonder how he knew we'd be here for dinner. What a coincidence."

Maksym glowered at her but didn't say anything because the waiter walked up with their pizza.

After dinner, he put on some old clothes and spent all evening crawling under his car with a flashlight looking for a tracker, but he didn't find one.

Report to Lord Kyrylo and Lord Cadence,

The meeting was scheduled to start at nine, and at fifteen minutes till nine, Lord Nicholas and Lord Freyja walked into the conference room.

-Subject Description(s)

Lord Nicholas was dressed in his RCMP blue serge officer uniform. He is approx. 195cm tall and of average weight for that height. He looks as if he works out. Ethnically, he is First Nation

Aboriginal. He is 53 years old, according to our intelligence, and is showing some of the changes we expect in a lord of that age, with hair that is approx. half white and ears showing distinct points. He is clean-shaven and has a regulation RCMP haircut. He looks very healthy. His eyes occasionally snapped a bright blue.

Lord Freyja was in a navy blue dress (I believe my wife calls it a "wrap" dress) with a short jacket with green trim on it, back knee boots with heels, a green purse, and a green beret. She is approx. 180cm tall and of average weight for that height. She looks very healthy and fit. Ethnically, she is far north European, possibly ancestry is Swedish or Norwegian. She is a full lord with stark white hair that was dressed in a single braid that reached her waist and fully developed lord ears that are mobile and point above her head by at least 4 cm. Her eyes are an intense emerald green and snapped and glowed during the entire meeting.

-Pre-Meeting

Lord Nicholas walked up to Commissioner Threader, saluted, and introduced Lord Freyja to him and then asked if he would do the honours of introducing the lord to the rest of the gathered attendees and of course, the Commissioner was more than happy to do so.

Lord Nicholas stayed with her as she made her rounds, but he stood to the side. Commissioner Threader introduced Lord Freyja to the Head of the DOEA Sloan (see addendum for names, titles, notes on participants), Lt. General Whittaker, CA, and to all of their aides.

Lord Nicholas did not introduce himself as a lord. From my observation, no one on the Canadian side has realised he is a lord.

Comm. Threader then introduced Lord Freyja to me, Lord Mordecai, and Lord Malachi and to my aides (Lds Mordecai/ Malachi did not have aides present). Both Lds Freyja and Nicholas were friendly and open. There was no coolness that I could discern.

The first impression is that Ld Freyja is a quiet, reserved person, but didn't seem at all nervous around people and was really very friendly – one could say charming.
Lord Nicholas was equally friendly, but there was a distance, too. He watches, listens, and I can see him making mental notes.

-Meeting

The meeting started on time, chaired by Commissioner Threader. The full transcript is attached to my report, so I'll just give highlights.

Welcome-
Statement of why we are meeting – To establish a cooperative framework for the protection of Lord Freyja and newly awakened/ raised elves.

Presentation of elf raisings – Introduced by General Whittaker and presented by his aide, Col. McHenry. How the EN and CA work together, how sites were chosen, what resources are used, what Ld Mordecai does, what Ld Malachi does, what Ld Adem does, and post-rise activities.

Lds Freyja and Nicholas were very attentive and asked questions, not for clarification, but justification of procedures and practices.

When the presentation was over, Lord Freyja had one question. "So you choose locations based not on the number of elves still underground but on what is best for border protection. Is that right?"

General Whittaker – "Yes, mostly, Lord Freyja. We have elf settlements in our capital because the EN wanted a settlement next to their embassy. The elves themselves expand wherever they want to. We neither stop nor encourage where they decide to wake their clan members."

Lord Freyja (nodded) – "Thank you, General Whittaker, but you must understand I have my own reasons for choosing a spot, and that is based on what I feel is best. Military or border security reasons aren't my concern. What is best for elves and my people, that's all that matters to me. I think it's a matter of quality v. quantity. You are looking for quality – a smaller number of elves, maybe, but in the perfect place. I'm looking at quantity – to get as many awake and back in this world as possible."

General Whittaker – "I hope, Lord Freyja, that by working together we can do both quantity and quality. But we'll take elves wherever you find them. Do you have a preferred location for the first raising we'll do together?"

Lord Freyja nodded, and Lord Nicholas gave the grid coordinates. (attached – TOP SECRET – CODEWORD with NTK Phased Release).

Lord Freyja gave a date (attached – TOP SECRET – CODEWORD with NTK Phased Release), and it was pointed out that it was a very short timeline for such a complicated operation.

Lord Freyja – "Possibly, but I think you guys can do it. We have done it alone so far, but you might as well be along for the ride. If you come, I can bring up more because we'll have more help. If not, if it's too short notice, then I'll bring up fewer, which is a shame, I think. It feels like a good site."

Lord Freyja was quite firm. She will be on site on the day. We (CA, EN) come along and help, or we don't. She's fine either way. She sticks to her timeline and will continue her walk after the raising. There was no indication of when or where her mission would end.

Presentation of the Logistics of the Day – Site security, training, food/water, transport, etc, were discussed by Lord Malachi with future meetings scheduled between Gen. Whittaker's staff and the EN.

Agreement in Principle – All parties agreed to cooperate as per previous awakenings and to meet with Lord Freyja and Lord Nicholas at the agreed day and time at the provided grid coordinates.

The meeting was adjourned.

Caddy

Caddy read the report. *"Lord Freyja was quite firm –"*

Indeed.

The EN and Canadians could be there or not. The lord was on a schedule, and everyone else would have to adapt to it. Caddy was very sure the Canadians would be there, and equally sure her people would be there, too.

Freyja, it seemed, was not one to be pushed around. She ceded nothing, not from what Caddy could see. Her date, her place, her show.

Caddy could appreciate that.

What was interesting was the statement, *"If you can come, I can bring up more because we'll have more help. If not, if it's too short notice, then I'll bring up fewer, which is a shame, I think. It feels like a good site."* If she could bring up fifty by herself, then what was a "good site"? Both Caddy and Dek could throttle back if there were too many for them to handle and leave some underground for the awakened elves to recover later. Obviously, Freyja could, too.

Caddy wondered what Lord Freyja's upper limit was. Caddy had once brought up a couple of hundred by herself, and it had wiped her out so badly that Kyrylo had put his foot down and said no more – limit of forty from then on. She and Mordecai once sang a duet that brought up three full clans. The best Mordecai could do was about thirty and usually ended up with twenty-five. Could Freyja do a hundred? More?

Mordecai and Malachi were both at the meeting. Their comments were attached to Jameson's and were simple.

"Lord Freyja is an Elemental. No doubt. Magic just flows around her, and she doesn't even know she's doing it. I saw her heat her coffee, move her purse when it got in her way, things like that, and there was NO flash, no effort, she doesn't even look at what she wants to affect. She just thinks, and things happen.

"Lord Nicholas is unripe, but his eyes are a very bright and intense blue, and he does things without thinking, too. He doesn't move things, but he moves himself. It's hard to describe, and we think humans see him move and think they just had a blink or jitter and discount it, but he will be in one place, and the next minute, he's three steps away. It's very easy to miss. We don't think he's porting. His eyes snap quite often, so he's doing something, but whatever it is, it's very subtle. Malachi thinks he could be a Warrior Lord if he's not one already."

Well, Caddy and everyone else in the lord world in both modern and Before Times had missed Adem's subtle but powerful gift. She would be damned if she would miss Lord Nicholas's ability. If she could just get them back to Aelfeham House, then Gerald and Victor could have some training time with both, and they'd figure out exactly what it was that Nicholas did.

Caddy wouldn't screw up again, not with these two. If Kyrylo didn't need her here, she'd be porting to Canada now; she'd love to be at that raising. She had a feeling it was going to be a doozy.

Gary

Richie and Wendell were on the move, and Gary knew they were going to meet up with Lord Freyja. He knew because they told him.

Lord Freyja was finally going to work with the CA and the EN and raise some elves. They had a date and a place, which they wouldn't tell Gary because he wasn't going and so didn't need to know. Gary begged the Rangers to let him come along, but they just fobbed him off.

"If Jameson says you can come, we'll take you, but we're not authorised to bring any guests. Raising elves is serious business. This isn't a jolly." Wendell was firm.

Jameson, the prick, said no. Lord Gary could stay at the compound, or he could go back to Aelfeham House; his choice. Privately, Jameson told Wendell that the last thing they needed was to drag along a lovelorn idiot to pester Lord Freyja on their very first cooperative venture. She obviously already had a boyfriend, and it wasn't Gary. If he could put Gary under house arrest, he would, but you can't arrest a lord for just being annoying; otherwise, Lord Chi would be under permanent detention.

Then Gary got this break. Richie was in the barracks'
Day Room, on his phone, telling some girl he had to go on Super
Secret Squirrel work and couldn't go out next Wednesday night.
From what he was saying, she was sure she was being jerked
around in favour of some other girl, and he was trying hard to
convince her that she wasn't without actually saying what it was he
was doing.

"Sweetheart, believe me, if I could be anywhere else, it
would be with you. Really. They're sending me to the middle of
nowhere; it's not even on the map. You don't have to worry about
other women, and that's the truth. I'll be sitting in the Halkirk
Hotel, all alone, thinking of you."

She said something, and he nodded.

"I'll be back on Saturday, no problem. Friday night if
they let me, but I'm riding with other guys, so it'll be up to them
—"

And that was all Gary needed. A quick check on his
phone and he found the Halkirk Hotel. All it took was a call, and
he found out from the helpful man on the other end that it was
totally booked up from Wednesday to Saturday. He offered a
discount if Gary could come next week, but Gary turned him
down. Something was going down and would be done by Friday
night. Freyja's elf raisings, according to the internet fan sites, were
always in the morning.

From what Gary knew about Mordecai, he always went
straight home and flopped in bed after a raising. Althea said he was
totally wiped out, and he slept for at least a day, and Gary could
remember walking into the TV room many times and seeing Althea
curled up with a book or watching a movie with the other women
because Mordecai was, she said, practically comatose, and she
wanted to let him sleep without her rattling around.

Freyja would be tired, too. She'd go back to wherever she slept and pass out, and she'd be alone. Surely that Mountie bodyguard wouldn't be sleeping with her the entire time.

Gary couldn't imagine that the EN people would be sleeping in a hotel, and the VIP Freyja would be roughing it. She had to be in a motel of some sort.

Comatose.

He called up all of the motels in a fifty-mile radius, and almost all were booked up for Thursday night, but all emptied out by Friday. Except for the Halkirk Hotel, they had people lodging all weekend.

Gary had been to one elf-raising, ages ago, before Adem made transport nodes, before elves could port them straight back home. The VIPs had rooms to stay in overnight because they worked the next day, breaking down the camp, but the redcoats there as observers and helpers were herded on buses and driven to the nearest elf clan for a serial port back home.

Freyja had no "back home" to go to. She would rest in a motel, probably for days.

The Rangers were leaving on Wednesday morning and driving up to Halkirk. No VIP helicopters for them!

If Gary drove up, he wouldn't have to go early for any pre-raising work; he didn't even have to go while the elves were being raised. He could go up on Friday, and by the time he got to Halkirk, everyone else would be packing up to leave, and Freyja would be sleeping, utterly exhausted. The Rangers would be gone, driving back to Lethbridge. No one would worry about Gary wandering around; he was a lord, after all, and he could wear his uniform. They'd think he was supposed to be there. Shit, he could probably volunteer to guard her door while the bodyguard went out to get a bite to eat while she slept.

Comatose.

He called up Alma to see if he could borrow her car on Friday morning. He wanted to go out to the pistol range and pop off some targets, and the Rangers were going to be gone.

She said Sure, if he'd drive her to work and pick her up, he could have the car until school let out at three.

Perfect, he said. And it was.

Tim

The girl, a corporal in a military police unit and a godly child, sent her contact a message that she was being called up for perimeter guard duty somewhere south of Edmonton, but she didn't know exactly where. That was okay because Tim had her phone number, and she had activated her FindMyPhone app. He could see where she was every minute of the entire operation, and wherever she was posted, he would know in real time.

All he had to do was call motels somewhere in the general area and see what activity was going on. Most had their available rooms online. That many people moving around in the middle of ranch and farm country, even military personnel who would bivouac on public land, would leave tracks, and he was right. The motels and hotels were filling up, and they were all clustered around one area.

He didn't look for a room for himself; that would leave its own tracks. And he fully intended to escape back to the US once the job was done. Tim was not suicidal, and God had further work for him, he was sure. Tim would sleep in his car. It wasn't like he'd never been to the field before, and compared to some of the ditches he camped in while he was in the regular Army, his car was a luxury suite.

Nick and Freyja

On Thursday, Freyja and Nick gathered the wolves at Big Knife and fed them. They were hungry, and when the helicopter came and dumped the carcasses (pork today!), it made them happier, but they were still a little upset. Freyja had been gone for days now, and while she was gone, they'd heard and felt more people in the area than they were used to, so they stayed hidden, which was no fun. All the humans running around on ATVs made them nervous because so many of them had guns. They could smell the weapons, and to the wolves, that meant ranchers and hunters who'd take pot shots at them.

Freyja told them not to worry because she knew who those people were, but to stay hidden. There was no point in being seen and risking an encounter with a nervous policeman or soldier who would shoot first and apologise later.

Tomorrow morning, they would have a whelping, and that would be fun, and they could run around.

Nick and Freyja walked to the site of tomorrow's wakening just to see what the wolves were talking about, and while they didn't see any people, they saw quite a bit of trampled grass and tire tracks and a few survey stakes with bits of bright orange plastic ribbons poking up through the grass. People had been scoping out the site.

Out on the road, soldiers were already setting up barriers.

"Well, this is going to be a discrete, low-key operation, I can see that now." Nick was not happy but resigned; the EN had done dozens, if not hundreds, of these awakenings over the years, and they had a system that seemed to work. Freyja was nonplussed, and while Nick was used to this sort of military operation, she'd never seen or even read about how the army did things. While she'd sat through the meeting describing it, to see even the tiny beginnings of the operation coming together was intimidating. Nick told her that by tomorrow, the area around the awakening site would be as crowded and busy as the powwow.

"There are lots of elves down there. I can feel them now. They're rousing because they can feel me walking up here." Freyja looked at her feet and kicked the dirt as if she was going to pop up an elf right then.

"Do you think you'll be bringing up forty or fifty?"

The lord looked up and smiled. "Oh, it'll be more than that. Since we're supposed to have loads of people here to help, and they know what to do, I'll bring them all up. Might as well. It'll tire me out, but you'll take care of me, and I can sleep all I need to afterwards." She nodded and looked around. "It'll really mess up this field, I'm pretty sure."

"Let's go then and find some lunch. We don't need to be here, and you can carb load. If you're going to run a marathon tomorrow, you'll need the fuel."

Gary

Friday morning dawned hot and clear. After dropping Alma off at her school, Gary took her car and her credit card and filled up the tank. She thought he was going to the shooting range with her pistol to get some target practice in. He smiled, kissed her goodbye, and waved to her at the elementary school front door. She waved back, and that was the last time she ever saw him.

Gary didn't hesitate and started the four-hour drive to Freyja. He'd be there right after lunch, and he was very sure the Rangers would be long gone on their own four-hour trip back to Lethbridge. He might even pass them on the road.

She'd be in her room, sleeping.

All he had to worry about was the bodyguard, but that was what the pistol was for.

Tim

Tim was up with the chickens, looked for the corporal's pin on the FindMyPhone map, and simply followed the line of military vehicles until they turned up 855. That confirmed in his mind that the hotel in Halkirk was the nearest decent place for the VIPs, and of course, the VIPs were the lords. He knew from his phone call that it was booked solid by one entity until Monday, "for a family reunion".

The little corporal's phone showed that she'd stopped moving at Big Knife Provincial Park, further confirmation that whatever demonic ceremony they were planning was nearby. Tim didn't even bother to go test the perimeter; he knew it would be almost wall-to-wall guards. Instead, he'd wait for the demon to come to him. If they went up 855, they'd come back down 855, and he could just park off the road and wait to see which way the vehicles turned and follow them to their final resting place.

He grinned; he liked the sound of that. Final resting place. Now that the kill was getting close, the old excitement was stirring, and he was in a good mood. It was a pity Angel wasn't around. He'd bang her until her teeth rattled. But it was okay; a good kill would keep him horny for weeks. She'd get hers.

Freyja

Freyja walked into the circle with Nick and looked around. She had never seen anything like it. There were tents lined up at the entrance to the site that created a mini-village, huge marquees that held water and food for the soldiers. There were buses and cars and military APCs and even an anti-aircraft battery. There were portaloos. There were drones flying overhead. On the outside of the circle was another perimeter, much further out, where soldiers and military police were watching for elf-parazzi, infiltrators, whoever was too close and too nosy.

She and Nick were stopped three times by checkpoints with guards demanding they show ID until she just gave up and took her hat off. If her damn ears weren't ID enough, she didn't know what was.

Around her was a massive ring of men and women, ready and waiting for the elves to push out of the ground, eager and excited to free them. Behind her was a scrum of VIPs from the Canadian Army, the Elf Nation, and the RCMP. If she wanted one, she was sure that they'd dig up a rep from the Holy See and another from Buckingham Palace.

She felt terribly underdressed in her shorts (a new pair, thank goodness) and hole-free t-shirt. She did wear a bra because she knew she'd sweat like a pig.

Mordecai was standing back there with his brother Malachi, who was on a *horse!* Where the horse had come from, Freyja didn't have a clue. He was a nice horse, though, and when Freyja walked by, he said hello.

She looked at Nick, her eyes like saucers. Nick looked at her, grinned, and shrugged.

"Man, I have no idea how we managed by ourselves if this is what the EN needs for a normal raising. I think there's one person per elf here."

Freyja smiled back. "Then I guess I'll have to raise a bunch of them. The wolves will be upset if they're left out."

She walked to the centre. Unlike both Cadence and Mordecai, she didn't wander around looking for a good spot. She just walked to the centre and looked around, and then started talking. She talked in what felt like a normal tone of voice, but everyone heard her as if they were standing right next to her. The magic was already starting.

"Nick and I want to thank all of you for coming today. This is, as you know, our first time with such an elaborate set-up, but we have been told you are experienced and know what to expect, which is comforting to us. I'm going to call the wolves in; they know what to do, too. Don't be alarmed if you see them go after an egg. They open up the sacs with their teeth, the way you open them up with your knives. If you see one digging, go help him. That means an egg is trying to break the surface, and you might need to help it. Oh, and when the wolves come in, don't pet them. They're not domesticated, and people make them nervous. I want everyone to leave here with the same number of fingers they came with. Are you ready?"

There was a ragged cheer, and Freyja smiled. "Well, I hope you are. Let's do this."

She whistled for the wolves, an incredibly loud, piercing trill that made people jump, and the wolves ran from somewhere, where no one could say. They had been watching and hiding in the grass all along, and no one had noticed them. They arranged themselves in a circle, and Nick had to cover a smile. The wolves weren't anywhere near as nervous as the people standing next to them.

Then, with no further prep, Freyja started singing. She rumbled in octaves so low and deep that at first the humans listening could only feel the vibrations, but Mordecai straightened up and looked at Malachi, his eyes wide. She was drilling with sound, straight into the centre of the earth. She didn't tell the elves to come to her. She was going after them.

Then she flamed up, a full ball of fire from nothing. No gradual increasing glow, no build-up, just fire, and then a full-throated, other-worldly song of command. If mountains or planets or stars could sing, this was what they would sound like. She soared into impossible notes, and with each word, her magic song scooped up and pulled the elves to the surface.

Come to me, Come to me, Come to me...

It's time to wake
It's time to grow
It's time to rise
And you must know
It's time to claim your ancient land
It's time to live,
To feel the sun,
We're clan.

Your blood has soaked.
This sacred soil,
Your wait is done
And you are home
It's time to claim your ancient land
It's time to love,

To greet the stars,
We're clan.

Freyja sang, and great waves of earth buckled and cracked over the hard, dry field. Then she stopped, listened, and while the people couldn't see her in the bright, enveloping light that surrounded her, they could sense she was smiling.

"They're coming."

And she burst into her welcoming song.

The ground began to vibrate, and under their feet, the humans and lords could feel the shuddering earth swelling deep underground. Then, about a hundred yards away, a geyser exploded almost four stories high, spraying steam, rocks and earth, and a fountain of boiling water from deep in the earth, and Malachi looked at Jameson and yelled.

"Jameson! GET TO 9 O'CLOCK, I'LL TAKE 12!!" And he smacked Gangster Jack hard on the rump and thundered off to the other side of the circle. Gen Jameson ran to his point, but before he got there, a great rift, a tear in the earth, split down the middle of the field, and out of the rift erupted the egg sacs of the elves. They exploded skyward, a volcano of huge, soft spheres shooting up twenty feet in the air and falling back to earth, where they bounced around like beach balls, to be chased by the soldiers and the wolves who set on them in a frenzy, tearing at the egg sacs and releasing the elves inside.

And they kept coming. More and more eggs poured out of the rift in the field, pulled up by Freyja's unimaginable magical muscle, straight up from their hiding place deep in the asthenosphere. She sang her welcoming song, a cry of joy, of exultation, of triumph.

And still they came. More and more until the field was knee-deep in discarded egg sacs, and even the wolves were starting to tire. Just when the humans and lords began to give out, she was done, and her last note faded away.

She stood in the centre of the field where she had started, and Nick held her up as she swayed, holding on to her bond-man's arm to steady herself, and listened.

"They're all up." She smiled up at Nick. "A good haul, I think. If you don't mind, I'd like to go back to the hotel now."

– and she collapsed.

Nick picked Freyja up and carried her glowing body off the field. As he passed a stunned Mordecai, he yelled over his shoulder, "I'm taking her back to the hotel to sleep it off. She'll be fine, but she needs her sleep. Let me know how many she raised; she'll ask when she's awake."

And that was the end of the awakening for Nick and Freyja. The burst of joy after every awakening, the utter exhaustion of the men and women who helped free the elves, the clean up and tear down – all that was handled by others. Nick put Freyja in the jeep and drove off without a backwards glance.

Tim

Tim could hear the music; Satan's siren song was wonderful to listen to, and he knew he'd remember it the rest of his life. But the temptations of evil were always offered in beautiful wrappings, and he wasn't going to be seduced into forgetting his job by a pretty tune.

He waited and watched the road. They'd be breaking up soon, and he was right. A lone jeep came down the road, leaving the last checkpoint, which was already closing down as it passed by, its job done. As it passed, he got a good look at the occupants and grinned.

The woman in the passenger seat was sleeping, her head on the driver's shoulder, looking for all the world as if she were passed out. It was the whore, he could tell by the glimpse he had of her ears. The witch was still glowing with the devil's fire. Tim pulled out as soon as he could and not be noticed by the jeep and followed them.

Nick

The old hotel's size was deceptive. The front was an old storefront, and there were some bedrooms upstairs, but in the back was a series of newly built log cabins surrounding a large, landscaped parking lot that looked rustic from the outside but were modern hotel rooms on the inside. Nick and Freyja had one of the cabins, and as soon as he pulled up, he jumped out to unlock the door and then came back to carry Freyja into the room.

He laid her on the bed, took off her boots and shorts, shoved her under the blankets, and kissed her. "You did good, baby, really good. Sleep now." Her eyes fluttered, and she smiled. "Love you, Nicky," and she rolled over and was out.

Nick smoothed her hair, tucked the blanket around her, and let out a deep breath. It was over, and the tension he'd worked under for the last week in anticipation of this awakening eased with each exhalation. He was nervous about the EN and army involvement, but more than that, he was nervous that she wouldn't reach the standards she set for herself, that she would be disappointed in her efforts. But Freyja had exceeded everyone's expectations, and that was a huge relief to Nick. He wanted her to be happy when she woke up, and he knew she would be.

So much magic, so huge an effort, and she had given it her all, and now nothing was left. Watching her, he was awed at the power, but more than that, he was proud of her – not just proud of what she could do but proud of the effort and passion she put into her gift. Freyja didn't have to do any of this; she could be playing in the backwoods with her wolves and singing to the wind, but she drained herself like an elite athlete going for an Olympic medal for a prize that wasn't for her; it was for the helpless elves locked deep underground, waiting to be released. She did it for them because it was the right thing to do. How could he not be proud of that?

She would be asleep now for a couple of days, and he could rest too. While she slept, he would plan the next leg. In the meantime, he'd take a shower and read a bit. He needed to rest, too.

Gary

Gary sat in Alma's car in the parking lot, slumped down and napping, waiting for Freyja to show up. He knew what room she was in because the girl at the front desk had told him.

It was amazing what that red uniform meant and, literally, what doors it would open. The EN had the entire hotel booked, and to the front desk clerk, he was just another member of that elite group, and she was happy to tell him the room numbers of his fellow lords. Lords Mordecai and Malachi were staying in the hotel proper until tomorrow; Lord Richard was checking out with Ranger Bunn this afternoon. Lord Freyja was staying in the far cabin through the weekend.

He was even able to inspect the room before Lord Freyja checked in, just to make sure it was suitable for her. It was, and a little strip of duct tape on the door lock made it even more suitable.

Something made a noise, and he jerked awake, upset that he had fallen asleep. A light was on in Freyja's room. He could see the yellow glow around the curtains even in the daylight. Damn! She had come back from the awakening, and he didn't even see her walk in. Just as he sat up, ready to kick himself for being such an idiot, the light went off again. No one left.

She was sleeping, just like Mordecai after an awakening.

Comatose.

Gary could hardly breathe; now was his chance.

Top level. End game.

He tucked the pistol in his jacket, picked up his bag with the duct tape and hood in it, and reached for the door.

And in a moment of sanity, he almost stopped. Almost. He could change his mind, leave, go back to Lethbridge and give Alma some wild excuse for not picking her up after school and putting six hundred miles on her car. Go back to being red-coat Gary, lord of nothing.

Instead, he got out of the car and started walking to the door.

Tim

Tim saw the lord walking to the whore's door and wondered what that was about. Was he delivering something in that bag?

This was one of the minor lords, a redcoat, and his hair and beard still had a lot of colour in them. Probably one of those who were so weak they were practically human, and he was just a delivery boy for the EN. Tim carefully left his car, keeping the rifle low and out of sight, and crouched between the parked cars to give himself cover, but he still had a clear view of the motel room's door. It was a perfect shot, really.

He debated shooting the redcoat, and while it would be nice to claim a lord, any lord, what he wanted was the big prize – the woman. He aimed at the door, right where her head would be if she opened the door wide. Tim knew when he popped her, he'd be able to get the redcoat on the next shot anyway. That would really be sweet.

But the redcoat didn't knock at the door. He looked around and then opened it just wide enough and slipped in.

Tim couldn't believe it. This redcoat guy was going to fuck her! The way he slunk in, the guilty set to his head, there was no doubt in Tim's mind. It wasn't as if Tim hadn't done the same thing himself before he met Angel. Find an unlocked female's room in the barracks and have a little fun when they're sleeping. They woke up in the middle of the rape and were afraid to complain because all Tim had to do was point out that they had left their door unlocked, and so it was consensual. No one would believe that he wasn't invited in.

That's what this redcoat was doing, grabbing some sleepy slut nookie.

Tim relaxed, watched the door, and waited. Whatever happened now would be interesting. When they finally came to the door, they sure wouldn't be looking for anyone in the parking lot. He'd get them both.

_____

Freyja

Freyja was asleep, the deep, dreamless sleep of the innocent and the dead.

Then she couldn't breathe. She turned her head, but something was over her mouth.

Someone was lying on her, and she couldn't breathe. Her eyes flew open, but she couldn't see; something was over them. Something was over her mouth and nose.

She bucked, trying to push the man off. She could feel him, feel his arms and legs, feel an erection, feel his body lying on her as he held her arm, pressing her down. Nick?

It didn't feel like Nick. Nick wouldn't do this. She couldn't breathe, and she tried to push him off, but she had no muscles; she was empty, and nothing worked. She began to panic.

Then he lifted his hand from her nose.

"Breathe, Freyja, BREATHE."

She gasped for air, a huge ragged gulp, and with all the magic she had left, she silently screamed for Nick. HELP ME!!

And then the man was gone. She twisted in the blankets, her hands suddenly free, and clawed at the duct tape that covered her mouth and eyes. Freyja fell off the bed, caught in the net of blankets and –

There was a tremendous crash.

Tim

The lord flew out the window. For a minute, Tim thought he was one of the flying ones, but no, he was one of the thrown ones. Something or someone threw the 190 lb man out of the window like he was a sack of garbage, which he was, and he landed halfway across the parking lot on the hood of a car that was just pulling in.

Tim knew from experience that, unlike what people saw in the movies, being thrown through a window was not something normal people walked away from. The glass shards were like knives and would gouge great hunks of meat off, and the force of landing usually broke bones. This guy exploded out of the motel room like he was fired from a cannon. That had to hurt.

Then suddenly, a huge man was there, half-dressed, furious, and grabbed the red coat and –

It was another lord! His blue eyes glowed laser bright with fury, great flashes of blue light burned from his body, and he punched the lord in the face, surely breaking his jaw. Then he methodically began to beat the lord to death.

Tim raised his rifle. The shot was too good, the opportunity to eliminate two lords too juicy to ignore.

A man got in the way, blocking the shot. It was one of those fancy pants Rangers; he was trying to stop the fight. There were two of them, one pulled at the redcoat, trying to get him away from the lord, and the other grabbed the lord's arm.

"NICK! STOP!" the ranger yelled, and Tim had to hand it to him; he was a brave or supremely stupid sucker to get in between the infuriated lord and his victim as he beat the redcoat to a bloody pulp.

The big man hesitated. Just a second, but it was all the ranger needed. "NICK! Where is Freyja? Is she –"

Tim had a clear shot at the big lord, and he took it. But the ranger moved, just enough, and caught the bullet in his back, right in the shoulder. He fell, and Tim took his second shot and hit the red coat.

But the big man was gone.

Shit! He was right there! Tim popped up to get a better view.

And the last thing he ever saw was the demon eyes of the devil lord as he twisted Tim's head off from his body and threw it across the parking lot.

Richie

Richie had Gary in his arms, and he was as close to death as a man could be. In front of him lay Wendell. All he could do for either was scream, "PORT! PORT!" and for a sickening second, nothing happened. He thought, "We're out of range. There are no elves, and Wendell is going to die."

Then a Warrior Elf ported in, still naked, mud-streaked, and exhausted from the awakening. He took one look at the situation and reached for Gary, but Richie screamed, "The Ranger, take Wendell!" What the lord commanded, the lord got. Wendell disappeared.

Then two more Warrior Elves ported in and took Gary.

Richie ran to the motel room. Inside, he saw Nick bending over the body of Freyja and sobbing his eyes out.

"Nick – oh shit – Nick –"

Nick looked up at Richie, tears running down his cheeks, and he bent over his bond-wife.

"Nick. I'm so sorry." Richie bent over Nick and put his arm around him.

"I'll be okay." Nick brushed away Freyja's hair from her face and gently pulled off the last of the duct tape where it was hanging from her temple. "She's fine. Once she got the tape off her mouth, she went back to sleep. She slept through the whole thing."

Freyja

Freyja woke up, and the first thing she saw was the white ceiling. It looked, she thought, just like the tall, ornately plastered ceilings at Aelfeham House.

She stretched and gods! She was hungry! She wondered where Nick was, and then he was there, a sandwich in his hand.

"Hey! Sleeping Beauty is awake!" He leaned over and kissed her, and then handed her the sandwich. Freyja grabbed it and wolfed it down, and Nick counted his fingers. Yep, all still there.

"Aelfeham House! What're we doing here!" Freyja paused long enough to look around and then finished the sandwich in about three bites.

He sat on the bed and told her everything. She had no idea what had happened after she got to the motel; she didn't even remember the attempted rape or pulling the tape off her mouth or going back to sleep. It was all gone.

The more she heard, the more upset she got, and Nick's constant assurances that everything, from their point of view, turned out okay didn't help. He had defended her and fought on his own. He could have been killed! And she'd slept through it all.

Gary had sneaked into the hotel room and tried to bond-rape her while she was passed out. He didn't know that Nick was in the room and about to get in the shower when he heard Freyja's mental cry for help.

But it wasn't just one murderous encounter; they'd had two people after them. An assassin was waiting for Freyja in the parking lot and shot Gary and Ranger Bunn. Both were still alive. Bunn had a shattered shoulder blade and suffered severe blood loss. It was touch and go, but between Althea and Dr Mandy, the healers saved him. They'd had to rebuild his shoulder, but he should be fine. He was on extended leave for now.

Gary was in detention on Príosún Isle. It was the same place where Lena was imprisoned, where she went mad after Lester's death, and where she later died. The elves patched him up, reluctantly, and only because Caddy told them to, but they weren't happy.

To an elf and to the Old Fart lords bond-rape was worse than killing a lord. It meant permanent, miserable enslavement to the rapist and eventual, inevitable death when the bond became too horrible to endure. The only way to free yourself was suicide, and the rapist would do anything to prevent that because that meant their own agonising death. It was bad enough to have an accidental bond, but bad did not begin to describe the horrors of having your forever life stolen from you and still having to endure being tied to a sociopath who wouldn't, couldn't release you.

Between Nick's beating and the bullet from the assassin (the elves refused to say which, but Nick suspected their refusal to say meant he did it), Gary had a permanent spinal cord injury from the neck down. This could be fixed if he were put in the cauldron, but Mandy wouldn't sign off on it, and neither would Althea. For one thing, the elf clan leaders were dead set against it. They'd keep Gary alive, they'd guarded and nursed him on Príosún, but they drew the line at the cauldron. He had no credit with the Elf Nation to pay for extraordinary medical treatment. And besides, who would talk to him while he was reforming? Who would sit in the room with him for two weeks and keep him anchored to this world? No one. Not Chi, not Alma, no one. He was despised by everyone who knew him.

The assassin, an American orc named Tim Snelling, was associated with a black operations unit in the American government. The day after he tried to kill the lords, a car bomb went off in Fredericton, New Brunswick, killing the Premier's two children and her husband as he was driving the children to school. Another bomb went off in Toronto on the subway, but no one but the bomber was hurt. It was thought that the bomb had gone off prematurely, and while the woman lost an arm, she lived, and through her, they learnt that both incidents were also connected to the same group that Snelling had belonged to. According to the subway bomber, the unit had decided on more attacks to "put Canada on notice not to fuck with the US and to stop waking imps."

The EN and Canada were still considering what actions they would take. The American public was on edge, and while some didn't believe that the black ops unit was really a part of the Executive Office ("Crisis actors! It's all fake!!"), everyone knew that the US was now in active conflict with Canada. The border was shut down, this time by the Canadians. The EN said nothing, but that just made the speculation and fear worse.

The secession movements in the American north-west built up steam, and in Utah, three state senators scheduled a secession debate in the statehouse. Yeah, the US Supreme Court had long ago ruled that a state couldn't leave the union, but if the people of the state voted to leave, they weren't following the rules of the American government any more, were they? Refugees were moving to and from the western states as people either fled Meechum's regime or joined it.

Freyja had slept for four days, and while she slept, the world lurched and pivoted and realigned.

She listened to all of that and became very quiet. Her elves, her people, were being threatened and attacked. Nick could have died, and if he had died, she might as well have never awakened. She would die with him, and in her mind, her death would be a blessing.

Nick continued, "But in the end, that Snelling man never got to you, and Bunn is going to be okay. Gary – I don't think about him any more. His life is what he made, and he deserves it. We can talk about our next steps later, after you think about all this. In the meantime, I think we need a couple of days of rest and thinking before we go back. It's safe here. The elves are taking care of the wolves. They're being fed, and I ported back for a couple of hours yesterday to check on them, and they're fine. Are you okay with that?"

Freyja nodded; yeah, that all seemed sensible.

"Then go take a shower, and we'll go to the Breakfast Room, and you can have a real chow down. I'm hungry, too!" He gently kissed her. "I missed you, babe; you're not a good conversationalist when you're passed out."

Freyja blinked back a tear. She loved him so much.

Freyja and Nick

Everyone was very nice. Super nice. Extraordinarily nice. Embarrassingly nice.

At lunch, Lords Jack and Alizah met them at the door of the Breakfast Room and introduced themselves as their mentors, and there was no turning them away. Alizah talked a mile a minute about everything and nothing, and Jack introduced them to every lord and elf in the room. Of course, they'd already had four days of conversations with Nick, so the introductions were for Freyja.

Lord Cadence and Lord Kyrylo came to see Freyja and Nick right after lunch, and she was quite blunt. They had screwed up last time. Freyja had not been treated according to the standards they had set for themselves when new lords came to Aelfeham House, and she apologised for that.

Caddy noticed that neither Nick (who had been there for four days) nor Freyja were wearing the bluecoat uniforms that hung in their wardrobes; both were dressed in what had been known as "business casual" in her old working days. They were guests but not a part of the Elf Nation, and when Kyrylo asked Freyja what her plans were, she immediately said that after her rest, she needed to go back to Canada and finish her walk. She had not reached her goal yet, and there were more elves to wake up. Plus, there were the wolves to take care of.

Kyrylo nodded and kept his own counsel. Now was not the time to lean on the two lords.

Both lords were friendly and polite, but neither showed the slightest interest in working in Europe. Both had found their soulmates outside of Aelfeham House, and while they seemed to enjoy the camaraderie of the lords' home base, they didn't need Aelfeham House in the same way as other lords coming in who longed to live with elves and their peers.

They had their own elves in Canada, and they had each other.

Freyja and Nick were, as Caddy said to Kyrylo later, a lot like the nomads who'd come over as a group and already had a social network set up. If Mongolia had been safe, they probably would never have left to go to rainy England. Some were already talking about moving permanently to Canada, where their camels were living on a ranch the EN had bought and where elf clans had already been established by Mordecai. The Elf Nation empire wasn't cracking or falling apart, but it was certainly diffusing, and the elves themselves didn't mind at all. In Before Times, lords had lived all over the world amongst the elf clans, not in one central location, and Caddy and Kyrylo would like to see that happen again one day. But diffusion had security risks of its own, and keeping the tiny tribe safe was their concern. A lone lord was vulnerable, even a powerful Elemental like Freyja.

And powerful she was. Mordecai was quite abashed when he reported back to Caddy about the elf raising. He'd thought he was pretty hot stuff, not an Elemental like Caddy, but pretty powerful. Freyja put both him and Caddy to shame. She'd raised eight hundred and seventy-three elves that day – by herself. There had been no elf left sleeping, so they really didn't know if she could do more than that. Yeah, she'd slept for days afterwards, but other than that, she didn't seem at all the worse for wear.

Kyrylo was eager for Gerald, the elf who trained lords in their magic, to assess and work with both Nick and Freyja so that the Warlord would know exactly what these new lords were capable of. Nick was doing weird things that the old lords who came from Before Times couldn't figure out, and Nick's bright blue eyes hinted that he was no slouch. Gerald wouldn't be able to work with either lord if they returned to Canada and roamed.

Nick had a few "play" sessions with Vrt and Malachi, and Victor had no doubt he was a fully capable Warrior Lord; he just needed to learn the sword and knife skills and some speciality weapons just to round things out. Like Berke, he'd had previous high-level military training, and Victor could see it.

In Victor's opinion, Gary was lucky that Nick went after him without the elf knife or sword training because what Nick did with his bare hands was lethal, and he'd known exactly what he was doing when he was beating the lord. Nick only hit Gary a few times before Wendell stopped him, and that was enough to cause permanent damage. And that orc assassin's head didn't pop off by accident. Some instinct in Nick told him that the orc had to be decapitated, and that was exactly what he did.

But, again, the extra training Victor felt Nick needed couldn't come if the couple were in Canada.

Alizah

In the end, it was Alizah who changed Freyja's mind. "Changed" might be too strong a word; maybe "nudged" was better.

They were sitting in the TV room, knitting, and Freyja was showing her how to double-knit the Fair Isle way. Alizah was determined to knit a jumper for the baby, and her ambitions far exceeded her talents. Nick poked his head in and was amazed that Freyja knew how to knit.

"How do you think I get sweaters? I didn't go to stores, and all I could buy at Wally's were jeans. But Lilly would go to the shops in Fairbanks and buy me wool and patterns, and she taught me how to knit. I knit a lot in the winter when it's too cold to go out and the light is low and I can't read." She looked at Nick appraisingly. "I'll knit you a sweater, but goodness, I'll have to buy a lot of wool!"

He grinned and told her he was going to have some sabre practice with Malachi. "See, I have talents, too! I'm a swordsman. I'll practise with you later!" He winked, and before the ball of yarn could hit him, he was gone.

"It's good he's practising with Malachi. Kai will teach him a lot." Alizah concentrated on the knitting, but she still shot Freyja a look. Freyja didn't say anything; she knew where the conversation was going. They, and by "they" it was all the lords, from the primaries on down, wanted Nick and Freyja to give up the elf awakening thing in Canada and stay with them. Knitting and sword practice, and doing fun things with friends, were all part of the wooing.

"Did you know that when I first met Jack, he was a one-eyed raven?" Alizah stopped knitting and looked out the window. "Jack's not a strong lord, not like you. I guess in today's lord world, he's about middling, but back in Before Times, he was considered really weak. He's a flyer, not a fighter, and when the orcs and humans were killing off the lords, he was cornered, and the only way he could escape was to shape-change into a raven. Even then, he was shot with an arrow and lost an eye. But he was too weak to change back, and for 3,500 years, he lived as a forever-raven, and until he saw Caddy, he was all alone except for other ravens. Jack was the first other lord Caddy ever met."

Freyja looked at Alizah but kept knitting, wondering where this story was going; the lord sat back, giving up on her knitting and instead rubbed her still-flat belly, lost in thought.

"Anyway, when I came here, I was a real mess. You have no idea." And her voice trailed off. "But Raven Jack took me under his wing –" and she grinned, pleased with the pun, " – and we fell in love. I guess we bonded in our hearts, if not for real, although back then I didn't know what bonding was. I mean, we didn't have sex or anything; he was a raven. I was fine with him being a raven and me being a woman. I didn't need him that way, and as long as he was a raven, he wouldn't go off and find another, better woman because, like I said, I was a mess.

But one day I overdid it. I took a solo flight to Ukraine that tired me out, and I got caught in a storm and got blown over to Russia into an orc nest and fractured my ankle. I was too exhausted to escape." She looked at Freyja, and there were tears in her eyes. "Jack flew over the wall in the storm to find me. He risked his life for me. He found me and saved me. They shot at us on the way out; he could have died. He was just a bird, and all he could do was fly.

After we escaped, I felt so bad, so 'orrible. Everyone on this side was risking their life for me." She sighed. "Anyway, as soon as we got back, Jack talked to Healer Mandy and decided to go into the cauldron and get turned back into a man. That was risky, too. He could've died or come back as a half-monster. He'd been a raven for 3,500 years, and Mandy was scared 'e couldn't become a man again, but 'e did.

"Y'know, I played dumb, like I didn't know the risk 'e took, but I did." She smiled. "I'm good at playin' dumb. Anyway, I couldn't put my foot down and keep him a raven because I was afraid of him runnin' off, could I? He had to change, to grow, and I had to accept that. He couldn't be a real bond-husband to me as a raven; he couldn't protect me; he couldn't protect himself the way he should. But he changed, and he's happier, and so am I. It all turned out for the good, and now we're having a baby. What's better than that?"

Alizah looked at Freyja and spoke in English, not Elvish. Her voice roughened, and the Cockney came out. "M'lovely, you've been a full lord fer most your life, and you grew up a lord in a safe place, in the forest. Nick's only been an unripe lord for a few years, and now he's changing and growing before your eyes. But 'is world is dangerous. 'e'll kill himself protecting you, and if 'e does, that'll kill you, too. That's why I think it's good 'e's 'avin' sword practice with Malachi. Everything 'e c'n learn will protect 'im and you."

Freyja looked at her knitting. If she worked, she'd have the baby sweater finished by the evening. Alizah, on the other hand, wouldn't be done this century, just in time for the kid to ripen into whatever it was they were destined to be. But that was okay; Alizah had finished what she set out to do.

Nick and Freyja

"Nicky, are you awake?"

Nick's eyes flew open. "I am now."

"Are you really tired? Do you want to go back to sleep?"

By all the stars, the woman was insatiable. So he rolled over, but she pushed him off.

"No, not that! I want to talk." Freyja sat up. "I've been thinking about my dream quest, and I don't know what to do, but I have some ideas and want to see what you think. I have to go back and finish my dream walk. Non-negotiable. But we only have two more stops, probably, before we get to Lethbridge."

Ah, the endgame discussion. Nick looked over at his bond-wife. "So, after we get to Lethbridge, what do you think will happen? I mean, realistically, Babe, I don't think anything will happen. I think the entire point of the dream was the journey, not the finish line. What do you think?"

He felt Freyja nod, a tiny vibration.

"The dreams said to wake elves, take care of my people, and live a happy life. That doesn't have an end. Lethbridge isn't a finish line, it's a starting point, I think." She patted his arm. "If I had never left Alaska, I would never have learnt about waking elves. I had to come here to learn about that. I had to get shot to come here. I would never have met you if I hadn't talked to Bruce and asked for help, so I wouldn't have a happy life because you have made me happier than I could ever be alone in Alaska. And serving my people, that's all part and parcel of both."

She paused.

"And if Gary and that Snelling man hadn't done what they did, you and I wouldn't be here today. Right now, we'd be on the last leg to Lethbridge. So if I follow the "meant to be" theme, you and I were meant to come here as part of the dream quest. So why?"

Nick let her go; he was pretty sure she had it figured out.

"I think you were meant to be here, not me. I need to be in Canada. You need this place now to learn to be a full lord, to become a Warrior Lord like Malachi."

Nick didn't like the direction she was taking, not at all, and he opened his mouth to say that, but she wasn't looking at him, and she just kept talking.

"So I can't and don't want to live here. I want to stay in Canada and wake elves and live a happy life. So, how to square the circle between your destiny and mine? I think about how Jo did it with Lily. She couldn't live in the cabin, and I couldn't live in the town, so he commuted. He shared his time between the two of us." Then it all came out in a rush. "Do you think that we can finish up Lethbridge and then come here for the winter? I don't think we can do the elf raising thing on our own now, not now that we know there are assassins and orcs after us, not after you having to protect me while I was sleeping and almost got killed."

"I didn't almost get killed."

"No, but it was too close for me. We need to watch out for each other, and while you were protecting me, I couldn't protect you because I was passed out. Anyway, I think we need to use the EN and Mounties all the time now just to be on the safe side. If we had stayed with them instead of going back to the hotel, we'd have been okay."

"I'm fine with keeping the circus, as Kai calls it."

"If we use them, it should be in the warm months; humans suffer in the winter, especially in a northern winter. So March to September, then, for raising. But as far as living here in England, I wonder if the EN would mind if we lived in the Yukon and asked Lord Adem to make a direct transport node to here, like the Primaries have in Ukraine. Caddy and Kyrylo, Jack and Alizah – they live where they are comfortable – why can't we? You can come and go with your Warrior Lord training, and I can come and go here when I need to. We'll find a place to live in the Yukon that has elves living there."

Nick considered this. "I think the EN will do whatever you want to keep you tied to them. They'd give you pink hot air balloons to live in if you asked for them."

Freyja smiled. "Well, I've been thinking about that, too. I don't want to 'tie in' with them in that I feel like I have to take orders from the Primaries. I work for elves and for my people, and my people are on another continent. I don't want to wear their blue uniform. We're not European. I'm fine with the EN representing all elves because it's the *ELF* nation, not the Lord's Nation. But I work for elves, not for Caddy and Kyrylo."

"That all sounds fine with me. I don't want to live here either; all I want is to be with you. But learning what Victor and that bunch know is good, and I'd be glad if we could work that out. So we talk to the Primaries tomorrow, hash all this out, and go back to Canada the day after tomorrow?"

Freyja leaned over and kissed him. "If you think I'm not asking for the moon, then this is what I want."

"We'll see what tomorrow brings. Love you, Babe."

"Love you, too, Nicky."

Caddy and Kyrylo

Caddy was not happy, but more because she didn't like being told what a new lord would accept when she was used to dictating the terms. There was no "my way or the highway" bluff with these two. They'd just leave and not look back.

Kyrylo told her to suck it up (although in a nice way). They weren't going to win Freyja's and Nick's hearts in a four-day charm offensive, and the two lords weren't rejecting Aelfeham House outright. And most importantly, they also weren't setting up an alternative power base.

From Kyrylo's point of view, if the two lords didn't want to wear the blue coats of the EN working lords because they weren't going to be working "for" the Primaries, that was a small thing. A niggle. After all, neither he nor Caddy could ever order a lord to do anything, and they had always said that. How would they enforce an order that a lord didn't agree with? Only with isolation, banishment, and imprisonment. They couldn't fire a lord or dock their pay.

He suggested that the elves design a "North American" uniform to wear whenever one was needed because uniforms were handy things, especially in a military environment. Freyja and Nick were fine with that, and Freyja whispered to Nick later that they could ask for uniforms that were comfortable and not out of that scratchy blue wool.

Freyja and Nick

When Nick called Commissioner Threader and told him what he and Freyja were thinking of the Commissioner was non-committal. But back in Ottawa, champagne corks popped. The Canadian government was going to end up with two lords permanently based in Canada who weren't under the thumb of either government but working with both. They might have lost Lord Ratna, but they were keeping Lords Freyja and Nicholas, and that was an excellent trade.

A week later, in Canada, another elf raising was in the rear view mirror with Freyja safely sleeping it off at Aelfeham House and Nick taking lord and Warrior Lord lessons while she recovered.

And then it was the last leg.

Nick steered them into farmland west of 36 and away from major roads. This part of Alberta was pretty densely populated from their point of view, but they'd spent the last night camping by Keho Lake, and then they walked cross-country over the ranches and fields to Lethbridge.

Freyja and Nick walked with the wolves down AB25 towards the Lethbridge city limits. As city limits go, it wasn't too exciting. They followed the grassy berm of a double-lane asphalt road towards a green overhead sign that said "East Lethbridge" with an arrow. They walked through flat prairie on both sides with barely a tree in sight, baking in the flat, bright light of the August sun.

And waiting at the sign were elves. Hundreds of elves, cheering and clapping.

Freyja took Nick's hand, and they walked under the sign to join her people.

"You go back to Canada to take care of your people, you protect the elves there, you wake more up. And while you're doing all that, you have a happy life. That will balance the books."

End of Book 8

Book 9

Heirs of Fixed Destiny

Continue the adventure!

This and all books in

The Return of the Tribes Series

are available for download on

Amazon Kindle
or
The Rum Lot Publishing

www.rumlot.com

E-Publishing, Hardback and Paperback versions of all books are
available on amazon.com

Please Donate
to the Excelsior Trust

If you enjoyed this book (and we hope you did!), please consider a small donation to The Excelsior Trust, a registered charity that is dedicated to preserving heritage fishing boats, in particular The Excelsior, LT 472, a wonderful fishing smack that is featured in Book Two.

As part of the trust's mission to preserve Britain's maritime heritage, they also subsidise unique training and sailing experiences for young people.

https://www.theexcelsiortrust.co.uk/

https://www.theexcelsiortrust.co.uk/donate
Registered Charity Number 285899

www.ingramcontent.com/pod-product-compliance
Lightning Source LLC
Chambersburg PA
CBHW060313260626
47160CB00007B/2587